LONG LIVE
the Beautiful Hearts

Beautiful Hearts Duet, Book II

Emma Scott

Acknowledgements

It's difficult to write about how this book came to be and acknowledge the person who needs to be acknowledged without spoiling certain plot aspects. I've saved the specific details for the Author's Notes at the end. PLEASE DO NOT READ those notes (or the Sneak Peek) until you have finished the book or YOU WILL BE SPOILED.

Thank you to Robin Renee Hill. There are no words to describe what you have done for me, including putting your own work on hold to get me through these last months, and then to complete this book. We did this together. It's our book, not mine. Love you.

Thank you to Melissa, for your gorgeous art, your covers that captured the books' spirit perfectly, and for being my conduit to the outside world and my comfort on the inside. I'd be lost without you.

Thank you to Suanne, for applying your editing genius again to this book, and for the hours of love infused within the pages and without. #labu

Thank you to Joanna, Sarah, and Joy for steering me in the right direction when I veered off course. Your input is invaluable.

Thank you to Dani for helping me to keep my livelihood afloat through tumultuous waters. I'm so thankful for you.

Thank you to Angela, for setting aside your time and artistry to make the book beautiful on the inside. You always come through for me, so thank you.

Thank you to Grey for always being one text away; love you.

Thank you to Dr. Colin Lenihan, M.D. for his valuable medical advice and expertise.

Thank you to MSG Mark Anderson, United States Army, for sharing his knowledge and experience through both these books, so I might create a realistic portrait of war, though any and all mistakes or liberties taken for the sake of the story are mine. And thank you for your service, sir.

Thank you to the author friends in my life, for your sisterhood and love: Kate Stewart, Kennedy Ryan, Katy Regnery, Shanora Williams, Raine Miller, Jade West, Rebecca Shea, Lisa Paul and Co., Nicky Grant, Desiree Adele, and Dylan Allen.

Thank you to my Entourage. There are not enough words to tell you how much you mean to me. I love you all.

Thank you to this community who still has not let go; I am still here and writing, in large part, because of you.

And thank you to the servicemen and women of this country. Researching these novels has brought me a deeper awareness for the sacrifices they and their families make for us every day, often with lasting repercussions. You have my utmost respect, appreciation, and love. Thank you.

Playlist

Switchblade, LP
Happier, Marshmello, Bastille
Love Me Like You Mean It, Kelsea Ballerini
In My Blood, Shawn Mendes
It Ain't My Fault, Brothers Osborne
broken, lovelytheband
Africa (Toto cover), Weezer
Natural, Imagine Dragons
You're Somebody Else, Flora Cash
Don't Speak, No Doubt
Recovery, LP
Something Just Like This, The Chainsmokers, Coldplay

Dedication

For Robin, who took my hand and is still holding on
For Melissa, who carries her always
For Robert, who stood up and said 'I will not let her go.'

And for Isabel
This and everything else I do with love, I do for you, baby. Now and forever.

LONG LIVE

the Beautiful Hearts

Beautiful Hearts Duet, Book II

PART I
Al-Raï, Syria

Prologue

Connor

My lungs sucked in air, bringing consciousness and chaos rushing back to me. And pain. A fuck-ton of pain stabbing into my left arm.

My vision was blurred as if I were underwater. I couldn't move, my body pinned down by something heavy on my chest. I could hardly gasp under the weight, reduced to shallow breaths. Gunshots, shouts and mortar fire distant through the ringing in my ears.

I blinked hard, forced myself to focus, and found the anchor pressing me down was Wes. He lay sprawled on top of me, his head on my chest, his helmet obscuring his face. His shoulders rose and fell—but was that him breathing or my breath moving *him*? I didn't know if he was alive or dead.

Alive. He has to be alive.

Terror ripped through me, carrying adrenaline on its currents.

"Wes," I croaked. "*Wes...*"

My gaze darted all over. I struggled to sit up and pain ground its steel teeth into my elbow, leaving me somewhere between puking and passing out.

"Fuck..."

I spit more curses between my teeth as I moved my left arm into my line of sight. A length of jagged shrapnel was lodged under the skin of my forearm. A wound so impossible, so ugly and *wrong,* it looked fake but for the pain that was howling up to my shoulder.

I turned my head this way and that, assessing our situation. Wes and I were exposed with no cover at the southern edge of the village. Figures moved through the blasted shells of homes, ghost-like in the smoke and dust. The fight was still happening but moving eastward.

My gaze snagged on a crater in the earth, smeared with blood. A little kid's sandal in the center. I remember running toward the owner of that shoe, trying to save him, to grab him and get behind some cover. I reached for him and then…

My memory had been blown to bits too, but I only had to look down to see my best friend lying motionless on top of me, covered in dust and blood, to guess what happened.

Wes chased me down. He saw what I didn't. He carried me away. He saved my ass.

Again.

A sob tore out of my constricted chest. Wes shielded me with his own body, taking multiple shots as we lay exposed.

And now he's dead.

"Wes," I cried. "God, no…"

Agony's jaws still locked on my arm, I scooted out from under him and gently eased his head to the ground. His eyes were closed, his mouth slightly open. I put two fingers to his throat. Tears stung my eyes when I felt his pulse, faint and way too slow, but *there.*

"Thank fuck…"

The relief was short-lived. As I walked on my knees, inspecting his wounds, a nauseous fear rose up in my throat. A bullet hole on the back of Wes's thigh had soaked his fatigues with blood, all the way down to the boot. My fingers moved around his waist and under his body armor and found three more gunshot wounds. But it was the shattered fragment of bone poking through his hip that got me in the gut.

"God, no, come on, Wes…"

I forced back the tears, digging deep for my training. We were exposed. The closest cover was a pile of rubble, maybe ten yards away.

I crouched on shaking legs and took hold of Wes's rucksack with my right hand. I gritted my teeth and pulled. Wes's deadweight

2

scraped across the gritty sand an inch.

"Come on…" I sucked in three deep breaths, clenched my jaw and pulled. Another inch. Fuck, he was too heavy and I was too weak.

Gunshots ripped the air open, followed by an explosion. Debris showered down and the adrenaline roared up in my three good limbs. Like the mom that lifts a car to get her kid out from under it, I grabbed Wes with my one good arm and hauled ass to safety. Once behind the rubble, I fell to my knees beside him.

"You stay with me, Wes," I said, sliding out my own rucksack. "You hear me? You fucking *stay* with me. Don't die on me, or I'll fucking kill y—"

My stomach heaved as my rucksack strap caught on my left elbow.

"Medic!" I screamed as I worked to get my aid kit open. "Wilson, goddammit…"

I dug into my rucksack and found my CAT. One handed, I fought to slip the belt-like tourniquet up Wes's right leg, getting it above the wound. I turned the clip around and around, tightening the belt until the clip wouldn't turn any more. Once the blood stopped flowing from the ragged hole in his leg, I strapped the clip into place.

"Medic!" I screamed. *"For fuck's sake, I need a medic!"*

I went to my aid kit again and grabbed my XSTAT. In training, we called them tampon shots. I tore the package off the over-sized syringe with my teeth and put the nozzle against the gunshot on Wes's hip. I depressed the plunger and the absorbent sponges filled the gaping wound, instantly soaking up the blood.

I was fighting for consciousness now. My vision grayed out and in as I assessed a bullet hole in Wes's lower back and another wound higher up, under his body armor. They needed tending but I didn't have the training or the strength. I sat on my ass, hard, exhausted. I sucked in one last deep breath and put everything I had behind it.

"Medic!" I screamed so loud my voice turned ragged at the end, a small pathetic scrap against the machine of war. "Jesus Christ, someone help him…"

Like a tree falling in slow motion, I lay on my good side, tight between Wes's body and the wall of rubble keeping us hidden.

"Wake up," I said hoarsely. "Wake up. Right the fuck now. Don't you die, Wes. Please…"

3

The world began to pull away. Even the pain in my left arm seemed distant. No more gunshots. Only a few faint shouts reached me now. Through the tinny ringing in my ears, I heard a woman's cries. I didn't know if we won or lost, only that each ticking second was bringing Wes closer to death.

I took his slack hand in mine. "You hold on, okay?" I said. "Listen to me. Don't go away, Wes. You stay and listen, okay?"

I shut my eyes for a moment, tears squeezing between my lashes.

"Stay with me, Wes, and remember…remember the time…we were about fourteen…hanging out in Jason Kingsley's rec room? Bunch of guys sitting…talking about girls. Trying to be tough?"

I swallowed hard, my throat full of glass and sand.

"We were all…boasting about whose ass we wanted to tap, and 'fucking that pussy'…as if we weren't all virgins." I chuckled tiredly. "But not you. You were shooting darts, and you…you had a crush on Kayla Murphy. I remember it…you kept shooting while telling us you wanted to kiss her. Kayla Murphy. I'll never forget it. You said, 'Kiss her in the little well of her collarbone, where her heart beats.'"

In my dimming vision, I saw shapes running toward us. Silhouettes of men.

"All the guys just stared at you," I said. "Remember? You turned around with a dart in your hand and your face was like *Fuck, what did I just say?* But instead of taking it back or making a joke…you just shrugged and said, 'Yep, that's what I'd do,' and went back to shooting those damn darts."

I chuckled as Wilson, Jeffries, and a couple of our guys surrounded us.

"Our friends had no idea what to make of that," I said, still holding Wes's hand because nothing would ever make me let go. "They just stared at you a good minute, then burst out laughing. Remember? They thought you were kidding. I laughed too, but I knew you weren't kidding. You weren't fucking kidding at all, were you, Wes?"

Time wandered away from me. When it came back, guys from our unit were loading us onto the chopper.

"On my three," Wilson yelled over the roar of helicopter rotors. He counted off and his team rolled Wes onto a stretcher. They'd removed his body armor and his midsection was now heavy with

LONG LIVE **the Beautiful Hearts**

bandages. As he was settled on his back, something fell out of his vest pocket. A bent, bloodstained notebook.

I stared through sand and wind being thrown around by the chopper. The pages of the little notebook fluttered in the hot gusts, looking like a wounded bird.

I grabbed it before it could take off and flipped through, stopping at a poem, scratched in ink. The words tear-stained and smudged with blood.

Wes's words.

Wes's tears.

Wes's blood.

At the bottom, his signature. Like a confession.

His name, not mine.

"Yes, Wes," I said, tears streaming down my own cheeks. "This is the truth. This was always the truth."

We climbed into the chopper, and more medics worked frantically over my best friend. Saline drip and an oxygen mask, but I saw one shake his head grimly.

Someone helped me buckle in and tried to treat my arm.

"Leave it," I barked. "Get me a pen."

"A what?" the medic asked over the din of the whirring helicopter blades. "A *pen*?"

I looked over to Wes, his eyes closed, his face a ghastly shade of white.

"*Give me a goddamn pen,*" I screamed.

The guy left my field of vision, then came back with a ballpoint and put it between my fingers. I held the notebook against my leg with my throbbing left hand—the arm which felt scarily numb—and scratched with my trembling right hand across the back of the notebook.

Autumn,

Wes wrote this and everything else. For you.

-C

I tried to write her address, but the pen fell from my fingers. I pressed the notebook against the medic's chest, my eyes falling shut under a wave of dizziness as the chopper lifted off.

"You have to mail this. Mail this…"

"What? Your arm—"

"Fuck my arm," I said. "You have to mail this.

Autumn...Autumn Caldwell. At Amherst University...Ridell Hall. No...Rhodes...?" My vision grayed out again and this time my eyes wouldn't open. "Fuck, I can't... It's Amherst. The school. You got that? Autumn..."

Then blackness came down.

PART II
Nebraska—July

CHAPTER

Autumn

The sunrise splashed across the horizon in molten gold and orange, pushing away the dark blues and purples of night.

"Look at that." Dad's voice was filled with awe. "Incredible, isn't it?"

I snuggled up closer to him on the porch swing, my cheek nodding against his shoulder. "I suppose it is."

"You see a sunrise like that... You can't help but feel something amazing is about to happen."

I peered up at his grizzled, gaunt face. His fine hair, once red like mine, had gone pure white since his quadruple bypass surgery last October. Under the plaid button-down shirt, his shoulders and chest looked narrower. He was tending the land again, although not as robustly as he used to.

"Something amazing," I said with a soft sigh.

I felt him look down at me. "How come you never want to talk about that boy, Connor? Not once this entire visit."

The name filled my heart with soft longing and pierced it with blinding fear. And every aching thought of Connor was followed immediately by deep, heated thoughts I didn't want to look at, much less give a name.

LONG LIVE the Beautiful Hearts

Weston…

"I'm scared for him," I said. "I've only gotten a handful of emails since his deployment. Nothing more than hi-how-are-you and basic news."

And not one word from Weston.

"War does terrible things to a man's heart and mind." My father shook his head. "You can't know how bad things are for him over there. Those emails might be all he's capable of."

"I know, but I just wish I knew he was truly okay. That he would talk to me."

Victoria Drake told me Connor called her frequently, whenever circumstances allowed. I heard more about how he was doing from his mother than I did from Connor himself.

Did Weston tell him what we did? Does Connor know I cheated on him?

It was the best explanation for both Weston's radio silence and Connor's terse, bare minimum communication. Before he deployed, Weston swore he wouldn't say a word about that kiss—a kiss that had almost led to everything else. He said it wasn't worth risking Connor's mental well-being when war was taxing enough.

The guilt must have gotten to him. Why else would Connor stop calling me?

"I think Connor's letting go," I murmured, swallowing tears. "And maybe it's for the best."

My father squeezed my shoulders. "Don't give up hope for your man or your love for him. It's too valuable. To both of you."

"Since when did you become so sentimental?"

Dad pointed toward the land, an ocean of corn stalks rippling green and tall under the gold of the spreading sunrise.

"Since I went into the hospital and nearly left all this behind," he said. "It showed me, more than ever, what's important." His hazel eyes looked down at me. "You, your brother, your mother. The people I love."

The men I loved were half a world away, facing unimaginable danger and I was stuck back here, not knowing if they were safe.

I sighed and leaned closer into him. I wanted to tell him everything. He'd listen and wouldn't judge. He'd still be proud of me and still be grateful for the money Connor had given to save the farm. But in my eyes, I had nothing to show for my junior year of college but barely head-above-water grades and another broken heart.

No, one that's torn in half.

I followed Dad's gaze over the cornfields and the rising sun, trying to find some peace in the world's beauty or a portent that something amazing was on my horizon.

"Everything's a mess," I said. *"I'm* a mess. Every day I pray that Connor and Weston will be all right, but I don't have much hope that there's something left between us."

All three of us.

My father pursed his lips. "I hear everything you're saying, sweetheart. And only you can know what's best for you. But I know that whatever we face in this life—good, bad, or worse—it only makes us stronger. Wiser."

"I just want to be in love with someone who loves me back. No games. No uncertainty. Just love."

Dad's eyes were kind and warm as he touched a calloused hand to my cheek. "You'll find it."

I checked my watch and got up. "I should go if I want to make my flight."

"I wish you didn't have to head back so early. The Fourth of July is coming up…"

"I know, but I'm going to get straight to work on my Harvard project and spend a little time with Ruby before she goes to Italy." I rubbed my eyes. "Ugh…and adjust to a new roommate."

"Too bad," Dad said, slowly getting to his feet. "I like that Ruby."

"I love her."

And I'm losing her as well. Everyone I love is gone or going.

The damn sunrise didn't portend anything amazing. Only loneliness.

In the kitchen, Mom was pulling breakfast rolls out of the oven. "For your drive to Omaha," she said, not looking up from stuffing them into a small Tupperware container. "Travis! Get down here. Your sister needs to get to the airport."

"I'm aware," Travis said, loping into the kitchen. Since graduating high school in June, he looked taller, bigger, more of a man. I was glad; Dad needed the help, and my little brother wanted nothing more than to work the land and keep the farm alive.

"You ready, Auts?" Travis asked.

LONG LIVE the Beautiful Hearts

"I think so. Bye, Mom," I said and ringed my arms around her sturdy shoulders. "Forgive me yet?"

"For what?" Then she pursed her lips. "We're not talking about that money. It's crass."

I'd wired the thirty-five thousand dollars Connor had given me straight into my parents' bank account at the beginning of summer. Had I handed over the check, there was a good chance my proud mother would've torn it up. *I* nearly tore it up, but no matter how badly it hurt, I couldn't watch my family's livelihood suffer needlessly along with my father's health. All summer Mom refused to talk about it, but I sensed her relief.

This is how it must've felt for Weston, I thought, *when the Drakes bought his mom a house. Relief and shame, both.*

"Love you," Mom said. "Drive safely. You hear me, Travis? *Drive safely*, there and back. Here." She put the container in my arms and shooed us out of her kitchen. "Go on. Scoot."

Dad walked us out to Travis's beat up blue pick-up truck where he pulled me into a hug. I clung to him, my eyes shut.

"I know you're scared for them, honey," he said.

I nodded against his shirt.

"They're in a dangerous part of the world right now, putting their lives at risk. But don't let the fear destroy your love."

My love. I didn't know what that was anymore.

Or who it's for.

"I'll try not to let it, Daddy," I said. "I love you."

"Love you, sweetheart."

I waved from the window as I watched Dad grow smaller. The scent of Mom's warm rolls wafted up to me from the container in my lap and suddenly, I knew where my love needed to go: to my family's farm and livelihood.

My Harvard project would focus on agriculture. The economic fairness for farming systems or investigating the potential for renewable biofuels. Neither stirred my passion, but the time had come to set aside my personal desires and emotions. They brought me nothing but heartache anyway.

And as we drove along Interstate 80 from Lincoln to Omaha, I firmed my resolve while the sunrise morphed into a golden day.

That is my something amazing. I finally know what I'm doing with my life.

11

But there were no accompanying fireworks of excitement in my heart. No *zing*.

I sighed and rested my cheek in my hand to watch the countryside slide past and tried to tell myself it was the right thing to do.

Waiting at the curbside pickup at Logan Airport, Ruby looked vibrant in a yellow sundress. Her caramel skin glowed as if she'd absorbed all the beauty of Jamaica during vacation.

"Aw, girl, what's the pout for?" she asked.

"It just hit me," I said. "I'm going to miss you so much."

"Me too, Auts," she said, giving me a last squeeze. She popped the trunk on her black Acura. "But I'll be back here to visit the parents for the holidays. Maybe some long weekends too. In fact..." She tossed my bag in the trunk and slammed the door shut. "I have a surprise for you."

"Lay it on me. I'll take anything you've got at this point," I said as I climbed into the passenger seat.

Ruby buckled up and navigated off the curb. "You, my friend, are not going to have to suffer a new roommate."

I blinked, then turned to her. "Are you serious? Wait, what do you mean?"

"I told Mom and Dad the situation with your stalled project and how your boyfriend being deployed to a war zone was threatening your big plans. They agreed that throwing in a new roommate might totally suck for you. So they bought out the room from Amherst for the year."

My jaw dropped. "Oh my God."

"Good, right?"

"Good? I'm having visions of quiet evenings studying without some stranger in my space. *Our* space."

Ruby beamed a megawatt smile. "Thought you'd like that."

"I love it. But Rube—"

"Don't even," she said in a hard tone. "Not a word about the cost. My parents love you. They wanted to do it. And Dad figures it'll

LONG LIVE **the Beautiful Hearts**

ensure I come and visit a lot. Which I will."

"It's so generous of them," I said, the familiar twinge of relief mixed with shame biting me.

Weston knows how this feels.

Ruby glanced at me sideways. "You look sad again."

I schooled my face back to neutral, erasing Weston from my thoughts. "Missing my family, I guess."

"How is your dad doing?"

"Better. But thin. He looks like he's aged ten years."

"Did your mom wig about the money Connor gave you?"

"In her own silent, fuming way. If Dad were healthy, I don't think she would've accepted it at all."

"Stubbornness runs deep in the Caldwell family."

Back at our place on Rhodes Drive on the Amherst campus, I rolled my suitcase in and surveyed the apartment with new eyes.

"All mine, huh?" I said, unable to keep back a smile as I thought of the peace and quiet I'd have to work on my agricultural project.

Ruby glanced at me and rolled her eyes, flopping down on the couch. "Oh God. I can already envision all of the wild parties you're *not* planning."

I sat beside her. "Amen. I figured out my Harvard project. Just this morning."

Ruby sat up. "You did? Good for you, sistah. What'd you pick?"

"I don't have all the details worked out, but I think it'll be about getting the government to give farmers better access and tax incentives for renewable biofuels."

Ruby's eyes glazed over. "That sounds...super interesting."

I laughed and shoved her arm. "It's important. For my family and for every farmer in America who's having a hard time right now."

"Then that's really great. Good for you."

"Meanwhile, you're about to spend a year on the Italian Riviera," I said. "The contrast of our lives is not lost on me."

"You should be proud, honey. You're going to save the world. I'm just not cut out for that." She patted my hand. "I'm so happy you found your calling."

"My calling," I murmured, still waiting for that *zing* that's supposed to come with finding your purpose.

Ruby cocked her head. "There's that look again. Have you heard from Connor recently?"

"It's been weeks." I turned my gaze to her. "I think it's over, Ruby. I think…"

I think Weston told him what happened the night before they were deployed.

God, I hadn't told Ruby that I kissed Weston—more than kissed him. He nearly tore my dress off and I couldn't get his zipper down fast enough.

I coughed. The words stuck to the roof of my mouth. It was wrong and yet it wasn't. How do I explain that?

Ruby leaned forward. "You think…?"

"I think it's better if we all move on. Connor and I. And Weston too." I plucked at the hem of my pale green sundress—a designer label I'd found at an estate sale in Nebraska that summer. "I've finally chosen my project, and they've got a serious job to do over there. Seems like we're all better off without the distraction."

Ruby pursed her lips, thoughts dancing behind her brown eyes.

"You don't agree?" I asked. "Or do you? I'm desperate for some advice. My dad says not to give up."

She held up her hands. "I don't know what to tell you, hon. But you spent all of last year trying to figure out where you and Connor stood. And it doesn't seem like a fun place to be."

"It's not. Maybe it's really over. Or should be."

Faced with actually losing Connor, my stupid heart clanged in protest.

"How can I break up with him while he's deployed?" I said. "God knows what they face every day."

"Still, it wouldn't kill him to tell you that you're important to him. How hard is that?" Ruby faced me straight on. "You deserve better than all this silence, Auts. You're not his penpal; you're his girlfriend."

"I know, but this is life and death." I went to my laptop on the desk by the window. "I'll send him an email. Tell him I'm thinking of him and that he can reply anytime or never, and we'll talk when we're face to face."

"Sounds fair," Ruby said. "But it doesn't solve anything."

"Maybe not," I said, clicking on my inbox, "but at least this way I can get to work. I—"

LONG LIVE the Beautiful Hearts

A strangled gasp tore out of me. The top email was from the United States Army, Dept. of Family Readiness. Sent this afternoon, not ten minutes ago.

"Oh my God..." My heart clanged so loud, I could hardly hear my own words.

"What is it?" Ruby said.

"Come here. Quick." My hand shook on the touchpad as I opened the message. Ruby moved behind me, her fingers digging into my shoulder. My eyes got as far as the second line and I heard a cry from somewhere. I think it was me. I swayed in my seat and Ruby put both arms around me as we read together:

Families and Friends of 1st Battalion, 22nd Infantry Regiment

On 13 June 20—, 1-22 IN was involved in an incident that resulted in one Soldier who was Killed in Action. The Soldier's primary next of kin has now been notified.
On behalf of 1-22 IN, I send my condolences to the Soldier's Family. We will hold a Memorial Ceremony for this Soldier at a time and place to be determined.
Please remember to keep all members of 1-22 IN and all other deployed servicemen and women in your thoughts and prayers. Thank you for your continuous support.

"That..." Ruby's words choked off and she tried again. "That's it? That's all they send? One killed in action, but they don't tell you who?"

"They tell family first," I said, my voice robotic. "The whole regiment goes on blackout until the immediate family is notified."

This explains why I've heard nothing from Connor lately. There's a blackout. Because he's dead. Connor's dead. Or Weston...

"Holy shit, Ruby..."

We sat in silent shock, the words washing over us again and again. *One soldier killed in action.* My thoughts drowned in a maelstrom of chaotic fear and driving back and forth between my men, my heart screaming and mourning and in terror for both of them equally. Each heartbeat was a name, Connor, Weston, Connor, Weston... Every exhale was a prayer for one of them.

Both of them.

I can't lose either of them. God, please...

My phone's ring shattered the silence and I nearly fell out of the chair.

"Jesus..." Ruby cried.

I rose on shaking legs and lurched like a zombie to my purse on the couch.

"It's Connor's mom." Slowly, as if I held a venomous snake, I put the phone to my ear. "Hi, Mrs. Drake."

"Hi, honey," she said, her voice heavy. "I have some news."

CHAPTER *Two*

Autumn

The plane touched down in Baltimore, and Ruby and I headed to the car rental counters.

Private First Class Samuel Bradbury.

Probably Sam to his family and friends.

Those family and friends were suffering now, gathered in grief over their lost soldier.

It could have been us, I thought at the car rental counter. Victoria Drake might've been making funeral arrangements right now. Miranda Turner could be on the floor, wailing and inconsolable for the loss of her boy.

It could've been me wracked with grief instead of hovering somewhere between sadness and relief.

Sam Bradbury.

Not Private First Class Connor Drake.

Not Corporal Weston Turner.

On the phone, Mrs. Drake told me everything she knew. The incident happened weeks ago, but the classified nature of the mission kept the Army from informing anyone until the men were flown out of the combat zone to Landstuhl Regional Medical Center in Germany. There, Connor's shattered elbow was put back together and he was treated for head injuries before being transported to Walter Reed Medical Center yesterday morning.

But Weston...

Weston was shot four times, and already he'd had two surgeries to his hip and back. A third surgery to remove the bullet that struck his gall bladder. A subsequent infection forced the doctors to put him in a medically-induced coma. He was set to be flown to Walter Reed, arriving the following day.

"His long-term diagnoses are unclear," Mrs. Drake said. "But he's more stable now. Doctors told Miranda he was on the edge of life and death for a while."

Life and death. Every soldier walked that edge. Connor and Weston stumbled over life. Sam Bradbury fell the other way.

"Hey," Ruby said, nudging my arm. "They'll be okay. They wouldn't have been cleared to fly from Germany if they weren't."

"I keep telling myself that, but I'm scared anyway."

"Me too."

Walking through the lobby of Walter Reed, my heart's heavy, dull thud of fear sped up to a rabbit-thump pulse with every step. In the elevator, Ruby reached out and took my hand. I gave her a grateful squeeze and didn't let go.

Connor had a suite on the fifth floor. In the private waiting area, Senator Victoria Drake, impeccable in a beige pantsuit, alternated between talking on her phone and talking to her team of assistants. Mr. Drake paced nearby, his expression grim.

"I'll call you back," Mrs. Drake said into her phone when she saw me. She approached with open arms and hugged us one at a time. "Autumn. Ruby. So good to see you."

"How is he?" I asked.

Mr. Drake joined us. "He's doing great," he said, as if willing the words to be true and not accepting anything else. "He's being evaluated to determine his fitness for returning to combat."

My eyes widened. "They might send him back?"

"I don't think so," Mrs. Drake said. "He was evaluated in Germany last week and they sent him here instead, which seems to indicate he won't return to his unit anytime soon. Thank God."

"How bad is his arm?" I said.

"His elbow's been replaced with titanium joints, but they're optimistic he'll retain full function. It's the head injuries that have the doctors concerned."

Mr. Drake smoothed the front of his suit jacket. "He's been having some blackouts and headaches. Episodes of anxiety and other signs of...mental distress." He forced these words out between his teeth, and grimaced as if they tasted bad.

"PTSD?" I asked.

"I'm not a doctor," he snapped.

Victoria touched his arm. "It's to be expected."

"He's decompressing from a dangerous situation," her husband said, nearly flinching from her touch. "Anyone would be emotional coming home from a warzone. Doesn't mean it's permanent." His phone rang and with a terse, "Excuse me," he walked off to answer it.

"Does Connor *want* to go back?" I asked softly.

Sighing, Mrs. Drake nodded. "The doctors told us that soldiers who experience trauma in the field often have an intense, urgent need to return to their unit. Not doing so is a dereliction of duty. They're abandoning their comrades still in harm's way."

"Survivor's guilt," Ruby said.

"Yes, exactly." Mrs. Drake's face was contorted in relief and worry as she lowered her voice. "Connor desperately wants to go back, but the doctors say most likely he'll be honorably discharged."

My chest caved in with a long exhaled sigh, then tightened with my next breath in. "How's Weston?"

Mrs. Drake's mouth hardened and she looked away. "His flight arrives tomorrow morning. Then they'll assess whether or not it's safe to take him out of the coma."

"He was shot in the back—?"

She put up a silencing hand. "It's too soon to tell what lies ahead for him and I'm not immediate family," Mrs. Drake said, almost snapping at me. Then she forced a smile. She nodded at Connor's closed hospital room door. "One thing at a time. After his evaluation is over, Connor will want to see you."

"Of course. I want to see him too."

God, so badly. All of the uncertainty and doubt I'd been feeling since they were deployed paled in comparison to these moments. To both men being alive. That's all that mattered.

"If you'll excuse me." Taking out her phone again, Mrs. Drake returned to her group, clustered on one side of the waiting room.

Ruby sank onto one of the small couches. "Connor's dad

sounded like he was giving a press conference," she said in a low voice. "As if Connor's mental health were a scandal."

"Just another example of Drake parenting," I said, collapsing beside her. "Nothing Connor does is ever good enough. Including being injured in combat."

I rested my head on her shoulder.

"It's going to be all right," she said, rubbing her temple against my hair. "Just breathe."

The door to Connor's room opened. Two doctors and an Army officer came out, all three wearing grim expressions. Mr. and Mrs. Drake strode to them. I strained my ears over the hospital's hustle and bustle but could only catch snippets of the conversation.

"Both evaluations indicate post-traumatic stress…"

"Dr. Lange in Germany advised the same…"

"…recommended for honorable discharge."

Ruby and I exchanged looks and our shoulders sank in a shared sigh of relief. The doctors dispersed after a few minutes. The Drakes had a tense, hissed conversation and then Mr. Drake strode away, his face unreadable.

Ruby and I got up to join the senator.

"Autumn, you can go see him now," she said absently.

Ruby put a hand on her arm. "Would you like to get a coffee with me, Victoria? Maybe something to eat while Auts visits Connor?"

"Yes," Mrs. Drake said with a sigh. "I'd like that."

Ruby shot me a soft smile as she and Mrs. Drake headed to the cafeteria. I sucked in a deep, steadying breath and knocked on the hospital door that had been propped open.

"Yeah," he said.

The room smelled of flowers and disinfectant. Connor sat on the edge of the bed, dressed in his own pajama pants and a white V-neck shirt. His left arm was encased in a bulky, complicated-looking brace of black plastic, Velcro straps and hinges. But it was his face that made my heart clench like a fist and stopped me from flying at him. His jaw scruffy and stubbled, his green eyes circled with deep rings. No trace of the megawatt smile I loved.

Alive and right in front of me, but his expression was withered, his smile dead.

War has stolen it.

For a long moment he stared at me. Confusion in his gaze,

almost bordering on mistrust. As if he couldn't quite believe anything his senses told him; as if the hospital room and everything in it were a dream.

"Connor?"

He raised his head. A spark lit in his eyes. His lips turned in the smallest of smiles. A small one, but I took it.

"Hey, babe," he said, his voice full of desert sand. "Come here. God, please come here…"

He stood up and I rushed to him. His right arm came around me, holding me tight, nearly crushing me. I buried my face in his chest and inhaled him, pulling him into my lungs. My hands skimmed over his T-shirt, feeling his broad back, the warm skin, the strong muscle; the feel of him convincing my beleaguered brain that he was alive.

"Babe," he said softly. Over and over, while I couldn't even speak. Only grab him in my hands and think, *You're here. With me. You're back…*

"Let me look at you," he said.

I pulled back and held his face in my hands. His skin had the thick tan that came from being sunburned over and over with a paler swathe around his eyes where tactical had shielded them. "Are you okay?"

A short jerk of his head, half nod, half shrug. "I'm better than they think. I get headaches and there are spots in my memory. But that's normal after being blown up, right?" His expression took on a pleading look. "They won't listen. They say I can't go back."

I nodded, swallowing hard. "I know."

Thank God.

He sagged a little against me. A long sigh, then he jerked upright. "Did you get it?"

"Get what?"

"I sent you something. A notebook."

"You did? God, Connor, when I hadn't heard from you in—"

"Did you get it or not?"

I flinched. His expression softened again at once, collapsing to regret. I wasn't experienced with PTSD, but it was easy enough to see that Connor didn't have a hold on his changing emotions. They bounced around like a ball on a Roulette wheel, and I made my voice the calm, steadiness he could focus on.

"No, I didn't get it," I said. "It might be held up en route or maybe lost. But it's okay." I put my arms around him. "It's okay, Connor. I'm just happy you're back—"

Connor stiffened in my arms and pushed me gently away. "You didn't get a package?"

"No, Connor. I didn't."

I sat on the edge of his hospital bed as he paced slowly, running his hand through his hair.

"You're sure?"

"I'm sure," I said, gently. "When did you mail it?"

He stopped, pinching the bridge of his nose with two fingers, his face drawn down with pain. "Right after...after the explosion. I think. I can't... I can't remember. Fuck. It's lost. I fucking lost it. I can't do anything right. Not one goddamned thing."

"Hey," I said, standing up. "It's all right. Come here. Come sit down again. It's a lot to take in right now. You're still processing it all. Go easy on yourself, okay?"

He sat hunched over his knees, his head bowed. I rubbed his back, and after a moment, his tearful glance slid to me.

"I did a bad thing," he said hoarsely.

"What...?" I said, then shook my head. "No. War is...terrible. You were put in a horrible situation and horrible things happen. You don't have to explain."

"Not there. Here. To you."

I sat back. "What do you mean?"

"And Wes." His broad back expanded and collapsed like bellows, forcing the words out. "I ruined his life. If he lives at all. I ruined him..."

Sobs rolled out of him and he covered his face with his good hand. I tried to hold him, but his shaking body was so big and powerful. It was like trying to hold a cracking boulder together.

"It's not your fault, Connor," I said. "No. No, it's not your fault. He signed up—"

"Because I did," he said, sucking in deep, hitching breaths. "He signed up because I did." He wiped his eyes on the shoulder of his T-shirt. "I have to get out of here."

He went to the door and was two steps into the hallway before nurses ushered him back in. Mrs. Drake and Ruby, both with Starbucks in hand, followed.

"I need to get the fuck out of here," Connor said, pacing the

LONG LIVE **the Beautiful Hearts**

room. "Back to my unit. They need me. And I can't be here when Wes...when he..." He held his head in his hands. "Fuck, these headaches."

"Take it easy," a nurse said, leading Connor back to his bed. "One more day of rest and a few more tests. Word is you'll be discharged tomorrow."

I moved out of the way as Connor lay back down and threw his good arm over his eyes.

"And Wes will be here tomorrow," Mrs. Drake said. "It'll be good to see him, won't it?"

"Good to see him?" Connor's bitter laugh was muffled under his elbow. "I'd rather be anywhere. Back in Syria, for fuck's sake."

"You don't mean that..."

The senator's words trailed away. As if he'd thrown a switch, her son was asleep.

"What just happened?" I asked.

"It's a survival tactic," the nurse said. "Combat soldiers can fall asleep fast—anytime, anywhere. Let's let him rest." The nurse ushered us out. "Dr. Mais wants to speak with you anyway, Senator."

The attending doctor—a short man with dark hair—met us in the waiting area and Mrs. Drake rounded on him. "Tell me the truth," she demanded. "How bad is the brain injury?"

"The concussion caused severe swelling," Dr. Mais said patiently. "Which subsided while he was being cared for at Landstuhl, enough that he was cleared to fly home. The headaches are to be expected, and they'll subside in time as well. The anxiety and emotional lability could be due to brain injury, but most likely they're from post-traumatic stress, as we discussed."

"What about the blackouts? He can't remember little pockets of time. And just now, he fell asleep in seconds. I don't care if it's a survival tactic. He just *went*."

"Senator Drake," the doctor said. "I've been at Walter Reed forty years and thousands of soldiers have passed through my care. I know PTSD when I see it and I feel confident the neurology evaluation will bear that out."

Mrs. Drake bit her lip, uncertain, and Dr. Mais put his hand on her shoulder.

"Look at it this way," he said. "Your son's arm was damaged and we repaired it with surgery, steel rods, and a brace. It's a war

23

wound. You must consider his emotional trauma exactly the same way. Does that make sense?"

"Yes." She nodded and drew herself up. "Yes, it does. I'm just so worried."

"Of course you are."

"My husband… I don't know that he views emotional trauma the same way."

"PTSD is an injury that deserves the same care and treatment, the same lack of judgment or shame that a bullet wound would warrant. It's imperative Mr. Drake understands that."

Mrs. Drake nodded, and I watched her morph back into Senator Drake. "He will. I'll see to it. Whatever Connor needs, he'll get it. The best care. I'll make sure of that too."

"I'm sure you will." With a last smile, the doctor excused himself.

"I need to go lie down," Mrs. Drake said. "I have reserved rooms at the Sheraton across the street. You girls just check in under my name. It's all taken care of."

"Thank you, Mrs. Drake," I said.

"I'll head over with you," Ruby said, then looked to me. "Unless you need me?"

"No, go ahead," I said. "I'll stay a little longer, make some phone calls."

And I need to be alone.

Ruby kissed my cheek. "Don't be too long. You look beat."

The senator gave me a stiff, one-armed hug. "Goodnight, Autumn."

I only had one call to make, to Edmond de Guiche, my boss at the bakery I'd been working at, going on four years. It was late, way past closing, and my call went to voicemail. I was treated to one of Edmond's trademark arias before the *beep*. I left a message telling him I would be a few days late to start.

I wanted to go back in Connor's room and curl up with him on the bed and tell him it was okay to feel undone. Tell him he did everything right, that it wasn't his fault—all the words his parents should be telling him. But it didn't feel right.

I did a bad thing.

"Me too," I said.

I had to come clean about what happened with me and Weston.

L O N G L I V E the Beautiful Hearts

No more secrets between the three of us. But I couldn't make myself walk back into Connor's room. Instead, I curled up in the waiting room chairs and fell asleep.

What felt like minutes later, a hand gently shook me awake. I blinked my eyes open, shards of morning light slanting through the windows. Ruby stood over me.

"Hey," she said, kneeling next to my chair. "Wes is here."

CHAPTER
Three

Autumn

The social worker assigned to Weston was a blonde, gentle-voiced young woman named Ellen. She led the Drakes, Ruby and myself downstairs to the ICU and Connor followed behind, looking like a man walking to the electric chair.

"They're situating Wes in the ICU now," Ellen said, showing us to a waiting area outside a set of double doors. "The doctors tell me he's in stable condition, all vital signs looking good. They're hoping to take him out of sedation sometime tomorrow."

"Thank you so much," Mrs. Drake said. She looked at her son, who sat apart from us, slouched over his legs. His left arm rested on his thigh; his right hand covered his eyes. His entire demeanor begged to be left alone. Every hunched line of his body made it obvious he'd rather be anywhere but here.

Guilt had a chokehold on the room and was slowly sucking out the oxygen. Strangling Connor. Me. Mrs. Drake who'd been left by her husband to manage this crisis alone. It was a wonder Ruby, the sole clear conscience, was even breathing.

"*More* waiting. That's all I get. Non-answers and 'please wait.' I'm *sick* of waiting."

Weston's mother burst into the waiting area. Miranda Turner

wore tight jeans and a purple-and-white Amherst sweatshirt. No makeup or jewelry and her bleached hair gathered in a sloppy ponytail. Paul Sheffield, the man she'd been dating for nearly a year, had an arm around her shoulder.

"Miranda, hi," Mrs. Drake said, rising to her feet.

Miranda burst into tears. "Oh, Victoria," she wailed, hugging the senator tight. "What did they do to my boy?"

"I know. Try to stay calm," Mrs. Drake said, now holding her at arm's length. "We need to be strong now for Wes."

Miranda caught sight of Connor and her face crumpled again.

"Oh, honey." She hugged him, mindful of his arm, then held his face in her hands. "Look at you. What happened to my boys? Your smile's gone, my Wes shot all to hell, and they won't tell me *anything*."

His jaw stiff, Connor pulled from Miranda's grip. She was too caught up in her drama to notice though, and started pacing the small space again.

"We're trying to stay calm, remember?" Paul said. He offered his hand to Connor. "Glad to have you back, soldier. And thank you for your service."

Connor sat a little straighter, a flash of pride sweeping over his expression. "Thank you," he said gruffly, shaking hands. The first words he'd spoken since leaving his room, and I sort of loved Paul just then.

I went to Miranda. "Hi, Mrs. Turner. I'm so sorry."

"Oh honey, you and me both," she said, giving me a hug. "Hi, Rube," she said over my shoulder. "What a mess. My poor baby. Three surgeries he's had already in Germany. *Three.* And then they put him in a *coma*?"

"For his own safety, Miranda," Paul said. "To keep him stable."

"Well, where is he? What's happening now?"

"They're setting him up in the ICU," Mrs. Drake said. "We'll be able to see him soon."

"That's what they keep saying and nothing else." Miranda turned to Connor tearfully. "What happened out there?"

Mrs. Drake stepped in between her son and Miranda.

"I think it's best if we all focus on Wes right now," she said. "Connor doesn't know anything more than what you've been told."

27

"He was with Wes on the battlefield," Miranda said. "He was with him in Germany. What happened, honey?"

There was no recrimination in Miranda's voice, but Connor flinched at every word. His horror-stricken face morphed into genuine pain, and his gaze was looking somewhere far beyond this room.

"A grenade happened," he said. "I couldn't get to the little boy. Couldn't save him. Wes ran to save me. Shielded me. It's my fault—"

"*Enough*," Mrs. Drake said. Beneath the glare on Miranda, her lips were trembling.

Miranda's eyes widened and she took a step back. "Okay, okay, you're right. Now isn't the time. I'm just scared, you know? I'm so scared."

She broke into tears. Paul put his arm around her and guided her to a chair.

"I know you are," Mrs. Drake said, easing a breath. She sat down and crossed her legs. "We'll see him soon and the doctors will answer all your questions."

"They've been telling me that for days," Miranda muttered.

Ellen returned to the room then. "Not long now."

"How long is not long?" Paul asked mildly.

"About an hour." She surveyed the room, her eyes landing on Connor. "Can I get anyone anything? Some water or coffee?"

Mrs. Drake leaned forward. "Connor, honey?"

But Connor was back in his hunched-over pose, head in his hand.

Mrs. Drake sat back. "No. Thank you, Ellen."

Hospitals, I found, measure time differently than in the real world. One hour meant three, and finally a tall doctor—6'3" at least—who looked to be in his late thirties, with a kind face and light brown hair, stepped into the waiting area. His smile was easy, but his eyes were sharp and full of intelligence, not missing anything.

"Hi, I'm Dr. Kowalczyk," he said. "Corporal Turner's ICU attending physician. You can call me Dr. K." He looked to Paul and Miranda. "Are you his parents?"

"I'm Miranda, his mama," Miranda said. "Paul is my boyfriend but should've been Wes's father and not the coward low-life he got instead."

Her words had less bite than usual, her ire melting under Dr. K's calm, friendly demeanor. How a man could exude such tranquility

LONG LIVE **the Beautiful Hearts**

and competency at the same time was beyond me, but it worked to calm Miranda at once and set my own heart at ease. At least Weston had a good doctor.

Dr. K sat in a waiting room chair next to Miranda and rested his arms on his legs.

"I know things have been hectic for you," he said. "Not to mention uncertain. But Corporal Turner—"

"Wes," Miranda said. "You can call him Wes."

"You got it," Dr. K said. "Wes's vitals look good and if he stays this stable overnight and gives us no surprises, we'll schedule him to be taken out of sedation sometime tomorrow morning. Once he's conscious again, we'll be able to run more tests to determine the extent and severity of his injuries. Okay?"

"His back," Miranda said. "He was shot in the back. They said one of his surgeries in Germany was on his spine…"

She left the rest of her fearful question in the air, hanging like a black cloud.

Dr. K pressed his fingertips together.

"That's true. The team at Landstuhl removed a bullet that fractured the third vertebrae in the lumbar region of his spine. It compressed the spinal cord but did not sever it. However, with the swelling and fracture, we're certain he sustained some damage. But to what extent, we don't yet know."

Spinal cord damage. The words slammed into my heart, and my vision was clouded with Weston crouched at the starting line of a race. The gun went off, but in my mind's eye, instead of him tearing down the track, he went down…

I shivered. *God, Weston…*

"The lumbar region?" Paul asked. "That's down low, isn't it?"

Dr. K nodded. "Yes, about here." He pointed to his lower back, just above his waist. "But as I said, we can't tell the extent of injury to the spinal cord until we can run tests with Wes's participation. Right now, our focus is on removing him from the coma safely and going from there. In the meantime, I'm sure you're all eager to see him."

"Yes, thank you, doctor," Miranda said. "It's been so hard."

Dr. K patted her shoulder and surveyed the rest of us. "All family?"

"They're like family," Miranda said. "All of them."

"We're going to need to keep it short and quiet, but you can all

29

see him for a few minutes. He's still under heavy sedation, so don't expect any interaction. Shall we?"

We followed Dr. K through the double doors and down the ICU hallway. I kept my mind empty, refusing to think about what Dr. K just told us. I vowed not to panic or let fear overtake me at the thought of what a damaged spinal cord meant for Weston.

The walls of the ICU were decorated with the American flag and large framed photos of notable moments in military history. Staff bustled about. Phones rang. We passed rooms with patients hooked up to machines, nurses and doctors tending, family sitting close by. I kept my eyes straight ahead out of respect for their privacy, but my heart was pounding.

The sense of walking that line between life and death was the same here as it was in Nebraska—a different kind of frontline, with the stakes just as high, and I couldn't help but think the doctors and nurses who worked an ICU were as brave as any soldier.

Dr. K stopped outside room 220. "Remember, nice and quiet," he said and stepped aside.

Ruby hung back and took my hand. "I'm going to be right here, okay? Go see him. If you need to freak out, I'll be here."

I nodded. "Yes, okay. Thanks, Rube."

The head of the bed faced the entry. Weston's feet pointed to the window. To his left, a giant bank of IV lines. A ventilator sighed and beeped. A monitor on the wall showed a pulse, blood pressure, and other colored lines making peaks and valleys I couldn't decipher.

Miranda's hand flew to her mouth. "Oh, my baby," she said behind it. "My sweet baby…"

My heart's pulse ratcheted up at her reaction, and my hands clenched at my sides.

Miranda, I swear to God… Shut up or I'll start screaming.

Paul guided Miranda around the bedside machines to make room for the rest of us. Connor glanced at Weston once, then went immediately to sit on the little padded bench built into the window. He stared out of the glass, mouth pressed in a tight line.

Mrs. Drake's lips were pressed just as tight as she looked down at Weston, and I stood beside her.

"I think he looks good," Mrs. Drake said. "Doesn't he? He's made it this far…"

She broke off and turned away.

LONG LIVE the Beautiful Hearts

I couldn't look away. Every vow to stay strong and stoic evaporated as I took Weston in. His bed was raised to a slight incline and he lay, pale and wan, against the sheets. His burnished blond hair dull and brittle. Tubes trailed from both arms and his stomach. A breathing tube was taped to his mouth and it pulled his lips into a grimace. His eyes—*those ocean eyes*—were closed. He lay utterly motionless. Only his chest rose and fell with the push and pull of the ventilator.

I pulled in a deep breath and touched his hand. "Hi, Weston," I whispered, nice and quiet. I sank into the small chair next to his bed.

The little room went as still as Weston. Nobody spoke, not that there was anything to say. Miranda cried on Paul's shoulder. Connor's gaze stayed fixed on the view outside the window.

"We should let him rest," Mrs. Drake finally said. "And get some sleep ourselves. Tomorrow is going to be a big day."

Miranda bent to kiss her son on the cheek. "You're going to be just fine, baby. You will. You have to be."

She and Paul shuffled out. Mrs. Drake started to follow.

"Coming, dear?" she asked.

"In a minute," I said, suddenly unable to bear the thought of Weston lying here alone.

"Connor?"

Slowly Connor's head turned. He looked at his mother, then, finally, at Weston. "Not yet," he said.

The door closed softly, leaving the three of us. Then Connor added, "I have to say goodbye."

CHAPTER
Four

Autumn

I whipped my head around. "What?"

Connor's shadowed eyes were still on Weston. "I did this to him," he said, shaking his head. "He's here because of me."

"Connor, it's not your fault."

"He signed up because of me. He signed up to protect me, which is exactly what ended up happening. He ran after me when I tried to save the kid. Wes knew it was too late to save him. I knew it too. But I needed to make something of myself. To *demonstrate responsibility*. Bradbury was dead. I was too late to save him. So I tried for the kid."

Tears filled his eyes and he turned back to the window, his right hand absently running over the heavy brace on his left elbow.

"It was futile but I didn't stop. I kept running and Wes ran after me. God, that guy could run. And he made it. A hundred pounds of gear on his back and I had a five-second head start, and he *still* caught me. And the kid died, because he was always going to die. It was too late to save him, but Wes saved me. Fucking tackled me away from the blast. Threw himself on top of me and took the shots. That's why I'm standing here and he's lying there…"

He broke then, bent over double, sobs shaking his shoulders. My own gaze blurred and wet, I got up and put my arms around him.

LONG LIVE the Beautiful Hearts

"I'm sorry," I said into his hair. "I'm so sorry."

"Sorry?" The word was half-sobbed, half-barked.

"For everything you've been through—"

"What I've been through is *nothing*. You don't know shit, Autumn. I was there. On the ground in Syria and in the hospital in Germany. I saw what they did to him. I saw his hip shattered and watched the blood pouring out of his leg. I saw the shot in his back and I know the score. I know what Dr. K's not saying about the *extent of his injuries* and I can tell you right now, Wes will never walk again."

The blood rushed loud in my ears as I backed away from the window seat. My legs bumped the chair by the bed and I dropped into it. An icy tingling sensation in my chest spread out over my skin, stealing my breath. My eyes froze open, unblinking as they remembered Weston running.

God, that guy could run.

Racing toward the hurdles in his three-step cadence, faster than I could count. Leaping with feline grace, one leg reaching, the other tucked tight. Lean muscles stretching and flexing under bronzed skin. Weston breaking away from the pack in a baton relay. No one had a prayer of catching him. He was too fast. Faster than anyone.

He had a hundred pounds of gear and I had a five-second head start, and he still caught me…

"No," I whispered, my hand reaching for Weston's. All that strength and power and speed now limp and weak in my fingers. I gripped it tight, shaking my head. "No, don't say that, Connor. We don't know—"

"*I* know," Connor said, his voice in shreds. "I know. I heard the doctors in Germany. He's not going to get out of that bed. He's not going to stand up or walk, and he's never running another race. Ever…"

My head wouldn't stop shaking. "*No.* You don't know that. They put him in a coma to stabilize him. There're tests they're going to do. It's not over. They can't know anything until he wakes up."

"I know what I heard. What I saw. What I made happen." Connor's head dropped. "He's done, Autumn. He's fucking done."

"Don't *say* that," I cried, gripping Weston's hand tighter. "He's not done. Whatever happens next, he's not done."

"Well *I* am. I'm done." Connor stood up and dragged the back of his hand across one eye, then the other. "And us. We're done."

A jolt of electric shock and guilt danced over me at the words and I snatched my hand from Weston's as Connor stood up and headed for the door.

"Wait. You're *leaving*?"

"I'm going back to Boston."

I flew out of the chair, blocking his path. "What are you talking about? You can't leave Weston now."

"I can't stay here and see him like this."

"But...Connor," I whispered. "He's your best friend."

"Yeah and look what I did to him." He looked down at Weston and a muscle flickered in his jaw. "I can't stay here," he said through his teeth. "I'm going home."

He started to take a step. I pushed him back.

"What about us?"

"Jesus, Autumn. There is no us. There never was."

The words slapped my face. "What the hell does that mean?" Knowing, of course, exactly what it meant.

No more secrets.

I squared my shoulders. "Weston told you, didn't he?"

"Told me what?"

"About what happened the night of your deployment."

Connor's brows came together. "I don't know what you're talking about. I was plastered that night." His upper lip curled in a sneer. "Why? Did I fuck something up then too?"

"No, I..." My mouth was dry. "Look, maybe now's not the best time to tell you. Everything is so messed up and confusing. But I can't deal with any more secrets. We kissed. Weston and I. The night of your deployment." I took a breath and forced the rest of it out. "It was more than kissing, actually. We didn't sleep together but..."

Connor went on staring at me a moment, his expression unreadable. He glanced at Weston, back at me, and then a harsh, mirthless laugh burst from his chest. "Jesus Christ," he said to the ceiling.

"I'm sorry," I said. "I'm so sorry, Connor. I was drunk and scared for you both. It's no excuse, but it's what happened. And I take full responsibility for my actions..." My words trailed at his angry expression. "He really didn't tell you?"

"He didn't tell me shit."

"I thought that's why you're so upset with me."

LONG LIVE **the Beautiful Hearts**

"Upset with *you*?" He shook his head. "You don't get it, Autumn. Wes and I…"

"What?"

His green, shadowed eyes met mine, weighing a thousand different thoughts. "Nothing. It's none of my business. It never was my business, turns out. Never me. But I made you my business and I'm really sorry for that, Autumn."

"What are you talking about?"

"We're done," Connor said. "And it's for the best. You can't see it now, but you will. Soon."

He moved to the door.

"Wait," I said. "Connor, please don't do this."

He paused with his hand on the doorknob. "I'm going," he said. "You stay with him."

"Please don't…"

"Stay with him. And keep holding his hand, Autumn. No matter what happens. Don't let go of him."

He strode out without looking back.

CHAPTER Five

Autumn

"Propofol discontinued at nine-oh-three," the anesthesiologist said, his eyes on the digital wall clock.

I sat on one side of Weston's bed, Miranda and Paul on the other. Ruby perched on the padded window seat. Every pair of eyes glued to the clock's red numbers, and when they flipped to 9:04, Miranda turned an accusing gaze on Dr. Kowalczyk.

"He's not waking up. You said once they stopped that drug, he'd wake up."

Dr. K's smile was patient as he un-looped a stethoscope from around his neck and settled the ear pieces. He leaned over Weston's inert body and pressed the disc to his chest, listening. A moment of breath-held silence, except for the steady push-pull of the respirator.

Dr. K leaned closer. "Hey, Wes," he said loudly. "Can you hear me? Can you open your eyes for me, Wes?"

Nothing.

"Well?" Miranda's eyes were wide, her hands twisted in front of her.

"It takes time," Dr. K said mildly, standing straight and taking off the stethoscope again. "It could be anywhere from a few minutes to seventy-two hours. Given that he's been sedated for almost a week, and unconscious since the initial incident in Syria, I'd guess later rather than sooner. And there may be adverse reactions, as well."

"Such as?" Paul said.

"Wes might experience agitation, anxiety, maybe even aggression upon waking. It's all perfectly normal, but you should be prepared."

Miranda flapped her hand at the respirator tube still taped to Weston's mouth. "Why does he still need that machine breathing for him? That's normal too?"

"It is. We need Wes to wake up to determine if he's strong enough to breathe on his own."

Dr. K spoke a few more words with the anesthesiologist, who nodded then left the room.

"I have to attend to another patient," Dr. K said. He gestured toward the nurse. "Rhonda will be here for the next ten hours. I suggest you get some coffee or something to eat. Maybe go for a walk. It could be awhile."

"I'm not going anywhere," Miranda said, echoing my own thoughts.

"Very well. I'll be back to check on him soon."

Miranda took her son's hand between hers. "He's going to wake up any minute. Aren't you, baby? We're all here waiting for you." She lowered her voice. "Well, almost all of us."

"Now, now," Paul said. "Connor needs to rest and heal too. And of course Victoria needs to go with him, just like you're staying with Wes."

"Heal?" Miranda cried. "This is a hospital, for chrissakes. He can't stay here and *heal* for however long it takes my boy to wake up?" Tears filled her eyes. "Wes is going to want his best friend here. He should be here."

"Miranda, they've been through hell," Paul said. "Not one of us can say how Connor's suffering. We can't force him to do something he's not able to do."

Miranda shrugged and said under her breath, "He got him into this mess. He can't stay to watch him come out?"

My stomach did a back flip and Ruby shot me a surprised look, eyebrows raised.

"This isn't Connor's fault," Paul said in a stern voice. "This is no one's fault. This is what can happen when you sign up to fight. Wes knew the risks. We can't go back, only forward." His tone softened. "Blaming Connor won't make you feel better, honey."

Miranda sniffed but didn't answer.

An excruciating hour passed. Then two. Weston showed no signs of waking and Ruby leaned over to me.

"Come on, Auts. You need something to eat. Or a coffee, at least."

"I shouldn't leave him," I said. *Connor asked me not to. And I can't anyway.*

"You should go, sweetie," Paul said. "Then Miranda and I will grab a bite. He'll never be alone."

I hated to leave Weston but I felt adrift after the frightening email from the Army had tossed me into this Baltimore hospital and caught me up in a sea of emotion and turmoil. Ruby was like an island in the storm, and I realized not telling her the truth about what happened with Weston and me had been a bad idea.

"Just a coffee," I said.

"You're such a sweetheart to stay with us," Miranda said. "I thought you'd go with Connor too."

"I… Weston's my friend," I said.

Miranda settled back in her chair. "Glad to know someone still understands the meaning of the word."

Down in the cafeteria, Ruby took a single sip of coffee and said, "Talk to me, Goose."

"About?"

"Why *are* you still here instead of with Connor in Boston?"

I sucked in a breath and said in a rush, "He broke up with me."

Ruby sat up, her eyes wide. "No shit? Last night? Is that why he left?"

"Partly," I said. "Mostly he left because he agrees with Miranda that what happened to Weston is all his fault."

Ruby rolled her lower lip between her teeth. "Oh damn," she said. "And there's all this talk about Wes having spinal cord injuries."

"I think it might be bad, Ruby," I said in a watery voice. "Connor thinks so, and he would know. He was there when Weston was shot and with him in the hospital in Germany."

"Poor Wes. God, and there was talk of the Olympics, right? Holy shit…"

I nodded miserably, then straightened. "But we don't know for sure. The doctors have to do more tests. And they're the professionals. I keep telling myself I'm going to wait for their word then I go back to the fact Connor was there."

Ruby pursed her lips doubtfully, then reached her hand to mine. "I'm sorry about you and Connor. I know things have been up and down for you two but I never thought he'd bail now." She cocked her head, studying me. "Are you super sad about it?"

"I don't know what I feel. I love him. Loved?" I ran my hands through my hair. "God, everything is so tangled up."

"No matter what, he should be here for Wes," Ruby said, shaking her head. "Guilt aside, I can't believe he took off."

"Guilt might not be the only reason." I cast my gaze to my coffee.

"Oh?"

I squeezed my eyes shut and blurted the words. "I cheated on Connor. With Weston."

When I peeked at Ruby, her eyes were wide and her mouth hung ajar.

"You…really? *You?*" She leaned forward, her voice laden with shock. "You fucked Wes? Connor's best friend, Wes?"

"Thanks, Rube. Because I don't feel shitty enough as it is. We only kissed, but…"

The memory of Weston's body on top of mine, his kisses bruising my lips, his hips grinding into me, my skirt rising up, his hand between my thighs, feeling how badly I wanted him…

I blinked and hugged myself against the pleasant shivers that slipped over my skin, even now. Even here.

"I was drunk and we kissed and it was going to lead to more but he stopped it," I said. "But I'm not going to make excuses for myself. It was wrong and Connor has every right to hate me for it." I raised my eyes to my best friend. "Do you hate me for it?"

Ruby loosed a laugh and a disbelieving sigh. "Oh my God, girl. You only *kissed* him?"

"It's still cheating, Ruby, and I wasn't the one who stopped it."

She blew air out her cheeks. "Wow. I'm shocked. You said you and Wes were chummy but I didn't think it was more."

More. That was the word. There was more between Weston and me. More feelings that made no sense, more electricity, more fireworks, and more *want.* Pure, unfiltered want.

"I didn't think there was either, but something clicked that night," I said. "Something fell into place when I didn't know anything had been *out* of place."

Ruby frowned. "What do you mean?"

I turned my mug around and around. "I don't know. Things had been so weird with Connor. He was so fluent and rich in his letters and poems to me, but in person? Nothing. Or hardly anything. I began to have a terrible suspicion."

"About?"

"About those letters and poems." I looked up to Ruby. "When I try to imagine Connor sitting at a desk, pouring his heart out to me, I can't do it."

"Neither can I," Ruby said slowly. "He just doesn't seem built for it."

"But Weston does," I said. "But it can't be that he…I don't know, helped Connor? How does that even work? Helped him write a poem, maybe? I can see that, but those letters? All those letters…"

All those beautiful words and the feelings that bled through behind them.

A cold shiver slipped down my spine. "I can't believe that they would do that to me. Manipulate me like that. My feelings." I lowered my shaking voice. "I slept with Connor because he made me feel a certain way with his words. I gave him my body and later my heart. If it wasn't real…if it was a *prank*…"

Ruby was shaking her head. "And to keep it going for so long. Through fucking *war*."

"It makes me sick to think about it. But my physical connection with Weston felt almost…inevitable."

"Tequila will do that to a gal." Ruby shrugged. "But seriously, maybe Wes is into you. Like, a lot. Maybe he's the one doing all the smooth talking and Connor's reaping the rewards."

"But that's so *fucked up*," I said and had to lower my voice as an older woman at the next table shot me a look. "Weston cares about me so much that he ensures I sleep with his best friend?" I shook my head. "My brain—and heart—keep trying to go there, but it's a dead end. I can't, for the life of me, believe Weston would do that to me. Or that Connor would take advantage. I just can't."

Ruby's head bobbed up and down, her eyes wide. "You're right. That's a whole lotta fucked up. But, look, if what you suspect is remotely true, then you have to ask them. Flat out."

"Connor won't talk to me," I said. "It's too humiliating, all of it."

"Is that why he left?"

I shook my head. "No. At least, he said it wasn't but I don't know why. He was hurting. He's just come from a combat zone and surgery and now he's being discharged from the Army." I sighed. "I don't think he fully knows how he's feeling."

"How are *you* feeling?"

I raised my shoulders a little. "I don't think it's hit me yet. But I need Weston to wake up and be okay before I can worry about anything else. There's nothing more important." I glanced at my small silver watch and started to rise. "Speaking of which, we should get back to him…"

"I have to get back to Boston too," she said. "I have a zillion things to do before Italy, and my dad's birthday is Sunday. I'm mostly here for you anyway. Wes hardly knows me." She reached for my hand again. "Will you be okay?"

"Yeah, of course," I said, my heart sinking. "You should go if you need to. And give your dad a birthday hug from me."

"What about you?" Ruby asked. "How long are you going to stay in Baltimore? Wasn't Edmond expecting you back at the bakery?"

"Yes, but I can't leave Weston. I need to be here when he wakes up. Especially since Connor isn't here. It feels wrong to leave."

"And you need to ask him about the letters and poems, yeah? Your feelings matter too. I think you keep forgetting that."

"Weston's life could be changed forever," I said. "I can give him whatever time he needs to wake up and get through any news the doctors might have. That's the *very least* I can do."

Ruby sniffed. "I hope he's worth it. If he played you with Connor…"

"I'll contend with that later," I said. "One catastrophe at a time, if you please."

We rose from the table, and at the end of the cafeteria, she gave me a hug.

"Get your booty back to Massachusetts before I leave."

"You're not leaving for three weeks," I said.

"True, but I know how you get. You're going to want to help out here as much as you can, no matter how much it fucks up your own life."

"That's lovely, Rube," I said. "Can I put that on my resume?"

She laughed. "Just get back soon. I'm going to be running around like a madwoman, but I need at least three full girl days with you in our old place, watching movies, drinking wine, and talking men. Or cursing their names, one of the two."

I nodded and gave her another hug and watched her go with a kind of strange nostalgia. What she'd described felt so normal and light, and as I headed to the elevators, back to the ICU, I had the sharp knowing feeling that nothing was going to be normal or light for a very long time.

Sixteen hours after the Propofol was turned off, Weston still hadn't moved independently. Paul sat across from me doing a crossword puzzle from a small book he'd bought at the newsstand. Miranda sat on the window bench, watching *The Real Housewives of New York* on the wall-mounted TV and giving the occasional snort at the drama. As one in the morning came and went, Miranda yawned and rubbed her eyes.

"Let's go to the family room and sleep," Paul said. "It's just down the hall. If he wakes up, we can be here in a minute."

Miranda reluctantly nodded and hauled herself off the bench.

"You going to get some rest, kiddo?" Paul asked me.

"No, I'm not tired," I said, lying. I was exhausted, but the fear of Weston waking up in an empty room was unthinkable.

Stay with him. Don't let go.

Keep holding his hand.

"You're an angel," Miranda said, cracking a yawn.

Paul patted my shoulder and mouthed the words "Thank you" as they left.

I laid my head on the bed next to Weston's hand, glancing up at him over the small hills and valleys of the white sheets.

"You have to wake up now," I whispered. "You might not want to. It must be so safe where you are. But please, Weston. Wake up."

LONG LIVE the Beautiful Hearts

His chest rose and fell, pushed by the respirator that breathed for him. I felt my inhales and exhales fall into sync with his. My eyes drooped. My thoughts broke apart and finally, sleep pulled me under.

CHAPTER
Six

Weston

The racers line up on the track. I take my place in a middle lane. Autumn is on my left, looking stunningly beautiful in a green dress. The sun is setting behind her, turning her hair to golden fire, just like that afternoon we walked home from the bakery. Then, I'd stopped to stare, capturing how the light made a halo around her red hair. I carried that mental snapshot with me all through our training. All through the hot dusty days in Syria.

Now she's here. With me.

You have to wake up now, *she says, expression serious as she plants her fingers onto the track.* Please, Weston. Wake up.

Over her shoulder, in the lanes beyond, my mother and Paul line up. Senator Drake in a pantsuit, fitting her heels into the starting blocks.

I look to my right, where Connor should be. Instead, it's a body lying facedown on the track. Full desert camo and gear, an AR-15 gripped in his hand.

Bradbury, *I think, even as a shard of fear slides into my heart. The soldier is too big to be Bradbury, and on his wrist is a scar. Just like the one Connor got in high school metal shop.*

No…

LONG LIVE the Beautiful Hearts

The call to set comes and then the gun.

An unseen hand flattens me and I can't move as Autumn and everyone else runs ahead. My cheek is pressed to the track, my head turned to the body that doesn't move either.

Connor, wake up, *I scream but no sound comes out. I squeeze my eyes shut and hear a child's crying, men shouting, and gunfire.*

It was supposed to be me...

A bomb explodes. No sound, yet the track erupts in a million pieces. Fire and smoke and blood. I'm blasted into a void where up is down. I fall up, *propelled by an explosion that turns my lower back into a burning knot of agony.*

Up into the zenith of the void, toward a tiny pinprick of light. Light that gets brighter and hotter and bigger. It sears my eyes and I'd swim away but I can't move. I'm flung up faster and faster until I crash into a wall of light and sound.

And more pain.

Weston, open your eyes.

Then I'm falling backward and the rough, rocky desert floor rushes up to meet me.

I'm going to crash.

Weston.

I'm going to die.

Wake up, Weston...

My eyes flared open and my body spasmed in a rictus of panic. Terror surged through my veins as I slammed into the ground.

Not the ground, a bed.

My brain registered white sheets, blinking lights, repetitive beeping. Then pain sliced me in half at the waist. I tried to scream but something on my mouth and down my throat pushed air into my lungs instead. I was drowning and being revived at the same time.

"Weston."

A voice in my head. Soft and green.

"Weston, look at me."

The voice was outside my head now. I reached for it. I needed it. I couldn't let it run away down the track without me, in a dress like spring but hair like...

Autumn?

I flailed after it, trembling and shaking, every tremor bringing another wave of agony.

"Easy, now." A different woman's voice. Harder. Authoritative. Hands pushed me down at the shoulders. "Calm down," she said. "That's it. Nice and easy. Don't fight the machine."

A low moan filled my head. Me. A guttural groan in my throat, squeezing between the inhales and exhales I couldn't control. All the while, thin slices of light came and went.

Those are my eyes. I'm opening and closing my eyes.

I'm in here.

This is me.

The pain. Holy fuck, the pain. A molten sledgehammer to my lower back, again and again.

"Weston," Autumn said. Cool fingers folded around my hand. "It's all right. Try to lie back."

Slowly my brain put things together. A bed with white sheets and beeping machines. This was a hospital. And Autumn was here.

"Autumn," I said. Or tried to. Whatever was in my mouth and down my throat blocked the word. I gagged as more air pushed in. A constant push-pull invasion I couldn't stop fighting.

"I'll call the attending," said the other woman, who must've been a nurse. "Just stay with him. Keep talking and help get him oriented."

Stay with me, Autumn. Forever.

My eyes fought to stay open. A plastic tube and white tape obscured my vision, but through and around it, I saw her. Standing over me with her red hair falling down around her shoulders. Like a beautiful, peaceful dream after months of a recurring nightmare.

"Hey," she said softly. Her little fingers twined with mine, her other palm ran smooth over my forehead. "You're all right."

No, I thought. *My back. Something is really fucking wrong with my back...*

"Just listen to my voice." Her touch so soft on my head. "You're on a ventilator. Okay? It's breathing for you. Try not to fight it. I'm right here. Keep listening to me. I'm going to tell you what happened. All right?"

I blinked my eyes because I was too weak to nod.

"You're at the Walter Reed Medical Center in Baltimore," she said. "You were injured in Syria. You were flown out to Germany first. Now you're here. The respirator is to help you breathe until you come out of the sedation. That's all."

Tears blurred my vision and I blinked hard, felt them slide down my cheek. Autumn reached out her hand and wiped one away, clutched it in her fist, as her own tears brimmed and then fell on the white sheet covering me. Despite her encouraging words, her beautiful face crumpled in pain.

Because Connor's dead.

I flinched at the thought and another bolt of agony lanced through my back. I couldn't cry out or curse at it, only manage a strangled sound past the goddamn tube in my throat. I pulled my hand from Autumn's and mimed writing in the air with an invisible pen.

"You want to write something. Hold on, let me look…"

Autumn disappeared from my line of sight and my hand fell back to the bed. The terror had receded, leaving my entire body heavy with pain and exhaustion. Immovable.

She reappeared and pressed a pen into my fingers. "Here."

She gently lifted my hand and I felt it rest again on a small pad of paper. The pen weighed a thousand pounds, but I scratched out the word.

Connor

Autumn read what I wrote, and her face contorted into horrified realization.

"Oh, God, I'm so sorry. You didn't know. Connor's fine. He's okay," she said quickly and blinked back tears. "He's here," Autumn said. "I mean, he's going home. He was discharged yesterday and his mother is taking him back to Boston tonight. His arm was broken pretty badly, but he's okay. He's all right, Weston, I promise. He's alive."

My eyes fell shut in soul-deep relief.

I did it. I won. Sock Boy is fucking dead forever.

I had only a moment to savor the triumph before my mother's screeching voice filled the room. Tears spilled over as she took my head in her hands and kissed my face. My mom. Memories of safety and love from my childhood played on fast-forward—scraped knees and the time I slammed my fingers in the car door. She was there for me. She was here now.

Over her heaving shoulders, I saw Paul, smiling tightly as he swiped at the corners of his eyes. He and Mom were here, Autumn was here, and Connor was all right.

"Hey there, Wes." A tall man in blue scrubs and a white coat was at the side of the bed now. "I'm Dr. Kowalczyk. Let's take a look at you…"

He shone a light in my eyes and all I wanted was to let go, fall away and sleep without dreams, but the agony in my back wouldn't let up, it was starting to gnaw my bones.

I fumbled for the dropped pen and scratched on the pad.

Hurts

"He's in pain," Autumn said, turning the pad around. "Can you give him something?"

The doctor shined a light in my eyes while talking about morphine with the nurse, and a few more chaotic minutes later, a warm wave smoothed over the broken, rocky shore of the pain, and I started to drift away. Far away, except that Autumn held my hand, so I knew I'd come back again.

My mouth felt strange around the breathing tube. I realized I was smiling. Or trying to. I kept drifting. Across the distance, I heard my mother speak.

"I want the truth. Is he going to walk again or not?"

Walk again…

Fear shot through my heart, deep and ugly. But I was drifting too far, too fast. I clutched at Autumn's hand, but I couldn't feel her anymore. She was disappearing down the track. My thoughts trying to run after her but breaking and scattering. Except for one.

Sock Boy wasn't dead after all. He was here, like a malevolent entity haunting a goddamn dresser drawer. Laughing at me as I floated and flailed, lost in space with no hand to hold.

I'm not going anywhere…and neither are you.

CHAPTER Seven

Autumn

Silvery light slanted into Weston's room when I slipped in the next morning, two coffees in hand. I set one on Rhonda's station and she smiled gratefully.

"He's sleeping," she mouthed.

I wanted to sit by him and hold his hand—*just like Connor asked*—but Dr. K ordered Weston's respirator taken out earlier this morning, an ordeal that left Weston gagging and exhausted. I sat on the window seat with my coffee and kept a tight vigil on his chest. It rose and fell evenly as he took his own breaths.

"He's doing great," Rhonda said.

I nodded with a faint smile. *For now.*

Later today, the orthopedic team would test the severity of Weston's spinal cord damage. Dr. K insisted we not panic until the tests were done, but Connor's words haunted me.

I can tell you right now he'll never walk again.

My gaze moved from Weston's chest to his long legs under the sheets, willing them to move or twitch, then making excuses when they didn't.

He's been through hell. He's on morphine. He's too weak right now.

My chest literally ached with the stress, and with Ruby back in Boston, I had no one to reassure me or commiserate with.

And I missed Connor. He'd been gone for months. I'd had him back for a handful of hours—full of pain and confrontation and ugliness. Now he was gone again. I needed him. Moreover, Weston needed him.

"Morning, soldier," Rhonda said softly.

Weston was stirring, head moving side to side and one hand rising briefly, then falling on his lap. His eyes opened at the scuff of my feet on the linoleum. The shadowed, haunted gaze followed me as I sat in the bedside chair. His cracked lips parted with an intake of breath, but I shook my head.

"No talking," I said.

My voice was scratchy with tears, yet an unexpected happiness crashed over me with the dawn of this new day where maybe something amazing would happen, like my dad always promised. Weston was alive. Horribly, maybe irrevocably injured, but alive.

"God, you're here," I said.

You came back to me…

He nodded faintly and all that he didn't know was suddenly between us, heavy and thick. My happiness soured and curled at the realizations awaiting him.

I'll be here for him. Whatever the news, I won't leave him to take it alone.

Weston's bleary eyes circled the empty room. "Where's Connor?"

"He's in Boston."

His gaze dropped down to his legs that were so impossibly still. Like a mannequin's. His fingers plucked at the sheet covering them.

"The doctors will be in soon," I said quickly. "With your mom. And I think your sisters are coming today."

With tired slowness, Weston's hand slid along one thigh and his finger tapped it.

"Tell me," he said hoarsely, his eyes wide and full of fear. The crack in my heart widened and went deeper to see the abject fear in his eyes.

"I'd better let the doctor explain."

Weston's head moved side to side. "I've lost time. I was in the desert. Now I'm here. I don't know what's happened to me and I can't..." His voice broke to a whisper. "Autumn, I can't move my legs."

"Weston..."

"Please." He swallowed hard. "Tell me."

My glance shot to the door and back, willing a doctor to appear and do this with professionalism and reassurance. I had neither. But Weston and I had always been ourselves around each other. Two scholarship kids who struggled to make ends meet and who hated taking charity but would freely give it. He needed the truth and I was the only one there to tell it.

"You were shot four times," I said. "One bullet pierced your gall bladder. One shattered your right hip. One struck your thigh. The thigh shot nearly bled you out. You had three surgeries in Germany. Then the gall bladder wound released toxins that caused a serious infection, so they had to put you in a medically-induced coma to keep you stable while they flew you home. It's a miracle you're alive."

"The fourth shot."

It wasn't a question. My heart crashed against my ribs.

I don't want to tell him, but I'm the only one who can tell him. I'm the one that's here.

"Autumn..." His eyes were pleading. "The fourth shot...?"

I drew a breath. Then the door swung open on a wave of sound. Miranda Turner and her daughters poured into the room like squawking birds, bickering with each other, while the desk nurse admonished them to quiet down.

"Don't you shush me," Miranda said over her shoulder. "Oh, baby, you're awake. Thank God."

"Hi, Ma," Weston whispered.

"Can't hardly talk, can you, baby? They said the breathing tube hurt your vocal cords on top of everything else. Can't talk. Can't walk. What's next, huh? I thought they were supposed to be making you *better*."

My teeth clenched and I had to fight the urge to throw my coffee at her.

Goddammit to hell, Miranda. Not like this. He can't hear it like this.

Weston stared at his mother. Not saying a word, but the beeping from the monitors sped up and the spiked lines registering his pulse moved closer together.

"Ma, shut up and stop freaking out." Felicia, Weston's oldest sister, looked tired in an old Sox sweatshirt and jeans. "We don't know the whole story." She bent down to give her brother a nervous peck on the cheek. "No matter what, you're alive. That's all that matters, right?"

Weston went on staring as his other sister, Kimberly, bent to kiss him. "You look good, Wes," she said through a smile stretched to the breaking point. "Really good." Both her voice and her grin broke and she turned away, stifling her sobs.

Weston's jaw was trembling now, his hands clutching white-knuckled around the bed sheet. I pried the one closest to me free and twined those tight fingers with mine.

Paul arrived then, thank God. Laden with Starbucks cups, he immediately read the situation and moved the Turner women away from the bed. Once he got them situated at the room's little table with coffee, he came back to Weston's bedside.

"How you doing?" he asked, his smile gentle. "Hanging in there?"

Weston didn't answer. He stared straight ahead at nothing. Or maybe at whatever future awaited. He stayed silent and still until the orthopedic team arrived.

"I'm Dr. Harris," said one doctor, older with a graying beard. "These are Doctors McCully and Anderson. We're going to conduct a few tests, which will give you answers I'm sure you've been waiting to hear."

Weston's beautiful blue-green ocean eyes were bright with fear. "What happened to my back?" he rasped out.

Dr. Harris pulled up a chair to sit eye-level with Weston.

"The MRI and CT scans taken at Landstuhl Medical Center showed a fracture of the vertebrae and compression on the spinal cord at the L3—or lumbar—level. Surgery to remove the bullet alleviated the compression, but they were not able to assess how much damage had occurred."

"Why not? Why is everything taking so long?" Miranda demanded.

Dr. Harris's calm gaze stayed on Weston as if he'd been the one to ask. "Typically, we conduct these tests within seventy-two hours from the point of injury. But you had other, more life-threatening injuries that needed tending first. In fact, it's something of a miracle you're with us at all. Whoever took care of you in the field saved your life."

"There was a blast," Weston whispered, his face pale. "I don't remember anything after that."

"Your platoon medic would have documented everything, I'm sure." Now Harris turned to address all the family members. "We're going to need everyone to step outside for a bit—"

"No way, José," Miranda said, crossing her arms. "I've been pushed around and kept away from my son long enough."

"Ma." Weston closed his eyes.

"I heard about these tests. You're going to poke him with needles and put ice on his skin or something."

"Correct," Dr. Harris said. "We'll be conducting pinprick and light touch tests to assess the nerve damage and which muscle groups are affected. And we'll be doing them privately and without distraction."

"He's my son," Miranda said. "I want to be here for him—"

"You are going to be here for him," Paul said. "In the waiting area. We're stepping out, Miranda. Right now."

I'd never heard him use such a tone with her. Miranda stared for a moment, then gave a quick nod.

"You're right," she said, getting up. "Of course. I'm just so worried. Come on, girls, Wes needs privacy." She bent to kiss his cheek as if both the tests and the stepping out were all her idea. Paul gave one last squeeze on Weston's shoulder before he followed them out.

I wanted to tell Weston everything would be all right, but it felt like a lie. Instead I pressed my lips to the back of his hand and gave him the one truth I had: "I'll be right back."

We gathered in the waiting area, no one saying a word. Connor's ominous prediction turned over and over in my head. Every time I tried to brush it aside and remain hopeful, the words swooped in like a gigantic hand, swatting at my tiny flicker of hope.

Paul leaned into me. "Would you hate me if I played Solitaire on my phone? If I don't, I'm going to Google *spinal cord injuries* and make myself sick."

"Go for it," I said gratefully. "I'll watch."

For an hour, every head stayed buried in a phone, numbing our brains with pointless, soothing crap. Finally, the orthopedic team emerged from Weston's room. They stayed huddled by the door a moment, conferring with crossed arms and unsmiling faces.

"Oh, God," I whispered.

Paul took my hand. "Whatever they say, Wes can pull through it. He's tough. He'll be okay." His warm brown eyes met mine. "He's lucky to have you here."

I took the smallest bit of comfort in that; comfort that ebbed away as the team joined us in the waiting area to tell us the results.

"We have good news and not so good news," Dr. Harris said, sitting in a chair. "The good news is the spinal cord injury is incomplete. Meaning the cord is not severed."

"Well, that's great," Paul said. "Isn't it?"

"It's what we expected after the MRI. But today's tests confirm the cord has been damaged. Wes is an ASIA B classification. ASIA is the impairment scale we use to gauge the level of damage," he said, answering our confused looks, then blew out his cheeks. "I'll be frank; there is damage and it's extensive."

"Jesus," Felicia breathed, and Kimberly burst into tears.

"Oh God." Miranda clapped her hand to her mouth.

"Wes has suffered what we call anterior cord syndrome," Dr. Harris said. "He retains some sensory function in his legs, though a pinprick feels the same to him as a feather brushing his skin. He cannot feel pain. He cannot feel temperature. He does retain proprioception, meaning he is aware of his legs' position in space. However…"

The word hung in the air. My heart pounded in my chest. The room was a train speeding toward a brick wall and Dr. Harris wasn't applying the brakes.

"At this time," he said, "Wes has no motor capabilities of any kind."

He'll never walk again.

"You mean he can't walk," Miranda said, her voice rising. "That's what you're saying? My baby can't walk?"

Paul's hand on mine tightened as Miranda collapsed on his other shoulder.

"No, he cannot walk," Dr. Harris said.

The train smashed into the brick wall in an explosion of metal and fire.

"We can't yet call this permanent," the doctor continued over

LONG LIVE the Beautiful Hearts

Miranda's low wails. "No two incomplete SCIs look the same. Wes might show vast improvement in one or more areas. We won't know the final outcome until after rehabilitation. But at this moment, the odds of him walking again without aid are extremely slim."

"So what's next?" Paul asked, lifting his chin. "You said rehab?"

My eyes fixed on the floor and my mind shied away from Harris explaining the level of care Weston would need from now on. Weeks of inpatient therapy, a urologist, a psychologist. Months of outpatient occupational and recreational therapy to learn to adjust to his paralysis and how to navigate life from a wheelchair.

Weston in a wheelchair.

His lean, tall, runner's body forever folded, his legs that carried him so far and so fast, forever stilled.

"He's alone right now," I blurted, standing up. "He shouldn't be alone."

Dr. Harris held up a hand. "Before you go, let me advise... I know this is hard to hear and incredibly upsetting. But most paraplegics go on to live fulfilling lives. When you go back to see Wes, go calmly. You're in as much shock as he is. Be truthful but offer as much optimism and support as you can."

My mind coupled *paraplegic* with *wheelchair,* and I had to fight the urge to run down the hall, Weston's family behind me. We went quietly back into Weston's room, filing around his bed.

"Hey, baby," Miranda said, kissing his head. "Mama's here. You're going to be just fine."

I took Weston's hand, gnawing my lower lip and fighting the urge to scream at her, *That's not true and he knows it!*

Kimberly turned away, her shoulders trembling. Felicia stared at her brother with her lips pressed together, shaking her head slowly from side to side. Weston stared straight up at the ceiling. More motionless and more silent than he'd been when he was in a coma.

A rattle of knuckles on the door and an Army officer in dress uniform stepped in.

"Are you the Turner family?"

"God, now what?" Miranda muttered.

"Yes, sir," Paul said. "Can we help you?"

The officer smartly held out a leather folder.

"It is my pleasure to inform you that Corporal Turner, in the name of the President of the United States, has been awarded the Purple Heart for his service and sacrifice."

Weston's hand in mine tightened, and his eyes fell shut.

"It is also my honor to inform Corporal Turner that he's been awarded the Bronze Star for meritorious service in a combat zone. Ceremony information, date, and location are contained therein."

"Thank you," Paul said, taking the folder. "Thank you very much."

The officer saluted Weston who kept his gaze on the ceiling and departed.

Miranda took the folder and opened it to show Weston. "Did you hear that, baby? A Purple Heart and the Bronze Star for heroic deeds in the line of duty."

"Whoop dee fuckin' do," Felicia muttered. "They take his legs and give him a little trinket instead."

"It's not even gold," Kimberly said. "Bronze? Isn't that, like, third place?"

"You both shut your mouths," Miranda said. "Show some respect."

"Everyone get out," Weston whispered.

The room was now filled with the Turners cawing and bickering, and only I heard him. I rose to my feet, but Weston's hand gripped mine hard and pulled until I sat back down.

"*Everyone out*," he gritted through his teeth.

His family ceased their noise and turned.

"What is it, honey?" Miranda asked. "You need something? Paul, go get him a drink, his voice sounds terrible—"

"I said, get out," Weston said, sucking air through his nose. "Now. Get out. All of you."

Miranda looked affronted. "Surely not me…"

"Out," Weston said, breathing hard through his mouth now. The beeping on the machines sped up.

"Come on," Paul said. "He wants to be alone. Let's go. All of you."

Gently but firmly, he shepherded the mutters and murmurs of protest, Miranda wondering out loud who didn't want their mom in a time of crisis…?

"Autumn?" Paul asked over his shoulder.

"Not her," Weston said. "She stays."

Something between approval and relief passed over Paul's face before he left. When the door finally shut, Weston turned his head to me, his eyes wide and lit with panic.

"I know, Weston," I said, scooting closer. "Breathe."

He shook his head, his chest rising and falling too rapidly, his breath gusting in and out of him.

"I know," I told him. "God, I know but breathe, Weston. Come on." I took his hand and laid it to my chest, over my heart, then put mine over his. "Breathe with me. Slowly. Inhale…exhale…"

Weston's chest rose under my hand in time with mine as he mastered his emotions. A warm tear slid down his cheek to my palm.

"I know," I said again, moving closer to him. "I'm sorry. I'm so sorry…"

I put my arms around him as best I could. There had always been a feeling between us—or maybe it was just me—that we'd known each other forever, and it erased the distance between us; even the silence during his deployment.

Nothing else matters. Not the kiss, not the confusion. The letters, the poems, the words, the silence. It's not important. This *is all that matters.*

He held me tight, clinging to my sweatshirt, his breath rasping in his nose. Anger at Connor suffused me all over again. Connor *mattered.* He was Weston's best friend. He should have been hugging him and making jokes to make him laugh. And if jokes were impossible, he should have just *been* there for him in these first terrible moments where a door in Weston's life slammed shut behind him, to remain locked forever.

Wes pulled away and wiped his eyes on the shoulder of his hospital shirt. Already his gaze was going back up to the ceiling. The moment of weakness was over and his armor was pulling around him. His defense made an electric humming in the air.

"You can go," he said.

"I don't need to—"

"Go. I need to be alone."

"Are you sure?"

"Yes."

I wiped my own eyes and stood straight. "All right. I'll be here if you need me. Right outside the door."

He said nothing, his gaze fixed upward.

57

"Okay," I said in a small voice.

I walked calmly to the women's bathroom down the hall, shut the stall door and burst into tears.

CHAPTER Eight

Weston

They moved me from the ICU to a regular room in the hospital. I had a view of the parking lot and twilight's amber light falling over the lined-up cars. I dozed now and then but didn't dream.

I thought that damn track dream that haunted me all through deployment meant I was going to die in Syria.

I did. I'm alive but my life is fucking over.

For the millionth time that day, I strained to move my legs. Bend my knees, wiggle my toes, *anything.* The disconnection to my limbs defied description. I could feel my legs were *there* but I wasn't in them. They were outlines of flesh and muscle and bone. A hyper-realistic sculpture. Dead weight.

Anxiety pressed a hand down on my chest. I closed my eyes and recalled the exam earlier that morning. The doctors held a sheet in front of my face so I couldn't see where they touched me or with what.

"Can you feel that, Wes?" Dr. Harris had asked.

I felt…something. A poke. A twinge. I pounced on it, full of hope, saying, "*Yes.* That. I felt something. That's good, right?"

Harris frowned. "Do you feel any pain?"

"No." From the look on his face, I knew it wasn't good. "Do it harder. Whatever the fuck you're doing, do it harder."

Then from behind the sheet, he held up a five-inch needle. "I depressed this three inches into your quadriceps muscle."

Fuck.

A needle three inches straight into muscle felt like faint pressure, nebulous and indistinct.

"Do it again," I said. "Do it somewhere else."

They did. The needle went into my shin, my calf, the bottom of my foot—and the sensation was the same. A feather touch when I should've felt pain.

They put an ice pack on my thigh and I felt only the faintest of pressure. No cold. They put a heating pad on my knee. Same. Pressure, but no temperature.

Incomplete SCI. Months of rehab to *maybe* someday walk with braces and crutches. I imagined my future self taking slow, halting steps, dragging scaffolded legs behind me as my arms struggled to carry the weight. And that was my *best*-case scenario. The more likely reality was me sitting in a wheelchair for the rest of my life.

You'll never catch that car now, Sock Boy.

The doctors reassured me that paraplegics went on to live happy, fulfilling lives, but the pitiful words were drowned out by the rushing of blood to my ears. I turned my gaze to the ceiling and stopped talking. Finally they left but then my family returned. With Autumn…

She held me through the first panicked grief, but then I had to let her go.

I have to let her go.

The sun was sinking deeper. I fixated on my legs again, clinging to the idea that I could feel them. But no pain. If only I could feel pain in my legs, I might be okay.

At my bedside table was a pad of paper, a pen, water cups, and a vase of flowers from Autumn. I stared at the pen and was getting an idea when one of the nurses, Gina, came in to check on me.

"Dinner will be served in about an hour," she said. "Your first solid meal, if you count yogurt or Jell-O as solid. You hungry?"

"No," I said.

"You need to eat," Gina said, checking IV lines and my temperature. "To keep your strength up so we can assess your bowel function. How's the pain?"

At the small of my back was an ache that throbbed in time to my heartbeat. I had plenty of pain but not where I wanted it. My gaze went back to the pen on the bedside table.

"What's your pain number?" Gina asked. "One to ten."

Ten going on a hundred.

"Wes?" She leaned a little closer.

I looked away from the pen and up at her. "Three," I said.

"Really?" Her smile widened. "That's great. After the hubbub of moving up here, I thought you'd be needing a stronger dose."

I shook my head. I needed to be able to feel as much as I could. My own little pinprick test.

Gina fussed with the tubes and lines and checked the piss bag strapped to the side of the bed. I kept my gaze locked on the ceiling.

"I'll be back when the food arrives. You let me know if the pain worsens. I expect you're going to want something tonight to help you sleep." Gina stopped her ministrations and touched my arm. "You sure you don't want any visitors? Your family is still here, ready any time you are."

I shook my head.

"I'll be back in a bit."

One last pat on my arm and she left. As soon as the door clicked shut, I reached for the pen, ignoring the flare of pain in my back. It was a cheap ballpoint. I clicked the nib out, threw back the bed sheet and stabbed myself in the thigh.

I watched with surreal detachment as an inch of the pen disappeared into my flesh. I felt absolutely nothing in my leg, but an icy hot sensation flooded my chest, so intense that my upper body went rigid.

I just gave myself a heart attack.

The monitors started going crazy, lighting up and beeping like pinball machines. Gina rushed back in, followed by Dr. K. The strange, cold fever went on burning a hole in my chest, leaving me nauseous and short of breath, yet all I could see was the pen buried in my leg. All I cared about was the *nothing* of it.

I feel nothing in my leg.

"Autonomic dysreflexia," the doctor muttered. He got in my face, kind but stern. "You can't do this to yourself, Wes. Your legs can't feel pain like this but your body can."

What difference does it make? I thought as they fussed over me and put something in my IV—I was suddenly being dragged into unconsciousness. Warm hands reached up from under the bed and started dragging me under.

There had been no pain. Not where it counted.

But the pain in the marrow of my being, in my soul, howled with unending force, even in the dark.

They took away my pen.

The pad of paper on the table was blank. A fitting metaphor, I thought, for what was left of me. I woke from the drug-induced sleep with the yawning realization that I'd lost more than my ability to walk. The pulsing need to write; the burning flame that hadn't been extinguished, not even in the desert of war, was dead now. Dead like my legs.

I was a runner with no legs.

I had paper but no pen.

It's gone. All of it.

Night had fallen outside the window, black and thick. The time on the wall monitor showed after midnight.

This is punishment for chasing after what wasn't mine. For using my writing to manipulate and deceive. To make Connor feel worthless. To hurt Autumn. I hurt the woman I loved when I swore I'd never do that.

Never love anyone.

I shouldn't love anyone.

The night shift nurse, Cynthia, checked my fluids, lines, and took my blood pressure. Since my adventures with a ballpoint, I was on a twenty-four-hour watch with a psych-eval waiting for me in the morning.

Cynthia wasn't like Gina. Gina was all soft smiles and warm words. Cynthia was no-nonsense and watched me like a hawk. She would've been at home at Basic Training.

"You should be sleeping," she said, adjusting the pillow behind my head.

"Who's in the waiting room?" I asked.

Tell me Connor's out there. Please. Tell me my best friend came back.

"Usual suspects. Sisters, mother, father—"

"He's not my father."

Cynthia pursed her lips. "I know you're hurting, but you might want to take a little inventory of what you still got."

"Who else?"

"A pretty red-haired girl." Cynthia raised her brows. "Your girlfriend?"

Autumn is my girlfriend.

The thought belonged to someone else, to a life that had nothing to do with me.

"Could you ask her to come in?"

Cynthia's lips pressed together in her version of a smile. "It's after midnight. But she's there, and I'm going to take this request as progress."

She went out. A few moments later, Autumn came in.

"Twenty minutes," Cynthia said. "Then he needs to sleep."

Autumn pulled a chair beside me. "Hey."

She looked like hell. Exhausted. And God, she was beautiful. Her hair in a messy ponytail, her face scrubbed of makeup, wearing soft pants and a T-shirt. All that worry and fatigue in her hazel eyes was for me. She'd stayed here all this time for me, and I'd never seen anything more fucking beautiful in my life.

Her gaze rested on my thigh, which bore four stitches I hadn't needed Novocaine to get.

"God, Weston…"

"I had to see for myself."

"Don't do anything like that again. Ever."

"I won't."

"Promise me."

"I promise."

The empty words cost me nothing. I wouldn't drive a pen into my leg again because now I knew there was no point.

"I'm so sorry," she said. "You're strong. You're going to make it through this—"

"Where's Connor?" I asked. "Tell me the truth this time."

"I told you the truth last time. He's in Boston."

I held her gaze. "Now tell me the whole truth."

"His elbow was shattered and they had to replace it. He had a severe concussion as well and he's showing signs of PTSD. He's been honorably discharged from the Army."

Good.

"Is the PTSD why he's not here?" I asked, mentally bracing myself for the answer. "It's bad?"

"I don't think it's the time to tell you."

"I'm not going anywhere," I said darkly. "Tell me."

She bit her lip, then drew in a deep breath. "He thinks this is his fault. What happened to you, I mean."

I stared at her a moment, then rolled my head to stare at the ceiling. "So why are you still here?"

For a split second, I indulged in a fantasy where Connor told Autumn our truth. He told her everything, she forgave him and she was here at my bedside because what Connor said was true. Autumn was in love with me.

She's in love with my soul, he said. *And my soul is you.*

I crushed the idea. There was no Autumn and me, no kind of *us*, fantasy or not. I was wrecked. If I'd had nothing to offer her before, I had even less now. Not even pretty words.

"I'm here because I'm your friend," she said.

"And you're Connor's girlfriend," I said.

"I'm not his girlfriend," she said. "He broke up with me."

My stupid fucking heart tripped over itself. I stared at her a long time before asking, "Why?"

"He wouldn't say. At least, he wouldn't give a reason that made sense." She ran fingertips under her brimming eyes. "It hurts more than I thought it would. Or maybe it hurts just the right amount. I loved him. And I thought he loved me." She sat back and leveled her gaze at me. "His letters made me think he did."

"He did," I whispered and stared at the blank pad of paper without a pen on the table beside me. "He loved you so much. But it's too late now."

"What does that mean?"

I shook my head.

"Weston." Her hand fell on my arm. "Look at me."

I did, falling into her hazel eyes. Emerald and gold flecks on velvet brown.

"Ever since we began dating," she said, "Connor was one way in person and another on paper. And I began to have this suspicion that…that I was being played. More than played. *Manipulated.* In the worst way. I can't believe it and yet I can't stop thinking about it. I don't know what to think. I'm *scared* of what I think. So now you tell me the truth. Did Connor write those poems and letters to me?"

Here it was. The truth, waiting to be set free. I heard the question behind the question.

Did you *write those poems and letters to me?*

I wanted so badly to confess. To let her hate me cleanly. But the hurt was bright and sharp in her eyes. The betrayal would cut her to the core. She'd slept with Connor because of me, and the wrongness of what we'd done crashed into me harder than a bullet.

"Weston?"

"It was him. I don't write," I said, giving her my new truth. "I can't write."

She held my gaze, studying me, and in that moment, I knew she believed me. Because we were friends. Because she trusted me. The sigh of relief, the tension leaving her shoulders told me I made the right decision. I may have lied to her face but it was better than hurting her with the truth.

I need to hurt her one last time, to keep from hurting her ever again.

"You can leave now," I said.

She nodded. "You're tired? You must be. I'll let you get some sleep."

"No. I mean you can go back to Amherst."

"I don't have to yet."

"I want you to."

"Classes don't start again for a few—"

"You're going to put your life on hold for me? No job? No place to stay?"

"I can figure it out," she said. "I don't want you to be alone."

I closed my eyes at her attempts to break down the wall with her soft words. "Go back to school," I said into the darkness. "Go save the world."

"Weston, what are you—?"

I whipped my head to her. "Did you hear me?" My voice—still scratchy from the breathing tube—raked across the air. "I said, get out."

Autumn flinched and sat back in her chair. "I know you're

upset," she said. "More than upset. You're devastated. I understand. But don't shut me out."

I said nothing. Stared at the ceiling.

"Weston, please talk to me. I can't take any more silence. From you or Connor."

It's better, Autumn. Better for you. Our silence is better than our lies.

I stared at a spot on the wall, putting my entire focus there so I wouldn't have to feel her pain.

"That's it?" she said. "You really have nothing else to say to me?"

I didn't. I left it all in a poem in the desert, written in blood and tears.

"Get out, Autumn."

She gasped slightly. I turned my head and forced myself to meet her eyes.

The night before deployment came roaring back. When I kissed her for the first time and every fucking wish of my heart came true all at once. I'd nearly taken her then and there on the couch with Connor passed out in the next room, because some part of me must've known it was my first and last chance.

You're out of chances, Sock Boy. Now finish it.

"Are you fucking deaf?" I said. "*Get. The fuck. Out.*"

Autumn shook her head. "You're trying to push me away. This isn't you…"

"This is me. This is exactly me and it's my voice saying in my words that you need to get the fuck out of this room."

And there it is, ladies and gents. The Amherst Asshole's triumphant comeback.

Everything soft in her face hardened and died before my eyes. All that was sweet turned sour.

It's better this way. It's better…

She pressed her lips together as tears spilled down her cheeks. "If that's what you want."

"That's what I want."

No! I want you…

"Then I'll go. And I wish you all the best. Please…take care of yourself."

One last time, our eyes caught and held. Unblinking.

LONG LIVE the Beautiful Hearts

Unrelenting.

Say goodbye to me, Autumn.

"Goodbye, Weston."

I forced myself to watch her go. The door clicked shut, like a key turning in a prison cell. The silence grew thick and suffocating.

With a primal scream of rage, my arm snaked out and swept the dinner tray of uneaten food to the floor, likely adding another entry in my psych-eval in the morning.

Cynthia came back in and surveyed the mess. "You're nothing but trouble, aren't you?"

I closed my eyes and willed the world to disappear. *I'm nothing but trouble.*

I'm nothing.

CHAPTER Nine

Autumn

Never again.

It was my new vow. My mantra I repeated to myself during the flight from Baltimore back to Boston and on the bus ride from Boston to Amherst. I had to keep my thoughts full of something, anything, but how much leaving Weston hurt.

I'd stayed at the hospital through the next morning, in case Weston had changed his mind or had gotten some rest after the first shock of his paralysis had dimmed a little. But he'd been adamant, and my heart tore in half again. For him, but for me too.

Never again will I let my heart become someone else's plaything.

Never again will I let romantic notions and longings dictate my actions.

Never again will I let a man—or men—come between me and my goals.

Never again will I love without feeling the fullness of that love in return.

No doubts, no questions, no uncertainty. If that takes a lifetime, so be it. In the meanwhile, I have work to do.

I let myself into my apartment, left my rolling suitcase at the

L O N G   L I V E the Beautiful Hearts

door and headed straight for my desk. Connor's letters were strewn all over. I scooped them together and carried them to the kitchen trashcan. The lid flipped open, waiting. I squeezed my eyes shut, still committed to my new vows, but I felt on some deep, instinctive level that if I threw those letters away, I'd regret it someday.

They're part of my history.

I let the trashcan lid fall shut and took the letters to my bedroom. From underneath my bed, I pulled the wooden keepsake box my mother gave me when I was ten. It had my name elegantly burned into the top and flowers and vines climbing over the sides. I set Connor's letters on top of photos and ticket stubs, letters from old penpals and a pearl necklace I'd inherited from my grandma. No trash here, only treasure.

I shut the box, shoved it back under my bed and returned to my desk in the living area. It was clean now, uncluttered and ready for real work.

I set up my laptop, arranged pens and notebooks beside it. Tomorrow after work I'd head to the library for resource material for my biofuels project. Classes at Amherst wouldn't begin for another few weeks, but I composed an email to my advisor to tell her I'd finally settled on a project.

My fingers hovered over the send button as I reread the email. It was a good plan. Competent. Solid.

And stirs nothing in my heart.

I snorted lightly. Following my heart had brought me loss and pain. I hit *send.*

I texted Ruby that I was back in Massachusetts and ready for our girl time before she left for Italy. She didn't reply. Left alone in a quiet, empty apartment, I heard the whispers of my heart telling me both Connor and Weston—especially Weston—were in pain. Their actions were born of all that they'd suffered at war, and I'd been selfish to leave them.

I didn't leave them. They pushed me away.

The urge to comfort or be there for them was one-sided. They didn't need me. Or want me.

And I was through being unwanted.

I decided a spring-cleaning-in-summer was in order. A fresh start to go with my fresh start. The apartment was already in good shape—I never let it get messy or cluttered—but I set to work vigorously.

All summer, my brother's country music had been pulling me away from my alternative songs with their honest lyrics. I tuned into a country radio playlist on Spotify and sang along loudly to "Love Me Like You Mean It."

"Amen," I muttered, scrubbing the kitchen counters until they were spotless. This was the perfect anthem for my new life.

My new, empty, quiet life.

When I got out of the shower the next morning, I noticed a new notification on my phone. Ruby left a voicemail the night before.

"Hey, girl, glad you're back. I'm still in Bean Town doing the fam thing, but maybe next week I'll head out west and we can hang. But call me when you get this. Any time, okay? Love you. Bye."

I frowned and listened to it again. Her normally loose and good-humored voice sounded tight and distracted.

I called her back, praying there was no more bad news.

Ruby answered on the first ring. "Hey, thanks for getting back to me."

"It's six a.m. and you answered the phone." I asked. "You okay?"

"I'm fine, but... Shit, I don't know how to tell you this. Or if I even should. But then I was like, fuck it, *of course* I should tell her."

"Tell me what?" I said, sliding onto the kitchen stool.

"Well." A sigh gusted over the line. "I flew back to Boston with Victoria and Connor."

"You did?"

"Yeah. He was pretty much on silent mode the first half of the flight. But then he had a couple drinks and kind of relaxed. We were talking and I got him to laugh a few times, so now Victoria thinks I'm the answer to all of her prayers."

"Okay," I said slowly.

"She invited me and my parents to her house for dinner sometime. Connor's really struggling and I think I should go, but I wanted to check in with you first. Best friend code and all."

LONG LIVE **the Beautiful Hearts**

I was quiet a minute, trying to figure out how I felt about it.

"Auts?" she said. "What do you think?"

"I think I'm jealous."

"You are?"

"A little," I said, with a short, watery laugh. "I mean, Connor won't talk to me. He dumped me and I'm doing my damned best to move on. But of course I want to know if he's getting better."

"I don't know that he's better," Ruby said. "It seemed like he was drinking more than a little. Victoria talked him into going back to school this fall. Or maybe forced him."

"I take it he doesn't want to?"

"Not at all. And he won't talk about Wes. Refuses to say his name and shuts down completely if you try."

I closed my eyes. *Stick to your vows.*

"Anyway," Ruby said, "I just wanted you to know the score."

"Thanks, Rube."

"My parents want me to visit some family in DC. I'll try to get to Amherst afterward. Can you live that long without me?"

"I'll do my best," I said, disappointed, but I reasoned the alone time would give me a better jump on my project.

"Atta girl. Love you."

"Love you, too. And Ruby, tell Connor..."

"Yeah?"

Tell him I miss him.

"Nothing."

"You sure?"

"I'm sure," I said. "Talk to you soon."

We hung up and I held the phone in my lap. I didn't like that Connor was drinking, but I couldn't fix him and he didn't want me around to try. He was done with me, and the only thing to do was to accept it. Stick to my vows.

I dressed in black pants and a white blouse and headed on my bike to the Panache Blanc bakery. The sun hadn't yet crested the eastern horizon but the air was warm and thick. The entire ride along Pleasant Avenue to Amherst's little downtown, I mentally prepared myself for Edmond de Guiche. I knew it would take him six seconds to read the story of stony resolve on my face, and immediately he'd try to talk, sing, or feed me out of giving up on love.

"Hi, Edmond," I called, stowing my bag under the counter. The bakery was filled with scents of warm, sugary pastry and fresh coffee. As I was tying my apron, Edmond burst out of the back doors, belting full-throated lyrics to some opera. In his white smock and black mustache, the big Frenchman looked from another time, where romance was easy, where men and women declared their love, were engaged the same night and stayed married forever.

"My darling girl." Edmond swept me into one of his trademark hugs and I resisted my trademark urge to melt into it. "I missed you so."

"I missed you too," I said. "I hope Phil wasn't overworked."

Phil Glassman was our other employee—nineteen now and still not accustomed to bakery hours even after working here for more than a year.

"Bah." Edmond waved his hand. "Philippe cannot be *over*worked. He is barely worked!" He laughed and then his eyes narrowed. "And how are you after your trip? How is your love, Connor? Safe?"

I nodded and started filling the napkin dispenser. "He had surgery on his elbow, but he'll be okay. And he doesn't have to return to combat."

"Ah, such a relief to hear. And Monsieur Turner? How is mon homme tranquille? My quiet man?"

"His injuries were more serious." I forced myself to meet Edmond's eyes. "He's been paralyzed. He can't walk. They think he'll be in a wheelchair for the rest of his life."

Saying the words out loud hammered at me all over again, and tears filled my eyes.

"Mon Dieu." Edmond covered his chest with a hand, his eyes wide. "This is so painful to hear. No more running?"

I shook my head. "No more running."

Before I knew it, I was suddenly engulfed in Edmond's hug and this time I didn't resist. I needed it.

"I am so sorry," Edmond said.

I nodded against his chest, then pulled away. "He's alive. They both are. That's all that matters."

"Oui," Edmond said. "And Wes is a strong man. He'll overcome whatever life sets before him, and he will triumph. This, I know."

"I hope you're right," I said. "For both his and Connor's sake."

LONG LIVE the Beautiful Hearts

Edmond's frown deepened. "I hear a goodbye in those words. What more has happened?"

I sucked in a breath and steeled myself. "Connor and I broke up and Weston has weeks of rehabilitation to get through. They both need to concentrate on recovery and they don't need me to do that."

"Says who?"

"Says them." Humiliation flushed my cheeks. "It's better for all of us, myself included. I can't compare what I've been through with what they endured in combat, but I know it's best for me that I focus on my work."

Edmond looked distraught. "Work? What about your love? Where does that go now?"

"To my school. My Harvard project."

Edmond shook his head. "You, with such a romantic heart and so much love to give—"

"It's not important."

"Not important?" If I'd spit in the cake batter, Edmond couldn't have looked more horrified. "Ma chère, it is the most important of all—"

"*No*," I said. "It's not. It's caused me nothing but pain. I care about both of them, but I have to care about myself too. And I don't want to talk about it anymore."

Edmond studied me a moment longer, his lips turned down. The oven timer gave a faint ping from the back room, and his eyes lit up. He went into the back room and returned with a tray of fresh cranberry scones.

"Eat, ma chère. To remind you there is sweetness in life. True love will find you and you will know no pain, only joy."

This time last year, Edmond had offered me the same warm food and words after I'd been betrayed by my ex-boyfriend. Then, I'd eaten and tried again. I'd stood at the edge of the cliff and jumped, despite all my fears and doubts and hurt. And I'd been smashed to pieces. Twice over.

I smiled faintly and shook my head.

"Thank you, Edmond," I said. "But I'm not hungry."

CHAPTER Ten

Weston

"I'm not hungry."

"Stop messing around, Weston Jacob Turner, and eat your food."

A spoon of oatmeal entered my field of vision, held in my mother's acrylic-nailed fingers. I turned my head away on the pillow and took my hourly inventory of the parking lot. There were thirty-six cars at noon; now there were thirty-three. The red sports car was gone, and a silver sedan was in its place.

"You haven't eaten in two days," Ma said.

A white SUV pulled into the lot. That made thirty-four.

Fascinating life you've carved out for yourself, Sock Boy.

"Wes. *Wes.* Goddammit, will you look at me?"

Ma slapped lightly at my cheek, but I kept my gaze on the lot.

"You still carrying on like this? You got to start rehab, or you're going to get worse. You want that? You want to get worse?"

The hospital door opened and I heard footsteps.

"How're things today?" Paul asked.

"Things are terrible," Ma said. "He won't eat." Louder, as if I'd lost my hearing instead of my ability to fucking walk, she said, "They're gonna put that feeding tube back in you if you don't eat. You want that?"

I closed my eyes.

"You see?" Ma said, her voice cracking. "He's starving himself. Is that what you're doing? Trying to kill yourself? You already stabbed yourself in the leg, for crying out loud. Why not just stab your poor mother in the heart? Where's a pen? Paul, get me a pen..."

She broke down crying, but her pain couldn't pierce the fog of apathy that descended over me, thick and colorless.

"Just leave me alone," I said, my tone almost conversational. "Can you do that for one minute, Ma? Leave me the fuck alone."

She gasped. I'd never spoken to her like that, not even in my rougher Southie days, when I used fists and acid insults on kids who thought I was an easy target.

Now you're a sitting duck, emphasis on sitting.

"Wes," Paul said in a more conciliatory tone. "The rehab therapist is going to be here in an hour. You're going to need your strength."

Yeah. Strength to get my ass into a wheelchair for the first time.

Like an automatic reflex, when I heard the word 'wheelchair,' I tried to lift one of the dead weights attached to my hips. I could feel my legs were there, but they wouldn't fucking *move*. It was like parking a starving man in front of a buffet he could never reach.

"No, thanks."

I opened my eyes. Shit, a tan Nissan had pulled into a spot while I wasn't looking. Thirty-five cars now? I started my count over again. Just to be sure.

Paul spoke again in his low voice. Ma screeched. I tuned them both out and started to drift to sleep. *Thirty-four, thirty-five...*

I woke to a gentle poke on my shoulder and opened my eyes to a middle-aged man with dark skin, salt-and-pepper hair, and kind brown eyes.

"Hey there, I'm Harlan," he said. "Your rehab therapist."

His hand rested on the back of a wheelchair. Just the sight of it made my intestines curl.

"No, thanks," I said to Harlan and his wheelchair and turned away.

He tried to cajole me with his friendly, professional demeanor but I was too busy to listen. I had cars to count.

I slept and woke. Another psychologist came around to try to talk to me. Then a social worker. A nurse tried to get me to eat. The sky darkened to night—time to stop counting cars and start counting stars. Only a handful; the city lights muted the rest.

Was Autumn back in Amherst, looking at the stars tonight? In Amherst, maybe, where the sky could shine its diamonds over her better than in Boston. Better than here. With me.

> *For you, I'd bring down the stars*
> *Wreath their fire around your neck like diamonds*
> *And watch them burn you with my lies...*

I dove into sleep. When I woke, morning light fell over me. My hunger was roaring in my gut, but I ignored it. No walking? Fine. No soup for you. A twisted bargain I'd made with my body. Something I could control.

Nurses warned they'd put a feeding tube in today if I didn't eat, but a blue sedan was driving into the parking lot. Another day in the life of Sock Boy. I had cars to count, people to ignore, naps to take. The nurses' threats and Harlan's visits with his little friend, the wheelchair, were crowding my schedule. How was a guy expected to get anything done with all these interruptions?

In the middle of midday parking lot inventory, Michael Ondiwuje strode into my room.

Like a ghost from a different era. An ambassador from my old life. The life when I still had decisions I could unmake, words burning in my heart, and legs that could carry me anywhere I wanted.

"Corporal Weston J. Turner," Professor Ondiwuje said, pulling up a chair to my bed. "I cannot tell you how much it gladdens my heart to see you alive."

My own heart beat faster, pushing something more than wasted apathy through my veins for the first time in days. I stared, hardly daring to believe this genius poet came to see me. He wore a sharp blue suit and a lighter blue tie. He no longer had dreadlocks but let his hair go natural, rings of tight curls brushing his shoulders.

"How did you know I was here?"

"The faculty in my department spoke of Senator Drake's son— your friend, Connor—returning from combat and re-enrolling at

Amherst to finish his senior year. I immediately thought of you and had hoped your tour of duty had ended as well. That you'd come back to us. I did a little snooping as to your whereabouts, and here I am."

Hearing his name awakened an ache in me I'd tried to keep buried. Like the hunger, except I couldn't ignore it.

"Connor's back at Amherst?"

"He is." Professor Ondiwuje clasped his hands in his lap, a gold wedding band bright on the dark of his skin. "And you? When do you return?"

"I don't."

He frowned. "They tell me you're refusing food and you don't show any interest in your rehabilitation."

"They tell you correct."

"You're giving up then?"

I turned my gaze to the window. "I'm taking some time off."

"You're running away, you mean."

I snorted. "I'm not running anywhere."

"You are running." Professor O tapped his forehead with one finger. "Up here. You've been running from who you are for years, haven't you? Though it's a terrible lesson to learn, I can't help but feel this is the universe's way of saying now you're going to sit down and take it. You're going to sit and be with who you are, Wes. Maybe for the first time in your life."

"Is this some kind of pep talk?"

"Straight talk," he said. "The universe doesn't make mistakes."

I thought of my recurring dream of the track race. I was *supposed* to die in Syria. Not live with my body cut in half.

My lip curled. "Preordained bullshit is still bullshit."

Ondiwuje sat quietly for a moment. I sensed him organizing his thoughts for another line of attack. Something to inspire me to get my ass out of bed. It wouldn't work. There was nothing left.

"Do you remember the last time we spoke?" Professor O said. "I observed you were a runner, a poet, and a warrior."

"I'm none of those now," I said. "I can't run, I can't write, and I got nothing to fight for."

To my astonishment, tears filled the man's eyes.

"My God, Wes," he said, his voice cracked. "Nothing to fight for? Fight for *you*. For who you are. At long last, fight for yourself and what you love. *Who* you love."

A silence fell, heavy and thick. I shook my head from side to side, tears stinging my own eyes as I thought of who I loved.

Autumn. And God, Connor. My brother…

"I ruined everything," I said. "I ruined my friendship. I ruined her love. If she knew what I did…" I swallowed the tears down. "Right now, she's heartbroken and it's our fault. He dumped her and I kicked her out. It's on us. We're the assholes and that's how it should be. Because how would she feel about herself if she knew the truth? I can't do that to her."

Professor O shook his head. "There is nothing that love can't forgive."

"She'd never forgive me, and she shouldn't."

"I wasn't speaking of her forgiveness. I was speaking of yours. To yourself. The fight you have to fight is for *you* so that the love you feel for *her* has a chance."

I started to protest, but Professor Ondiwuje clasped his hand over mine.

"I'm going to tell you a story, Weston," he said. "Close your eyes and listen and I won't ask anything else of you today."

I closed my eyes, only because if I looked at his kindness another minute, all the weak scaffolding around my wasted heart would collapse for good.

"This story is about the Once Born and the Twice Born," Professor O said. "The Once Born man walks the path of life, and when the path takes him into the dark forest of hardship and trauma, loss or pain, he stops, refusing to take another step. He tries to flee the way he came, but it's closed forever. So he lives his life certain the world is unfair and harsh. Others around him point to the scratching branches and looming shadows and say 'Yes, life *is* hard and unfair. See?' And they make camp among the hardships, instead of continuing on the path ahead. The way out."

His deep, melodious voice crafted words of air and sound that landed gently on my chest, seeping into my bones.

"But there is the Twice Born man, Weston," he said, his hand tightening on mine. "The man who walks into the dark forest of his life and suffers. Sometimes unimaginably. The way back is forever closed to him, but the Twice Born man walks forward. The path becomes more twisted, the hardships seemingly impossible to overcome. But he keeps going until one day, the shadows lift. The branches cease to scratch at his skin and they part for him. He'll regard the scars with pride as he emerges from the forest reborn. Stronger for what he has endured. Wiser. Transformed. And grateful for the lessons he learned."

Tears seeped from under my closed lids.

"It's so dark where you are now, isn't it?" Professor Ondiwuje said. "But here is the secret: every Once Born is a Twice Born who hasn't yet discovered their strength. I've seen your heart and heard your words, Wes. You will survive this. You're a poet encased in warrior's armor. You will come out the other side, but you must take the first step forward. There is no other way."

I lay still a long time, listening to the sound of my own breath and the cadence of my pulse in my chest. A drum beat, a pendulum marking the moments of my life.

I drifted, and when I opened my eyes, Professor Ondiwuje was gone. The chair empty. Beyond it, in a corner of the room, the folded wheelchair waited to take me through.

I inhaled, and on the exhale came words in a weak, ragged whisper.

"There is no other way."

PART III
August

CHAPTER Eleven

Autumn

A thriving new market for corn, grains, soybeans, and other agricultural crops now exists in the ethanol and biodiesel industries. In 2015, for the U.S., alone...

I blinked and rubbed my eyes, as if that could make the words on the page more interesting. Or rub some fire into my blood for the material. I glanced from the textbook to the TV. All night it'd been shamelessly tempting me with the entire first season of *The Crown* on my DVR, while a pint of Cherry Garcia called to me from the freezer.

"No. I can do this," I muttered. "It's important."

If Harvard accepted my project, it would be my life.

The entire rest of my life.

I blinked, focused, and took up the textbook again. Just as my eyes were starting to glaze over, a Gmail notification popped up on my phone. My heart skipped a beat to see it was from the U.S. Army Human Resources Command.

God, what now?

I opened my laptop to read it more clearly.

Families and Friends of 1st Battalion, 22nd Infantry Regiment

It is with great pride that we inform you that on Saturday, 16 August, 20—, there will be a Purple Heart ceremony for 3 members of 1-22 IN:
Medic Specialist Kyle P. Wilson
Private First Class Connor Drake
Corporal Weston J. Turner
Corporal Turner will also be awarded the Bronze Star for meritorious and heroic actions in a combat zone.
The ceremony will take place at:
1 City Hall Square,
Boston, MA 02201
4:00 pm
All friends and family of I-22 IN Soldiers are welcome to attend.
Thank you for your continuous support.

Apparently, I was still on the 22nd Infantry's friend and family email chain. I searched the email for an unsubscribe link. I needed to get off this list and unsubscribe to whatever Weston and Connor and I had been.

My eyes strayed to the line about Weston. Promoted to Corporal and now earning the Bronze Star. Pride for him welled up in me along with missing him. My heart ached for Connor breaking up with me, but the absence of Connor in my life felt like an old bruise that was healing fast. The void where Weston had been grew bigger every day.

Because we're friends and friends miss each other.

Except we hadn't been friends since the night before deployment.

We'd broken the boundaries of friendship on the couch that night. Shattered them with wild kisses and grasping hands, as if we were desperate and starving for each other and had been for a long time.

Kissing Weston was the completion of something I didn't know had started.

The thought sat in my psyche like a thorn, immovable and painful. As painful as Weston kicking me out of his hospital room and out of his life.

LONG LIVE the Beautiful Hearts

I shut my laptop and went back to my textbook.

Cellulosic ethanol is often referred to as a second-generation biofuel. Also in this category is renewable diesel, including hydroprocessed esters, and fatty acids...

I propped my chin on my hand, and within moments, the words morphed into blurred nonsense. If I didn't get a grip on it soon, I'd have to switch one of my majors to chemistry.

A key turning in the lock jolted me. Ruby stepped into the apartment, looking beautiful and vibrant in jeans and a bright yellow blouse.

"Hey you," I said. "I wasn't expecting you until tomorrow night."

I gladly abandoned my desk to give her a hug.

"I come for our promised girl time," she said, kicking her rolling suitcase aside and hoisting a paper bag of groceries. "Wine, ice cream, and I hear *Ten Things I Hate About You* is making the rounds on cable. Let's do this.'"

"You're my hero."

I grabbed wine glasses from the kitchen while she pulled four bottles of cabernet out of her bag.

"I hope that's supposed to last us all four days," I said.

"We'll see. You've been dumped twice. Double-whammy. Desperate times call for desperate measures.

"Weston didn't dump me. We weren't even together."

Ruby shrugged. "Irregardless—"

"That's not a word."

She stuck out her tongue. "*Irrespective* of the particulars of your salacious affairs, I have enough wine and chocolate to get us through the next few nights until I depart for bella Italia."

"Can you take me with you?"

"I wish." She jerked her chin toward my desk. "How's your corn gasoline project going?"

"Great," I said, ignoring the 'corn gasoline' jibe. "Fine. Making progress."

"That bad, huh?" We took our cabernet and my pint of Cherry Garcia ice cream with two spoons and flopped on the couch.

"Not great," I confessed. "It's super boring, actually."

"Shocker," Ruby muttered, scooping a bite of ice cream. "Hate to say I told you so…"

A disgusted sigh heaved out of me. "God, Rube, I don't know what I'm doing. For once I don't have any man drama to distract me, but now the project feels so empty."

"Yeah, about that man drama," Ruby said slowly. "My parents and I went to dinner at the Drakes' last week. And Connor…"

"Tell me," I said, bracing myself. "How is he?"

"Not great, honestly," Ruby said. "He drank a lot and complained of headaches. Mostly he just seemed desperately unhappy, especially when the talk turned to Weston's rehab experience."

"What do you mean?"

She took a pull of her wine. "He went on a bit of a hunger strike. They put him under observation."

My face drained of blood. "A suicide watch?"

"Sounded like it."

"Jesus. And they talked about Weston being suicidal in front of Connor? Knowing he probably took the blame for that too?"

Ruby nodded. "It sucked. I talked to Connor after dinner. Tried to get him to laugh a little, you know? His parents…they just don't get it. They refuse to see how he blames himself. It doesn't matter that it's not his fault; he *thinks* it's his fault. But they don't address that. Same with his PTSD. They want to believe he'll just get over it." She shook her head, her dark eyes uncharacteristically heavy. "They basically railroaded him into going back to college. He didn't even say he wanted to go. They declared he would and he's going along with it."

"So, did Weston finish rehab?"

"Indeed," Ruby said. "He pulled himself together and barreled through it, according to Victoria."

"Has Connor tried talking to him?" I asked. *They need each other.*

"I assume so," Ruby said, "seeing as they're going to be roommates again."

My eyes widened. "What?"

"Weston's re-enrolling for senior year."

I'll see them. Both of them.

For one pure second, warm happiness filled my chest. Then the tangled, cold reality crashed back in just as quickly.

You don't even know what each man means to you, and they

don't want to see you anyway. Stick to your vows.

"The Drakes fixed up a new apartment for them in Amherst," Ruby was saying. "You know, one that will accommodate Wes's wheelchair and other needs."

"But this is good news," I said. "I mean, for their friendship. Connor wouldn't agree to live with Weston if they weren't on speaking terms."

Ruby shrugged, topped off her wine glass. "I suppose, but he still refuses to say Wes's name. I honestly don't know what he's thinking. I don't think *he* knows what he's thinking, but I sure as hell wish his parents would get a clue before he does something rash."

"God, Ruby, don't say that."

Ruby turned to me and took a breath.

"I know everything that happened between the two of you—and Wes too—hurt you a lot. Connor broke your heart. I don't blame you for wanting to protect yourself, but I feel like a lot of shit went down when these guys were hurting the most. They were fucked up and neither one of them knew what the hell they were doing back at Walter Reed. Shell shocked, you know? Maybe things are a little better and you can—?"

"Can what? Try to get back together with Connor? I have no idea what it even means to be with him. And I don't know what I feel about Weston except that for a few drunk moments, I wanted him so badly I thought I'd die. Where did those feelings come from?"

"Tequila gets my vote."

"I thought so too but… It was more than that."

Ruby opened her mouth to speak but I cut her off.

"No, I'm done. I care about them both, but…"

"But you're still a little bit shell shocked too," Ruby said. "I can see it. And I'm not suggesting you get back together with anyone. But I do feel like it couldn't hurt to talk to them."

I sighed, plucked a stray thread off a throw pillow. "The Army's Family Unit emailed me. I'm still on their list. Connor and Weston have a Purple Heart ceremony in about ten days."

Ruby nodded. "Victoria invited me, but I'll be long gone. Maybe you should go. It's a formal ceremony, right? No one's going to freak out. You show up, you say hi, you wish them the best, you get some closure. Otherwise, you're going to drive yourself crazy every time you step foot on that campus, wondering if you're going to run into one of them. And you will. Amherst is a small town."

She leaned over and patted my hand.

"I know you're gung-ho about moving on, but given all that you went through with Connor—and whatever the hell happened between you and Weston—I think you deserve an adult conversation. Even if it's just to acknowledge you're still there and you have every right to be, you know?"

I nodded. "The way things were left with both of them was so…ragged and raw. But I don't know if it's worth it."

"It's more than a week away," Ruby said, fishing on the coffee table for the TV remote. "You have time to think about it. In the meantime, you're mine for the next four days and *Ten Things I Hate About You* isn't going to watch itself."

"I was thinking of watching *The Crown*."

"Snooze. I need some Heath, may he rest in peace, and I need him now."

I grinned and curled up beside her.

We drank wine, finished off the ice cream, and watched the movie. And for a few blessed hours, my thoughts were solely with my best friend and how much I loved her and would miss her. And how, even though she'd be halfway around the earth from me, I'd still have her. Always.

CHAPTER
Twelve

Weston

The western Massachusetts countryside flew past the windows of Paul's silver sedan.

"I'm really proud of you," he said from behind the wheel. "I know I must sound like a broken record, but I am. Not just for finishing rehab but for going back to school."

I made a non-committal grunt in my throat. "Ma was right about one thing," I said acidly. "The Reserves *do* help with college."

My tuition was paid for, I was set up with six weeks of outpatient therapy through Amherst's Phys Ed department, and given a shit-ton of prescriptions. All on the Army's dime.

"I give you a lot of credit for getting back out there," Paul said. "More than you give yourself—"

"Yeah, well, I'm only finishing my Econ degree because what the fuck else am I going to do? Get a job?"

"You could."

"Doing what?"

"Doing any number of things. You have so many talents."

I snorted. The only things I'd been good at were running and writing, and both of those doors were slammed and locked shut forever.

"I'll get a desk job somewhere pushing numbers," I said. "Who needs to walk when I can sit at a cubicle for the rest of my life?"

Paul glanced at my dark expression. "You busted your ass in rehab. You're doing better than you think."

I ignored him.

He tried again.

"Autumn's coming back to Amherst too, right?" Paul said.

I shrugged a thousand-pound weight on my shoulders. I should've transferred to a different college to give Autumn a chance at moving on without seeing my worthless ass rolling all over campus.

"I don't know what happened the night Autumn left Walter Reed, but I hope you two—"

"There is no 'us two,'" I snapped. "She's better off staying far away from me."

"And what about you? Are you better off without her?"

"Does it matter?"

"It matters to me," Paul said. "She's a lovely woman and she cares about you."

I ground my teeth together. "I have nothing to offer her. Less than nothing."

"Not even friendship?" He shot me a small grin. "Granted, you're not exactly Mr. Sunshine at the moment."

No, I'm the Amherst Asshole 2.0 with a meaner mean streak than before.

"Anyway, Autumn strikes me as the kind of girl who wouldn't—"

"Mind being saddled with a paraplegic?" I finished.

"You're not a burden to anyone, Wes," Paul said, his tone grave. "You have to know that."

"Do I, Paul?" My temper, already on the shortest of leashes, snapped. "I'm a fucking burden to *myself.* Shall we count the ways my life is completely fucked? I have to stick a tube in my dick six times a day to piss. I have to massage my asshole every other morning to take a shit. The urologist said I'm probably infertile and can't have kids. Kids? I can't even fuck. I might never get it up and if I do, I might not come. And if I manage to come, so fucking what? I can't feel it anyway."

"Wes..."

"Or how about the most obvious—I can't walk. I can't run. I

can't *stand up*. I can't get out of that fucking chair."

The wheelchair rode in the backseat behind me. A sleek, lightweight folding model to the tune of $2,000, courtesy of the Drakes. A ball and chain I could never escape from and could get nowhere without.

"You might be able to do many of those things," Paul said. "You're conveniently leaving out what else the doctors said. You have an incomplete SCI. You have possibilities. You have *hope*."

I snorted and turned my gaze out the window. After Michael Ondiwuje's visit, I'd climbed out of a fog of apathy into a fiery pit of white-hot anger. I'd busted my ass for four weeks of rehab, only because the mean streak in me had been awakened. The Southie temper of my childhood that viewed everything—including paralysis—as an enemy to be conquered.

I learned how to transition from bed to wheelchair, or wheelchair to toilet, or wheelchair to another fucking chair, because that's all I'd ever do for the rest of my life: sit in a goddamn chair.

Harlan and his team of therapists worked with me strengthening my arms and torso. They taught me how to catheterize my limp dick. How to dress myself without needing someone to get my jeans over my useless fucking legs. How to monitor my diet, my blood pressure. How to manage the bizarre muscle cramps that felt like a weaker version of pins and needles in a limb that had fallen asleep.

I made it through rehab out of pure spite, and the lesson ingrained the deepest was that I was sick of people who weren't in my position telling me how I should feel about being in my position.

"You don't know jack shit about hope," I said.

"You don't know jack shit about me," Paul said. He shot me a look, eyebrows raised. "How 'bout them apples?"

"Fuck, whatever," I muttered.

The scenery rolled by and my anger melted into shame. Paul didn't deserve my wrath.

"Anyway, thanks for picking me up at Logan," I said tightly.

"My pleasure."

"Why did Ma want to drive to Amherst with the Drakes?" Not that I missed her screeching in the car ride, but her absence made me suspicious.

"I don't know," Paul said. "She hinted at some big surprise, but I couldn't get it out of her. Her lips were sealed."

"That's a first."

As the sedan approached the Amherst exit, my pulse jumped in my chest.

"You sure Connor is up for this?" I asked. "Or are the Drakes forcing him? Ma talked a good story about him being better, but I want the truth."

The pause before Paul spoke told me everything.

I threw up my hands. "Ah, fuck."

"Connor's a grown man," Paul said. "He wouldn't agree to live with you if he didn't want to. Whatever disagreement you had probably seems less important now. Time," he added with a small smile, "is the universal healer of all wounds."

I doubted that but bit back my retort. Connor hadn't spoken to me since...

Since Syria. Since the blast...

Not a phone call, not a text, not a word passed on from someone else. And now he'd agreed to be roommates again? Pick up where we left off? Ma and Paul wanted me to get back to my old life as soon as possible, as if nothing had changed. The Drakes pushing Connor to do the same—like they'd pushed him to do everything else—made sense.

But everything's changed. Every last fucking thing.

Paul drove past my street.

"You missed the turn," I said.

He frowned and nodded his chin. "The apartment's up on Milton Street. Isn't it?"

"No. Grant."

"This is the address Victoria gave me." He tapped his phone's GPS mounted on the dash, turned toward him.

We pulled into a lot marked by an elegant sign reading Pleasant Glen Estates.

"Is this a quarantine for disabled persons?" I muttered. "Or a retirement home?"

"It's a condo complex," Paul said. Frowning, he peered through the windshield. "I have a feeling this is the surprise your mother was planning."

Nervous anxiety tightened my body from the waist up as Paul pulled my wheelchair from the backseat. He unfolded it, locked it, then stood off to the side, his back to me. As if I were taking a shit and needed the privacy.

Carefully, I transitioned from the car to the wheelchair—ass first—then lifted each leg and set my feet on the footrests. The sun was brilliant in the late summer sky, but I wasn't sweating from the heat. My heart pounded faster and my breath was short. Aside from the airports, I'd never been in the chair in public before.

I pushed the chair through the lot and onto the smooth, winding pathway that led into the complex. Paul walked beside me, tall and easy, as if it were nothing. Because it *was* nothing to him.

Walking is the fucking easiest thing to take for granted.

The enormity of it—a lifetime in a chair—swamped me just then, making my hands shake as they pushed the wheel rims. The psychologist at Walter Reed warned the grief might come in waves. Not waves; gigantic fucking monsoons. Accepting the fact I'd never walk again was like trying to cram a boulder down my throat. Impossible to swallow and yet it wouldn't relent. That impossibility, coupled with the unyielding reality, created a rift in me. I couldn't accept it and I couldn't escape it, and living in that limbo was fucking torture.

I was better off counting cars in the hospital parking lot.

"This is it," Paul said, as we arrived at #4, a ground-level unit with a wide walkway.

Ma threw open the door before Paul could touch the handle. "You're here! Hey, baby." She bent, grabbed my face in both hands and smacked a kiss on my forehead. "Oh my God, I can't wait for you to see this."

"What's going on?" Paul asked as Miranda kissed his cheek.

"The Drakes came through yet again," she said, her eyes shining. "Look at your new place, Wes, baby. Come in."

I pushed my chair over the threshold and into a wide living area on hardwood floors. The entire place smelled of fresh paint.

Victoria and Allen Drake stepped forward. "Welcome home, Wes," Victoria said, her hands twisting. After a false start or two, she bent and awkwardly pecked my cheek. "You look fantastic. Doesn't he look fantastic?"

"Good to see you, Wes." Mr. Drake offered his hand and I shook it absently, my eyes fixed behind him.

Connor stood in the state-of-the-art kitchen, leaning against the marble counter, blue t-shirt and jeans, a beer in his hand. A heavy, intricate brace wrapped around his left elbow. He met my gaze while he took a long pull, then looked away.

I couldn't look away. The last image I had of my best friend was burned into my psyche. Him lying on the ground beneath me, motionless with his eyes half open, both of us painted in blood and ash, screams of dying refugees and explosions filling my ears. I'd thought he was dead. I'd been shot and dragged into oblivion, believing he was dead.

But he was right here, standing on two feet with open eyes.

"Con…" My voice was a croak, thick with threatening tears. It took every ounce of will I had to swallow them down.

"Connor, baby," Ma said with a nervous laugh. "Come over here and say hi, for crying out loud." I guessed she no longer blamed Connor for my injuries—given the look of this condo, it cost too much for her to stay angry at the Drakes.

Connor set his bottle down and slowly moved from the kitchen to the living room. My chin raised as he got closer and loomed over me.

"Hey," he said.

"Hey," I said.

Our gazes caught and held, and the deep bond forged in Syria was like a telegraph. Pain, anguish, guilt and anger all coming through his eyes, once so bright and full of laughter but now shadowed and bloodshot.

"You've both been through so much," Victoria said into the silence. "But you have all the time in the world to catch up. Come. Let's show Wes his bedroom."

"This place is ours?" I asked Connor.

"Yeah," he said bitterly. "So we can pick up right where we left off. Before I fucked everything up by joining the Army."

"Connor," Mr. Drake said in a low tone.

"*Father.*" Connor imitated his tone, then snorted a dry laugh. "I'm getting a headache. Going to lay down."

He strode to the kitchen, grabbed his beer off the counter and retreated down the wide, wheelchair-accessible hallway. A door slammed.

"His doctors say it's residual PTSD from the combat," Mrs. Drake said. "We're providing him the best care. And if you need anything, Wes, say the word." Her eyes, shining with tears, followed where Connor had gone. "We want nothing but the best for both of you."

"Aren't they amazing?" Ma asked. "Just look at this place, Wes. They've spared no expense."

"Miranda..." Paul began but she hushed him with a wave of her hand.

"Come on, honey. Come look around. It's all set up for you."

My mother and the Drakes led me on a tour of the condo that had been modified in every way possible to be wheelchair accessible. Every sink in the bathrooms and kitchen had the faucet on the side instead of the back. The freezer was a unit adjacent to the fridge instead of on top of it. Connor had a row of high cupboards, mine were low. My bathroom was wide, with rails everywhere, providing easy access to the toilet from my wheelchair.

"And look," Ma said, leading the procession to my bedroom. "They really spared no expense."

The room had lots of wide spaces, two low bookshelves instead of one tall one, and on the king-size bed was a body pillow.

"It's to prevent bedsores and numbness," Mrs. Drake said. "And this is really quite special."

She took from a chair by the window what looked like an elaborate electric blanket, wires coming out that attached to a small tablet device.

"This is a Bremen Blanket," she said. "The newest technology out of Germany. You wrap this around your legs while you're watching TV or taking a nap, and it sends electrical impulses that help increase circulation. It helps keep the muscle tone in your legs from... I mean, it helps maintain muscle tone."

"Isn't that something?" Ma crowed. "That blanket isn't even on the market yet. It's special. Everything here is so special. Just for you, baby."

I nodded slowly, the weight of this brand new condo and everything in it pressing on me as we moved back to the living room.

"We wanted to make your transition back to Amherst as smooth as possible," Mr. Drake said.

"It's a lot," I said in a low voice. "You didn't have to do this."

I looked back toward Connor's closed door. I could hear a TV blaring *Madden* from behind it. Because he had a headache.

God, what did Connor think of all this? What *could* he think of it but that his parents were making up for his supposed mistake? His guilt. Covering for him.

I clenched my teeth to keep from screaming. Or grabbing a lighter out of Ma's bag and burning this place to the ground. I didn't give a shit about any of it. I just wanted Connor to fucking look at me.

"You could've told Wes first," I heard Paul say to Ma. "Give him some warning."

"Warning? This is a surprise," Ma said. "Isn't it wonderful, Wes? So perfect to accommodate you. Get you back on your feet."

"Back on my feet," I murmured. "I'm really tired," I said, louder. "I want to rest now."

"Of course," Mr. Drake said. "We'll go and leave you to it."

"We'll go grocery shopping for you both," Mrs. Drake said. "When we come back, perhaps some dinner? At the Rostand?"

Paul glanced down at me. "Maybe. We'll play it by ear, Wes?"

Ma smacked a kiss on my cheek. "Please, baby," she murmured in my ear. "The Drakes spent a lot of time and money setting this place up for you. Couldn't hurt to show some gratitude."

I raised my head to make eye contact with these four people. Once, in another life, I'd been taller than all of them.

Those days are over, Sock Boy. Now be polite and thank the grown-ups for all the nice things they got you.

"Thanks," I muttered.

"Nothing to thank us for," Mrs. Drake said, picking up her purse from a chair. "Anything you need, Wes. Say the word."

"Are you sure you can be alone, baby?" Ma asked. "You need any help?"

"He's not alone," Paul said. "Connor's here."

Yeah, right. He's here. Just down the hall, nursing his headache by playing video games at top volume.

Finally, they all shuffled out and the door shut. A few minutes of silence passed, and then Connor's bedroom door opened.

"They're gone?" he asked, striding into the kitchen.

"Yep."

He went to the fridge, grabbed another beer and popped the top off. He leaned against the counter and took a long pull, looking anywhere but at me. The tension in the air felt like lightning about to strike.

"So you're going to finish your degree too?" I asked.

"It's what *they* want," he said, jerking his head toward the front door. "To pretend like everything is back the way it was."

I nodded. "Ma's that way too. As if the louder she talks, the more things will be normal. Did you know about this?" I asked, indicating the apartment.

Connor snorted. "Of course." He took a long pull from his beer. "You're surprised? They're always cleaning up my messes."

"Connor…"

"I gotta go. Shit to do."

He set his half-empty beer bottle on the counter and went past me, a hundred feet tall and too fast for me now.

"Connor, wait."

At the door he stopped, his back to me. "What?"

"Nothing. It's just good to see you, man."

He flinched, his shoulders rising. Then he went out and shut the door without a word.

CHAPTER
Thirteen

Weston

Ten days later, I was back in the silver sedan with Paul, this time on the way to Boston City Hall for the Purple Heart Ceremony. My mood was shit to begin with, but after two hours with Paul Sheffield and his relentless kindness, the fuse inside me was just begging to be lit.

"You all right?" he asked, as we rolled into the city proper.

"Why did I agree to this?" I muttered to the window.

"Because it's important," Paul said. "And you deserve to be recognized for your sacrifice."

My sacrifice. What a crock. He meant my penance for fucking with Connor and Autumn. For not handling my shit and taking care of Ma so I'd never have considered the Army Reserves. I planted the idea in Connor's head. He was hurting because of me. I fucked it all up and they were going to pin a medal on me for it

"There's a CVS near the City Hall," Paul said. "Do you need help filling any prescriptions?"

I recoiled. My urologist had given me, among other things, a script for Viagra. Paul had seen the damn thing on my counter when he'd come to pick me up and acted as if it were the most normal thing in the world for a twenty-something guy needing help getting his dick hard. And for who? There was only one woman I wanted to be with in this life, and I could never have her.

"No, I would not like you to help me," I snapped. The fuse was burning faster toward the bomb with every one of Paul's acts of kindness. "I don't need your man-to-man pep talks. I don't need you carting my ass back and forth across Massachusetts. I don't know why you bother in the first place."

"I *bother* because I care about you," he said, pulling into a parking space at City Hall. He shut off the engine and turned to me. "Wes, I've been with your mother a year now—"

"You're not my father," I said. "Let's get that straight right now. You can date my mother for years, for decades even—God help you—but it won't make you my father. Not now, not ever."

Paul held my gaze for a long, hard moment before answering, "I would never presume."

Then he got out of the car.

"Fuck me." I slammed my fist into my thigh. It resonated with a faint pressure but no pain.

The pain was everywhere except in my legs.

Paul and I traversed the parking lot in silence. The Purple Heart honorees had been instructed to wear our dress uniforms for the ceremony. The late summer sun beat down on the heavy wool and a rivulet of sweat slid between my shoulder blades, adding to the discomfort. When I saw my mother and sisters gathered in front of the building, I nearly stopped the chair and turned around. I couldn't take it. They could drop my medals in the mail. Or better yet, the nearest dumpster.

"My God, you look so handsome," Ma said, clutching her heart. She wore a yellow blouse and jeans. "Look at him in that uniform."

"You look great, Wes," Kimberly said. "Really good. Better every time I see you."

Felicia snorted and ground out her cigarette under her tennis shoe. "All of twenty-two years old and a veteran. My brother the veteran."

"Hey," Ma snapped. "You watch your mouth and show some respect."

"Jeez, Ma. Who said I—?"

"Don't 'jeez Ma' me. He sacrificed for this country. What are *you* doing?"

I tuned out their bickering and watched a limo pull into the parking lot. It parked, and Mr. and Mrs. Drake, Connor's brother Jefferson and his wife Cassandra stepped out. Connor followed with three of his baseball buddies.

I'd hardly seen him since we moved into the new condo ten days ago. He stayed out until all hours, drinking at Yancy's Saloon, stumbling in at three a.m. and locking himself in his room. He wouldn't talk to me. Barely looked at me. He caught my eye now from across the parking lot, then turned his back to sling his dress uniform jacket over the bulky elbow brace.

Subtle, Drake. Real fucking subtle.

Slowly, the party migrated across the parking lot to join us. The moms hugged. Paul and Mr. Drake shook hands.

"Good to see you, Wes," Jefferson said, crouching down to offer his hand.

Cassandra's smile was full of pity. "It must be so difficult for you. I admire your tenacity."

"Thanks?"

"You really do look wonderful, Wes," Mrs. Drake said.

And that makes you feel better, doesn't it?

I swallowed it down hard because the senator was looking at me with tears in her eyes. As if she were taking in my Army uniform and coupling it with the wheelchair for the first time. She swiftly bent to hug me.

"Thank you for what you did for him," she whispered. "Thank you so much."

Over her shoulder, Connor's expression verged on horrified, then crumbled with regret. I watched him take the flask from his pocket and take a pull, not even bothering to hide it.

"Goodness, today is making me emotional." Mrs. Drake dabbed at her eyes with the heels of her hands. "Let's get a few photos."

"Great idea," Ma said. "Let's get one of you two together. Connor, baby, scoot closer to Wes."

Connor left his buddies and stood next to my chair.

Ma and Mrs. Drake snapped photos with their phones, like proud parents on the world's most dysfunctional prom night.

"Hey, man," I said.

He kept his eyes forward. "Hey."

LONG LIVE the Beautiful Hearts

It was more than he'd said to me in days.

"How are you—?"

"We done here?" he asked the moms loudly, already moving away. "Let's get this over with."

Okay. Good talk.

Inside City Hall, members of the press gathered along with spectators and a few soldiers. I couldn't see much—my new vantage point put me flush with other people's asses.

I followed a whirr of camera shutters clicking to where the press was taking photos of Kyle Wilson, our platoon's medic. He stood with his family, leaning on a crutch. His left leg was wrapped in a brace from hip to ankle.

Wilson spoke a few words with Connor first, then limped over to me.

"The Iceman," Wilson said, shaking my hand. "Telling you, dude, I didn't think you were gonna make it."

"To the ceremony?"

"Out of Syria."

"Thanks to you," I said.

"Just doing my job. But it wasn't me who did the heavy lifting." He jerked his chin at Connor. "Anyone tell you what happened out there? What Connor did?"

I sat back. "I read the After Action report. All it said was that you treated me in the field and we were airlifted out of the combat zone."

"True," he said. "But you'd have bled out if it weren't for Connor. I just finished what he started." He shook his head. "You really didn't know?"

"No."

"I told our CO but it was a fucked up flight out of there. Harried as all hell. But hand to God, man, Connor saved your life."

Now it was me shaking my head. "Well, shit. Connor deserves the goddamn Bronze Star. Not me."

Wilson shrugged. "He did what any infantry in the field is trained to do. You, on the other hand, ran toward an oncoming grenade to save a fellow soldier's life."

"How is that different?" I asked. "We were trained to do that too. He'd have done the same. Anyone in our unit would have."

"Dude. They don't hand out Bronze Stars like Halloween

candy. You earned it." Wilson's gaze went down to my still legs. "We left a lot out there on the field, you especially. Take what you can get in return."

The Army liaison officer approached us. "We'd like to get started." He led us to the front of the room while press and spectators took seats on folding metal chairs.

"Attention!"

Every soldier in the room, including me, snapped ramrod straight, eyes forward as Major General Robert Eckhart stepped into the room in full dress regalia.

"Good morning," he said, a faint southern accent tingeing his words, his hands clasped behind his back. "Thank you, friends and family, for being here. It's my honor to bestow the Purple Heart to three of our own. It's the one award you hope never to give, and the oldest medal we have. It goes to heroes, plain and simple."

The Major General came to stand in front of Kyle Wilson. A uniformed soldier held out the medal—a brass heart hanging from a purple ribbon.

"This medal symbolizes a hero who's given a part of their soul or body against an enemy who wants to defeat our way of life. Recipients know valor and sacrifice for both the nation and for their fellow soldier."

He pinned the medal on Kyle. "By order of the President of the United States and certified by the Secretary of the Army, for wounds received in action on June the Thirteenth in the theater of war, I do hereby bestow upon you the Purple Heart."

Major General Eckhart did the same ceremonious presentation for Connor and me, pausing between each to pose with us while our families snapped photos and the audience clapped.

Then the Major General was handed a bronze starburst on a ribbon of red, white and blue.

"I'm honored now to bestow an award that we're *always* proud and humbled to give." He stood beside my wheelchair. "For meritorious service in a combat zone, for exhibiting extreme bravery and self-sacrifice under fire, I award Corporal Weston Jacob Turner the Bronze Star."

The Major General bent to pin the medal on my coat, and an old memory infiltrated my brain: a track and field judge laying an All-Around gold medal around my neck at a championship two years ago.

L O N G L I V E the Beautiful Hearts

I'd been so fast. So fucking fast...

The crowd applauded and Ma whistled between her teeth.

"That's my baby!"

I kept my eyes straight ahead. Beside me, I could feel the tension radiating off Connor's body. Over the telegraphic lines of our bond came the pain and guilt that I'd traded my legs to save his life and was being rewarded for it in front of his family.

I wanted to rip the medal off of my jacket and crush it under the wheels of this fucking chair. To show Connor it broke my soul that I'd never walk, but I had no regrets. I'd do it again. I'd been *ready* to do it all along because I wasn't supposed to come back. The fucking dream told me I'd die over there.

I'd been ready to die for him. I didn't need a goddamn medal to prove it.

We adjourned to an adjacent room for refreshments. I followed Connor, letting him carve a path through the crowd, determined to make him talk to me if I had to mow him down. And that's when Autumn Caldwell stepped out of the crowd.

Jesus, my goddamn heart...

In a white dress printed with orange, blue, and yellow watercolor blooms, she looked like a bouquet of wildflowers. Her hair was half-pulled up, the rest fell in coppery red over her shoulders. She clutched a small purse in front of her with both hands, her smile uncertain.

"Hi," she said.

Both Connor and I stared at her. I had no idea what he was feeling because my conduit to him was broken and all I knew was Autumn.

I wondered if Connor's heart was pounding in his chest like mine at the sight of her. If he were staring at her gemstone eyes, or her full lips; remembering how her mouth tasted like cinnamon when she let you in to kiss her. If he were marveling at her, feeling strangely proud that this woman was going to dedicate her life to helping fix what was broken. To give her heart and soul to something—and someone—worthy of her.

"I'm not here to cause any drama," Autumn said. "I heard you were both coming back to Amherst, which means we might run into each other on campus. Things ended abruptly between the three of us, so I thought it would be better if... I don't know. We broke the ice here?"

When neither of us spoke, she stood up straighter, her chin jetting forward.

"But truthfully, I needed to see with my own eyes that you're both okay. And I'm so glad you are. You both look amazing." Her eyes went to me and her voice softened. "You look incredible."

My hands gripped the wheels of my chair, aching to push myself out of it, to stand up so I could fall at her knees and beg forgiveness. A thousand words tangled in my heart, none escaping for fear of hurting her more.

"So that's why I came," she said. "To see you, say congratulations...and thank you for your service."

Then with a small parting smile she turned and walked away.

Don't go, I thought, staring after. *Please don't go. Please turn around. Please let me look at you one last time...*

At the door she stopped, turned, and shot a small glance over her shoulder. The expression on her face looked like longing. Then she was gone. Like a dream, a step out of time where there was beauty and kindness and not ugly rage and guilt.

My scalp prickled and I looked up into Connor's glare.

"What?" I demanded.

An outsider might interpret the grimace of disgust as directed at me, but I knew self-loathing when I saw it. It'd been staring at me in the mirror since the day my dad drove away.

"You haven't told her," he said.

"Why would I?"

He stared at me a moment more, his lip curling, then shook his head and went to join his three baseball buddies. Clapping him on the back, they closed ranks, surrounding and absorbing him.

How long was he going to ignore me? The entire rest of our senior year? While we were living in the same goddamn house?

Ma and Paul asked if I wanted to head back to Amherst or go out and get some dinner.

"You go. I'll get my own ride home." I didn't wait for an answer, just rolled to where Connor and his friends were standing. I caught someone suggesting going to Roxie's Roadhouse that night.

"What's up, fellas?" I asked with mock friendliness. "Going to Roxie's? Sounds good. Count me in."

Connor stared at me, then took a pull from his flask.

LONG LIVE the Beautiful Hearts

"You up for it?" one of the guys asked, glancing me up and down.

My mouth still works, dumbass.

I put on a bright smile. "Hell, yeah, I'm in. Let's do this. Connor? Whaddya say, buddy?"

He met my gaze, peering straight through my bullshit friendliness. I didn't back down.

Fuck this, Drake. Whatever you're doing, it ends tonight.

"Sure," he said. "Let's go."

CHAPTER
Fourteen

Weston

The Drakes let Connor take the limo for the night. On the drive west, he and his friends cleaned out the limo's mini-bar. They were loud and stumbling by the time we got to Roxie's forty-five minutes later, which was crammed for a weeknight. Apparently, a dollar drink special had brought out a bunch of locals.

Connor and his buddies headed straight for the pool tables at the back. One at the rear turned to offer help, but I irritably waved him off, and then regretted it. I could hardly maneuver through the crowd and was cursed at a dozen times for bumping into heels or rolling over feet. I wondered if I'd been this oblivious to wheelchair users when I wasn't trapped in one. I couldn't remember a single interaction.

Going to the bar to order a drink was out of the question. If I managed to push my way through the crowd, the bar top itself was on a level with my chin. I'd be like a little kid peering over the side trying to get the bartender's attention. No, thanks.

I saw a small table near the pool tables and headed for it, stopping twice to move aside chairs in the narrow path. I caught a guy at a neighboring table nudging his two pals. He had an impressive beer gut beneath a red shirt, and he rolled his eyes, as if my very presence irritated him.

LONG LIVE the Beautiful Hearts

It was hot as fuck in here. Connor and I had left our uniform coats in the limo, and I'd stripped out of my dress shirt too, down to a white undershirt. A waitress in cutoff denim shorts and a midriff T-shirt stopped by the table.

"Boilermaker," I said. "Two of them."

Connor racked up the balls at the pool table, getting ready to play the guy in the red shirt, and laughing. I could see the change in him, even if they couldn't. His laugh had a harsher edge to it and his smile wasn't reflected in his eyes. He laid his left arm with the brace on the table and made a crack about how he could still beat everyone there, brace or not.

The waitress came back with two shots of whiskey and two beers. I plunked a twenty on her tray and took her arm before she could move away.

"Two more," I told her. I had no idea when she'd be back and I needed to get good and drunk.

"You might want to think about slowing down," she said.

"You might want to think about minding your own fucking business," I muttered to her back.

Connor finally glanced my way and I held his gaze as I downed both of the whiskey shots, one after the other. Instead of dousing the fuse, the shots were gasoline on the flame.

Fuck this.

I rolled over to the rack of pool cues and grabbed one off the wall. Connor's opponent watched me the whole time.

"I got this one," I told Connor's friend, who shrugged.

"You gonna play?" the red shirt asked, dubiously.

I ignored him and rolled toward Connor. "Whaddya say, buddy? Just like old times?"

He scowled into his beer bottle but shrugged. "Sure."

Red shirt wouldn't let up. "There's hardly room to stand."

"Your concern warms my heart, but I'll be okay," I said.

"So much for getting a good game in. Why would you even come to a place this crowded?"

"Hey," Connor snapped. His eyes were dark and bleary with alcohol. "He can go wherever he wants to, asshole. It's a free country."

"No shit, he's allowed," the guy said. "I just don't get why he'd *want* to."

Connor set his beer down, his jaw hard.

"Let it go," I told him.

He ignored me. "Same reason as anyone else," he said, standing at his full height. "And I'll tell you how he got in that chair, asshole."

"Connor, don't," I said. He was finally acknowledging my existence, but I knew where it was headed—to his own goddamn guilt.

"He got in that chair by sacrifice. You wanna know where we just came from?"

The red shirt snorted. "The Special Olympics?" His buddies laughed.

Connor's eyes flared with rage. "United States Army, 1st Battalion, 22nd Infantry."

The laughter stopped.

"That's right," Connor said, pointing at me with his beer bottle. "They gave him a Purple Heart and a Bronze Star today. Because he's a fucking hero who runs at live grenades to save dumb pieces of shit who got him into combat in the first place."

The whiskey roiled like fire in my gut. "Jesus, Connor, shut the fuck up."

The red shirt held up his hands. "Hey, man. Sorry. I didn't know—"

"That's right, you didn't know," Connor said, his entire body coiling and itching to fight. "Because you're a dumb piece of shit who needs to be taught a lesson."

The guy's chagrin was morphing to anger. "I said I was sorry. You need to calm down before you get yourself in trouble, son."

Wrong choice of words.

The word 'son' hung in the air for a split second and then Connor charged the guy, fists cocked. A beer bottle shattered on the ground as they grappled, and the sound was like the starting bell to a prize fight—the guy's friends and Connor's baseball buddies went at each other in a flurry of swinging fists and grunts.

I moved my chair to the center of the brawl, waiting for someone to take a shot at me, or smash a bottle over my head. I was ready for it. Welcomed it. I sat in the eye of a tornado of guys grabbing at shirt collars and throwing clumsy punches, but no one touched me. No one looked at me. I was invisible, even to my best friend who was defending me.

The fuses that had been burning down all day, lit.

LONG LIVE the Beautiful Hearts

The red shirt guy had Connor pinned against the wall; Connor using his elbow brace to keep him at bay. I picked up the nearest beer bottle and with a scream of rage, hurled it at my best friend's head.

My dart skills hadn't been diminished by booze or my shorter vantage. The bottle hit right where I put it, smashing on the wall just above Connor where it rained beer and shards of glass over him and the red shirt.

"Fuck," the guy cried, and Connor used the distraction to give him one last shove, sending him sprawling on his ass.

Then Connor stared at me, breathing hard, his hands clenched into fists.

"That's right," I seethed, beckoning him to me. "Come on, I'm right here."

With amber drops of beer and bright green shards of glass dusting his hair and shoulders, he took a menacing step toward me. I'd never seen his eyes so full of rage.

"You want to take a shot?" I sneered. "Do it. I'm right here. *I'm right fucking here.*"

He hesitated, and I threw another bottle that smashed at his feet.

"Come on!"

The roadhouse went quiet as Connor and I stared each other down, the pain radiating between us. Then he sagged and turned away, shaking glass out of his hair. I looked for something else to hurl at him, but I was out of ammo and the bouncer was kicking us all out.

The night was sticky and hot. Connor's buddies, some of them bruised and bloodied, laughed and slapped each other on the back, pumped with adrenaline and alcohol. Connor stalked to the limo and climbed in.

We drove back to Amherst and dropped off Connor's friends, then drove to our new, modified condo, arriving sometime after midnight. Amber cones of light from tall lamps lit the condo complex's walkways. I followed Connor down the path, my arms working hard to keep up with him, but it was useless.

I was too slow.

Connor headed straight for the kitchen. I slammed the front door shut and moved to the center of the living room, watching him pop a beer. I sat, motionless, staring. Waiting.

Finally Connor shook his head. "What? Just what the fuck do

you *want*, Wes?"

"What do I want? Are you fucking kidding me?"

"Jesus, you threw a bottle at my head."

"I missed on purpose. But now that I have your attention, you're going to fucking talk to me. Is this about Autumn?"

His lip curled. "Is it about Autumn? About how you and she nearly fucked ten feet away from me the night before our deployment?"

I sat back in my chair. He knew and the betrayal hurt him; of course it did. That explained everything. I nearly sighed with relief.

"Yeah, man. That happened. But it was all my fault, and I'm sorry—"

"Jesus Christ, Wes, *shut up*. You honestly think I'm pissed about *that*?"

"You just said—"

"I don't give a shit that you almost fucked her. I wish you had." His eyes dropped to the beer bottle in his hand. "You forget that I know everything. How you feel about her."

I shook my head. "I told you. I wrote all those letters for you. For you and her. Whatever I felt for her died in Syria."

"That's a goddamn lie."

I started to protest, but he barreled over me.

"How did it go? *I'll bring down the stars for you...*"

I stiffened. "You... You read that?"

"Sure did," he said mockingly. "I can't remember all of it. My memory's full of gaps. But I remember the important parts. You loving her with your hands tied. Writing how you love her but putting someone else's name at the bottom of the page. My name."

"I...I thought that notebook was lost..."

He scoffed. "Well, it is now. I tried to mail it to Autumn, but I fucked that up too."

The blood drained from my face. "What do you mean, you tried?"

"I should've just kept it. Held on to it and put it right in her hands when we got back. But I was messed up out there. My head... I thought I was dying."

"What happened to it?"

He shrugged. "It's gone. I told someone in the chopper... I can't remember who. I told them to mail it to her. If she hasn't gotten it by now, then she probably won't."

I eased a sigh of relief, even as I mourned the words I'd never get back. The last poem I wrote before being blown to hell.

The last words I'd ever write.

"So she doesn't know," I said. "Do you still love her?"

"Does it matter?"

"Do you?"

"Even if I did, she's yours, Wes. She loved my *soul*, remember? That's you, not me. She loves you. I'm just an empty vessel. You poured your words into me and she drank it up." He took another pull from his beer. "How's that for poetic?"

I wheeled my chair closer to him. "You don't love her? I'm not asking for me, I'm asking for Autumn. She's—"

"You're asking because you're so desperate for it to be true, I can practically smell it." He gave another bitter laugh. "The irony is, you're the one sitting in that chair feeling *inadequate* or some shit, but it turns out, I'm the half-man. I'm the asshole with no depth. No soul worth loving except the one you gave me."

"That's not true," I said. "You're talking drunk bullshit right now."

"Am I? I'm not enough for her. I never was. You think I'd give it another shot, knowing all she'll be is disappointed when I can't come up with the right words? *Your* words?"

"That doesn't mean you don't have a soul, for fuck's sake." I rolled into the kitchen, feeling short and pinned to my chair while Connor towered over me. "Look, it was a dumb idea and we took it too far, but you wanted it, man. You wanted her, and you were willing to do anything—even join the goddamn Army—to prove yourself to her. You can't just walk away—"

Connor barked a harsh laugh. "I've spent my entire goddamn life trying to prove myself to everyone."

"That's bullshit too," I said. "You were happy being yourself until you tried to be someone else—"

"Not *someone* else. You. I wanted to be you."

I sat back in my chair.

Me?

Connor Drake wanted to be the poor bastard whose own dad didn't think he was worth sticking around for?

"I wanted what you have," Connor said. "To think on deeper

levels. To turn women on with my thoughts and words. To be *more*. Everyone wants me to be more than what I am and I fail them. Over and over, I just fail everyone." Connor hung his head, the anger draining out of him. "Especially you."

"You didn't fail me," I said, moving closer to him.

"You'd still be able to walk if it weren't for me."

"You saved my life out there. They told me. If it weren't for you stopping the bleeding—"

"Saved your life?" Connor scoffed, shaking his head over a sip of beer. "I set the house on fire, then pulled you out. What a fucking hero."

"I signed up on my own free will. And on that dirt road, I did what I was supposed to do. As a soldier and as your friend." I clasped my hand on his arm. "I'd do it again in a second, man. I would."

Connor stared at me with red-rimmed eyes. "It's over, Wes. All of it."

"What's over?"

"Her and me. Me and you. Amherst. Boston. This…" He gestured at our apartment. "It's over. I'm done."

He walked into the living room, and I followed. "Connor, wait."

He turned around suddenly. "You know, when we saw Autumn today? The way she was looking at you? I nearly told her everything."

The way she was looking at me…

"But I was scared of fucking that up too. I didn't have the words." His expression softened with his voice. "You have them, Wes. You can tell her the truth so she'll understand. Tell her you love her. Take a fucking chance at being happy for once in your life."

"It's too late," I whispered. "She'll hate me."

"Probably. For a little while." Connor sighed. "Whatever, man. Do what you want. I'm done fucking shit up for you." He started down the hall toward his bedroom.

"Jesus, Connor, *stop*. You didn't fuck anything up."

"It's a nice thing you said just now, about how you'd do it over again. But the fact is, you wouldn't be sitting in that goddamn chair if it weren't for me and everyone knows it." He looked back, his eyes shining. "That's the truth, and God, I can't even look at you, Wes. I can't fucking stand the sight of you."

I stiffened, feeling cold all over as he turned his back and continued down the hallway.

"Connor, wait. Talk to me. Or talk to someone. You were injured too. The shit we saw over there? It's messing with you. It's…"

Turning you into someone I don't recognize.

His bedroom door shut, not with a slam, but a resigned *click*. I wheeled after him and banged on it.

"Connor, come on. Talk to me. Open the goddamn door."

No answer, only the sound of dresser drawers opening and closing. Fear sunk claws into me. Did he still have his service revolver? Was he looking for it? Were things this bad and I didn't see it?

I tried the knob, then pounded on the door again.

"Drake, I'm not fucking around. It doesn't matter what anyone else thinks. Only what I think. No one forced me to sign up. I needed those benefits. I signed the papers. It's my injury and *I* get to say how I got it. No one gets to fucking tell me how to feel about it, including you. And I say it's not your fault." My fist slammed again. "Dammit, Connor, *open the door.*"

The door swung open and a sigh gusted out of me. In my friend's hand was a duffel bag, not a weapon.

Connor studied my relief and his lip curled. "Jesus, Wes, did you think I was gonna off myself? Really?" He barked a harsh laugh and stepped around my chair.

I wheeled after him. "So you're leaving? At one in the morning?"

Connor shrugged, gathered his keys and wallet from the front table. "Keep the condo. I'll let my parents know I'm okay, but that's it."

"Connor…"

"They gave me my trust fund. Six million dollars. I guess I *demonstrated* enough *responsibility*. Finally. I put some money into your account. You can use it for school or…not. Whatever you want to do."

"I don't want your money."

"Too late," he said. "It's what I'm good for."

"That's not true. Where are you going?"

He grabbed his coat off the hook. "I'm done trying on different lives other people want for me. I'm tired of living with what I've done. I'm starting over. I'm erasing all the words, Wes."

I grasped at something, anything to get him to stay. "You think running away will fix everything?"

"I can't fix a goddamn thing," Connor snapped. "That's the fucking problem. And I can't live seeing what I did to you every day."

"I'm okay," I said through gritted teeth. "Or I will be. But don't do this. Don't…"

Don't go.

I clenched my jaw, my throat thick. "You're my best friend."

Connor flinched, then opened the front door. "Tell Autumn the truth. She'll be pissed. And hurt. But only for a little while. She loves you. And once she realizes she's had your soul all this time, she'll be so happy… Tell her I'm sorry someday." He raised his eyes to mine. "Because I am. Sorry. I'm so fucking sorry, Wes."

Then he left.

PART IV
September

CHAPTER Fifteen

Autumn

"Hey, look who it is."

"Holy shit. The Amherst Asshole."

With a jolt, I picked up my head from an almanac of United States agricultural history. The whispers came from two girls at the next table. I followed their gaze across the library and saw Weston a few aisles over, wheeling his way past chair legs and backpacks. A scowl twisted his chiseled features, but he still looked sharply beautiful in jeans and a black T-shirt.

"The rumors speak true," one of the girls said behind her hand.

"Right?" her friend said. "I thought it was just talk. But nope. Paralyzed."

Weston had come to a halt, unable to get around a guy whose chair was pushed back into the aisle.

"Having a hard time choosing a table to sit at?" Weston said, loud enough to make a half-dozen heads lift up from their work.

The guy glanced around. "What?"

"You're in the middle of the goddamn aisle. Pick a table and shove the fuck over."

"Sorry, man." The guy scooted his chair closer, and Weston pushed through the narrow aisle to a spot at the end of a table. He parked his wheelchair, then reached around for his backpack. He dumped it on the table, roughly setting up his study materials.

"Still an asshole," murmured the girl at the next table. She twirled a lock of dark hair around her finger. "And still ridiculously hot."

"Amen," said her friend.

You should taste one of his kisses, I thought.

"Too bad though," the dark-haired girl said. "There's probably nothing happening downtown." She indicated her lap.

"I know. Such a shame."

Anger made the words on the almanac pages blur before my eyes. I was about to inform them that nothing was shameful about serving one's country, when a familiar feeling came over me. Identical to a sensation I'd had last year in this same library. An electric tingle shivering over my skin. I looked up.

Weston was looking at me. Our eyes met but he didn't see me. Or rather, he was seeing all of me at once, past memories filling his eyes as he looked at me here and now. The full force of his attention was a shot of *zing* straight to my heart that spread over my chest and melted into a low heat. We both looked away.

All right, calm down, I told my pounding heart. *It's a small school. You knew this was going to happen.*

But I didn't know it would take everything I had to keep my eyes from seeking his again. Or how my body remembered his hands on me, his mouth on mine, and the weight of him pressing me into that couch. How I'd spread my legs to feel more of him.

A few more moments and I would've had all of him…

I pressed my knees together and shifted in my seat. Slamming the almanac closed, I opened a new textbook and turned its pages, repeating my vows.

Never again will I let my heart become someone else's plaything.

Never again will I—

The electric tingle came again and I looked up to see Weston looking at me. His gaze immediately slid away.

Dammit.

Stronger than the physical memories of Weston was the friendship born in this library. The talks we'd had. The feeling I could be myself and he understood me. Was there any greater gift from one

115

human being to another than understanding? I doubted it.

I missed it.

I had my vows and I meant to keep them, but I missed Weston. That one drunken detour on the couch aside, he'd always been my safe haven.

I gathered my things, rose, and started down the aisle. A glance at Weston showed him steadfastly *not* looking at me...until I veered course for his table. His eyes widened and met mine, and the lure of falling into the depths of his ocean eyes was tangible, but I wasn't the same person I'd been a year ago. I wanted to make sure he was okay, but I had to be okay too.

"Hi," I said.

"Hey."

"Can we talk? I won't keep you."

He hesitated, then nodded. Once.

I set my books on his table, sat down, and rested my arms on them. "How are you doing? Truly."

"Okay," he said. "Getting on. Class, rehab, doctor appointments. Rinse. Repeat."

"How's it been adjusting?"

"Basically wheelchair life sucks ass," he said. "No aisle is wide enough. The sidewalks are all cracked. Everyone stares at me, but no one looks me in the eye."

Except I was. And the pain in those ocean blue depths was miles deep. Sadness seemed embedded into every fiber of his being. He sat in the wheelchair, resigned. Weighed down. As if he couldn't stand up even if he were capable.

And I couldn't stop looking at him.

"They're not staring at you because you're in a wheelchair," I heard myself say.

"No?"

They're staring at you because you're beautiful.

"You stand out, Weston," I said, my cheeks burning. "I'll just leave it at that."

"Yeah, I'll bet I do."

"So." I gestured at his books. "Econ major. Still going to be a Wall Street vulture?" The joke fell flat now. Like it belonged in another time. The Before. I waved my hands. "Don't answer that."

He shrugged. "I suppose that's where I'll end up. In an office somewhere, pushing numbers around."

"Is that what you want?"

He smiled bitterly. "If it's in a wheelchair accessible building, what more could a guy ask for?"

A lot, Weston. You could ask for a lot out of this life.

"What about you?" he asked. "Did you pick an emphasis for your Harvard project?"

"I did," I said. "I'm going to work in agricultural technologies, and my project is going to be bringing new legislation in front of Congress to increase farmer accessibility to biofuels and offer better tax incentives for those who use them."

"Uh huh," Weston said.

"Ruby calls it my corn gasoline project."

"How is Ruby?"

"Fantastic, as usual. Living it up in Italy." I smiled ruefully. "I miss her. Even if she can't stop making fun of my project. She thinks it's boring as hell."

"Doesn't matter what anyone thinks about it but you," Weston said.

"Exactly, thank you."

He held my gaze for a moment, searchingly. I broke first with a sigh.

"My corn gasoline project is boring as hell."

His mouth widened in a smile and he chuckled, low and throaty.

"Don't laugh at me," I said, laughing.

"Sorry, but for a second you just looked so..."

"What?"

"Nothing." The smile faded as he lifted one of his legs, adjusting it. "Muscle spasm," he said to my concerned look. "It's nothing. Anyway, I imagine it sucks being bored with your life's work."

"I just haven't found my groove yet," I said. "But I'm not giving up. I can't. I've lost enough time already."

His eyes grew heavier and he nodded. "Yeah, you did."

I hesitated. "How's Connor?"

"Your guess is as good as mine," Weston said. "He took off before the school year started. Haven't seen or heard from him since." A grimace flitted over his features at my alarmed expression. "Let me rephrase: *I* haven't heard from him, but his mother tells me he's been in contact. He's okay but he won't say where he is."

"He just…left?"

"After the medal ceremony." Weston's lip curled. "The Drakes gave him his trust. I guess they figured almost losing his arm and suffering God-knows-how-much PTSD was worth six million dollars. I just hope he's not using the money to drink himself to death somewhere."

"Jesus, me neither." I shivered at the thought. "I'm so sorry."

"For what?"

"That he left. He's your best friend."

Weston waved a hand. "Doesn't matter."

"It matters to me. How you're doing matters to me, Weston." I heaved a breath. "Look, I'll be honest with you. I didn't come over here to make small talk."

"Good. I hate small talk."

"Me too. And I really hate it with you. We were always *more* than that."

"Yeah," he said slowly. "We were."

I leaned over my arms, my gaze on my hands. "So I'm going to confess something to you. It's going to sound terrible."

"Okay."

"I miss our friendship more than I miss being Connor's girlfriend."

The blue-green of his eyes lit up for the first time. "Autumn…"

"I do. And that night on the couch—"

"Don't."

"I have to." I pushed on. "That night was exactly what you said it was. I had too much to drink and I was lonely and scared. And—let's be real—you're extremely good-looking and I'm a mortal female."

He frowned, confused, as if the compliment didn't make sense, even as his pulse pulsed a little faster in the hollow of his throat.

"I always felt we had a connection," I said. "I'm going to do my work and finish my project and go to Harvard. That's non-negotiable. But…it wouldn't suck if we could still be friends."

He sighed and ran his hand through his hair. The heaviness returned to his eyes and when he spoke again, his voice was low, as if it were burdened too.

LONG LIVE the Beautiful Hearts

"I'm not…much good for anything right now," he said. "Or any time soon. It's why I was such an asshole to you in Baltimore."

I twined my fingers tight to keep from taking his hands. "I know you were upset at the hospital, and I feel like I gave up on you too quickly. You told me to leave and I left, but I regret it. A lot."

He was shaking his head from side to side. "Don't waste your feelings on me, Autumn."

"What does that mean?"

"Look, I'm glad you came to talk to me just now. It's really good to see you but I can't do this to you again."

"Do what?"

"Hurt you. I'm not in 'a good place,' as the psychologists like to tell me. I don't want to drag you down too."

"You're not dragging me down," I said. "Being there for each other is what friends do. No matter what."

"Not 'no matter what.' Not at your expense."

"It would cost me more to walk away."

"But you should. For your own sake."

I shook my head. "Everything that happened to you is still new. You haven't had time to process anything."

His eyes flared with anger.

"I don't mean to tell you how to feel, but—"

"Then don't. I've *processed* enough to know this *sucks*. Half my body doesn't work the way it's supposed to anymore. It already feels like I've been pinned here for years and I've got the whole fucking rest of my life ahead."

"But you don't have to do this alone." Now I did lean forward and take his hand. "I want to help."

"Of course you do," he said. "Helping is in your blood. It's who you are." The longing as he looked down at our clasped hands put a fresh crack in my heart. It widened when he slid his hand out from mine. "I don't want your help. I was an asshole to you in Baltimore and I'm so sorry for that. But I meant what I said."

"Weston—"

"Please," he said, his voice turning gruff. "I can't get up and walk away. You need to."

His expression and voice hardened even as the pain swam on the surface of his eyes, making them shine.

"You need to do what I can't do, Autumn. Get up and walk

away."

CHAPTER Sixteen

Weston

November

"Such a fancy restaurant," Ma said. "Are you sure you can afford this?"

"Yeah, Ma, I got it," I told her for the hundredth time that night.

Thanks to Connor, I could afford to take her and Paul out to The Rostand every night of her life for the next decade, not just this Thanksgiving. The night he left, Connor told me he'd put some money in my bank account. "Some money" turned out to be a quarter of a million dollars.

I'd never seen a number that large outside of my Econ textbooks, and months later, it still made me queasy. I hadn't told a soul because I hated it. I hated it, but I needed it, and needing it made me hate myself more.

I wasn't confident I could get a job yet. Adjusting to the wheelchair and training my body for constant sitting, was a slow, agonizing process. Constant physical and mental effort to keep me upright and keep my balance. I worked hard in therapy three times a week, but aches, pains and muscles spasms were a daily occurrence.

And Jesus, my hands were a mess. My wrists constantly smudged dirty from rubbing against the tires as I turned the hand rims. My palms and the tips of my fingers were perpetually blistered.

Dirty hands and chronic pain. Who the hell would hire me?

"Still no word from Connor?" Ma asked, dipping a shrimp into cocktail sauce. I shook my head and she chewed around a disbelieving look. "I can't believe he hasn't come back yet. I can understand taking some time off, but it's been months."

"He's hurting," Paul said. "He should take whatever time he needs."

Ma picked up her water glass to gesture at me with it. "Wes hurts a heck of a lot worse and here he is, busting his butt in rehab and working hard at school." She took a sip of water. "Anyway, I'm proud of you, baby, for not giving up."

"I second that." Paul raised his water glass and clinked it to Ma's.

Not for the first time, I wondered what in the hell Paul Sheffield got out of being with my mother. He laughed with genuine mirth at her jokes and when she leaned over to wipe his mustache with her napkin before planting a kiss beneath it, true happiness shone in his smile. And in hers.

I guess not all men are trash after all, are they, Ma?

My mood grew blacker. I might've been something good for a woman had I not grown up believing I was as shitty as my father.

Pity party, Sock Boy? You fucked up royally with Autumn, so maybe Ma was right.

The entrees were served, and Ma and Paul dug into filet mignon while I had the chicken Kiev.

"You're awfully quiet tonight, Wes," Paul said. "How are things with you?"

"Fine."

Paul pursed his lips. "Anything you'd like to talk about?"

"Nope."

Yep.

The eternal solitude of my life—an empty condo, classes, rehab, back to the condo—was growing oppressive. I was the one who suggested Thanksgiving dinner at a restaurant. Not just because Ma's little house in Boston was a wheelchair-user's worst nightmare, but because I wanted to talk. I wanted to have words in my life again.

LONG LIVE the Beautiful Hearts

Have a conversation that ran deep and lasted for hours. Where I could say anything and be understood. Or say nothing and that was okay too.

Autumn.

Her name, the answer to my heart's every question.

I pushed the thought down with the rest of the pain, but Paul, who had an uncanny sense of timing, pulled it right back up again.

"How's Autumn?" he asked. "Is she in Nebraska for Thanksgiving?"

"I don't know," I said, pushing my food around. "I haven't talked to her in a while."

Fifty-six days, thirteen hours and forty-three minutes. Give or take.

"That's too bad," Paul said. "When I saw her at your Purple Heart ceremony, I thought you two had—"

"We haven't," I said. "She's busy. She has to work on her Harvard project."

"How is she taking it that Connor's gone?" Paul asked, then shook his head. "Never mind that. How are *you* taking it that he's gone?"

"I miss him," I admitted.

It's like a missing limb. A piece of myself. Like being paralyzed all over again.

Ma snorted. "Who needs him? To up and leave like that? To throw away so many years of friendship?"

"It's more complicated than that," I said in a low voice.

"Seems pretty cut and dried to me. You took the worst of what happened over there, and you're okay."

"I'm not—"

Ma beamed. "Which is why I'm so proud of you."

"Stop saying that," I said, my hand clenched around my fork. "You say that a hundred times a day."

"So? It's true. And anyway, I—"

I slammed my fork down. It clattered across my plate and hit the floor. "Jesus, Ma."

She stared in shock. "What'd I say?"

"Nothing, that's the problem," I said, my Boston accent thickening to match hers. "For once in my life can you say something honest? Something real?"

Ma looked at me as if I were crazy. "What in the hell are you talking about? I'm telling it like I see it."

"Then see *me*, Ma. Look at me when I tell you everything is not okay. *I'm* not okay. Nothing is fucking okay."

She sat back in her seat. "You going to talk to your mother like that? When I've done nothing but try to take care of you after your piece of shit father up and left?"

"Miranda," Paul began.

"Don't," I snapped at him. "Don't try to smooth it all over. Don't talk to her like she's your wife and you're my..."

Piece of shit father.

I bit off the rest of my sentence and swallowed it down. "Never mind. Forget it. Forget I said a goddamn word."

"Well, sure, let's do that." Ma dabbed the linen napkin to the corners of her eyes. "Let's pretend the beautiful evening isn't ruined. It's Thanksgiving for crying out loud."

I scrubbed my hands over my face. "Ma, I'm sorry." I reached my hand for hers. "I'm sorry. I didn't mean it."

"You know what we forgot to do?" she said, looking at us both. "We forgot to go around and say what we're thankful for. I'll start. I'm thankful you're still here, Wes. Connor's gone, but you... You're still here. And I'm thankful. How's that for real?"

I looked at her then. Tried to *see* her as I'd begged her to see me. To notice and remember how she held things together since my dad left us. Plugging holes in a leaky dam, one after the other, trying to keep the whole thing from collapsing. To survive another day with a roof over our heads and the lights turned on was a victory. If I was alive and could breathe and eat and talk, that's all that mattered.

"It's fine, Ma," I said, the anger deflating completely and leaving shame in its wake. "More than fine. Perfect. Thank you."

Paul turned to me then. "I'll just say one thing. If you need help, ask for it. It's both the hardest and easiest thing in the world to do. But ask."

After dinner, Paul and Ma dropped me off at the condo and drove back to Boston. I went back to my empty place, and though it was only nine o'clock, exhaustion had seeped into my worn-out muscles and I was ready to hit the sack.

I struggled out of my clothes and into sweatpants and a T-shirt. In the bathroom, I catheterized myself and taped a plastic bag to my thigh so I wouldn't piss myself while I slept. I transitioned from chair

L O N G   L I V E the Beautiful Hearts

to bed, wrapped the special circulation blanket around my legs and used the body pillow to prop me on my side. The skin around my tailbone had developed an irritation that would turn into a pressure sore if I wasn't careful.

What a fucking life.

Ask for help.

Paul probably was referring to himself, or maybe a therapist, but there was only one person who could help me.

I squeezed my eyes shut against the ache in my heart. I couldn't impose my life on Autumn. It was unfair and selfish after pushing her away. But the loneliness around and inside me was hollowing me out. I was starving to death without her. I needed to fill my eyes with her beautiful face. I hungered to see her eyes light up when she spoke of something that moved her. I wanted to gorge myself on her laugh, or better yet, *make* her laugh. Fill the empty places in my life with her voice that always spoke words of goodness, kindness, and compassion.

I hugged the body pillow tighter.

My writing was dead, so what did it matter if we were just friends? I'd never have to tell her the truth about the letters and poems because there wasn't going to be any more letters or poems. There was nothing to hide.

Without your words, you have nothing to give her in return. Not one damn thing.

Except that she said she felt she could always be herself around me. Maybe that was worth something.

It wasn't much, I thought, as I drifted off to sleep, but it was all I had.

The Panache Blanc bakery was crowded as hell on Monday morning. In my past life, I'd have taken my place in line like everyone else without a second thought. Now I was self-conscious about so many people around me, paranoid I'd bump someone with my chair, and feeling short when once I would've towered over everyone.

How little people looked at me now that I was in the chair.

Most of the time, their glances flicked once and darted away. Other people stared as if trying to figure out what was wrong with me. Some talked to me as if I were mentally slow. Men called me "buddy" or "pal." Women smiled at me with pity when they held the door for me, never attraction or possibility.

Those days are over.

My heart crashed in my chest to see Autumn looking vibrant and beautiful, her hair pulled up in a bun with tendrils down. She was working the registers, running back and forth to fill pastry orders. My pulse thudded hard when she bent to grab a croissant from the display case and our eyes met through the glass.

Her eyes widened, her lips parted and for a split second, a smile lifted the corners of her mouth. Then her beautiful features hardened and she returned to her customer. She kept shooting dark, confused glances at me as the line progressed, until it was my turn to order.

"A coffee, please," I said.

A faint pinkness touched her cheeks as she stared me down in my black turtleneck and jeans. "What are you doing here, Weston?"

Asking for help.

"I want to talk to you."

"Now? I'm a little busy."

"After your shift."

"That's in four hours."

"I'll wait."

She frowned, put her hands on her hips. I could see a million thoughts running behind her hazel eyes, not the least of which was how many times she was willing to put up with me pushing her away. But I knew her. I knew her heart.

One last chance. That's all I ask.

She pursed her lips, then turned to pour me a coffee and handed it over. "You're going to wait here for four hours?"

"Yes."

"The place is packed. There's nowhere to—"

"Weston! Mon homme tranquille!" Edmond de Guiche came around the counter to hug my shoulders. "So good to see you, my friend."

"Good to see you, Edmond."

The large Frenchman beamed at Autumn. "This is good, non?"

LONG LIVE the Beautiful Hearts

She tucked a lock of hair behind her ear. The customer behind me sighed loudly.

"What can I do?" Edmond asked. "What do you need? To sit at a table?" He assessed his crowded bakery. A man occupied the large table by the door that was reserved for the disabled, his laptop and books spread out. Edmond pounced.

"Oi! Sir. If you would be so kind…"

"Edmond, wait," I called. "We can share it…"

Too late. Edmond rousted the guy from the table and offered it to me with a flourish. My face burning, I took my coffee.

"I'll just be right over here, then," I told Autumn.

She pressed her lips together to conceal her smile, then tilted her chin stiffly. "If you insist."

"Ah, yes," Edmond said, as I parked my chair at the table. "This, I like."

He pinched my cheek as he began a booming aria that filled the bakery and returned to work behind the counter.

Since I had four hours to kill, I took out my own laptop and books to study. I was ditching class to be here, but it was worth it if Autumn was willing to hear me out.

I'd drop out if it meant sitting across from her one more time.

I pretended to be interested in my econ work, but the numbers and facts were blocks of incomprehensible text. My eyes kept straying to Autumn. Despite the crowd, she never looked harried or impatient. She greeted everyone with a smile, and every now and then she caught me watching her. On the third time she lifted her eyebrows and planted her hands on her hips.

I chuckled into my book. As if I could help but stare at her.

You're extremely good-looking and I'm a mortal male.

An hour later, the morning rush died down and she came from behind the counter to refill my coffee.

"Are you hungry?" she asked. "Can I bring you something?"

"I'm good."

"Are you, Weston?" she asked. "Are you really good?"

I looked up at her intense, searching gaze. "Autumn, I—"

She waved me off. "Don't answer. Not until I can give you my full attention." She checked her watch. "Which won't be for three more hours."

"I'll wait."

"You'll wait," she repeated. "I'm sorry, I just…"

"What?"

"Why are you *here*?"

I opened my mouth and she flapped her hand again, adorably flustered. "Don't answer."

I chuckled as she stormed off. Two hours and fifty-five minutes later, she plopped down in front of me.

"Well?" she said.

"Can I talk now?"

"Yes."

"You sure?"

She narrowed her eyes at me, and I laughed. God, just being in her presence was breaking up the black cloud hanging over my head.

"It's not actually funny," she said, crossing her arms. "I'm happy to see you but that doesn't mean this is easy. Whatever this is."

My smile faded. "I hurt you."

"Yes, you did."

"I'm sorry. I have no excuse except you were right. I wasn't in a good place when I…"

Her eyebrows raised. "Kicked me out of your life? Twice?"

"Yes." I leaned back, both a sigh and a laugh gusting out of me.

Her eyes flared. "What's so damned funny?"

"You. No matter how much of an asshole I am—"

"And we know you can be," she said.

"It's kind of my thing," I said, actually grinning. "Everyone but you talks to me like I'll shatter if I don't hear a hundred times a day how strong I am."

"A mere shell of a man but *somehow* persevering?" Autumn said with a hesitant smile.

"Exactly," I said. "Although 'shell of a man' isn't that far off the mark."

"You're not—"

"I miss our friendship, too."

Her gaze jumped to mine. "You do?"

"Yeah, I do. Basically you're the only person I want to talk to. The only person who says what she means. Everything you say is something good and real."

Autumn held my gaze unwavering, her gemstone eyes looking

at me, and I knew she really saw *me*.

"I wouldn't blame you if you wanted nothing more to do with me," I said. "If you want me to go, I will, and I promise I won't bother you again." I swallowed the jagged lump in my throat as I realized how much was at stake in this moment. "I don't deserve it, but I hope you'll give me one more chance."

She glanced down at her hands on the table and was quiet for a long moment. Then she glanced at her watch and my heart sank.

Conversation over. She's done with me. She has work to do and classes to go to and—

"It's past lunch time," she said. "I'm kind of hungry and you've been waiting here *four* hours." She looked up at me, a beautiful smile on her full lips, her eyes warm and full of forgiveness. "Do you want to go get something to eat?"

"Yeah," I said, my voice gruff. "Yeah, I do."

CHAPTER
Seventeen

Autumn

December

"I'm sorry, Autumn," my advisor said. "I know this isn't what you wanted to hear."

"No, it's not." I clutched the phone tighter. "What am I going to do?"

I wasn't asking her so much as myself. Harvard had rejected my biofuels project, and the news sank to the pit of my stomach like a rock.

"Look," Ms. Robinson said, "you're already looking at a late application for next spring or even next winter. You can modify the project and try again or come up with something else. Or you might want to think about taking some time off. Refocus your efforts."

I heard the subtext loud and clear: *Take some time off and get your shit together, girl.*

"Yeah, okay," I said. "I'll think about it."

"You're still on track to graduate Amherst with honors, so chin up, dear, and Happy Holidays."

"Thanks, you too."

We hung up and I let my phone drop in my lap.

L O N G   L I V E   the Beautiful Hearts

"Crap."

Months of painstaking, laborious work down the toilet. The apartment was too quiet to contend with the news alone. I picked up my phone again and texted Weston.

I need to talk. :(

There was no immediate answer. I texted Ruby the same message, realizing she'd moved from being my first phone call to my second. After Weston.

Makes sense, I thought. *She's thousands of miles away, while Weston and I see each other practically every day. That's all.*

She texted back: **What's up?**

Harvard rejected my project. Can I call you? I typed. **It's been awhile.**

A pause then, **Sure.**

I dialed her number at the villa in La Spezia. The funny ring buzzed three times before she answered.

"Hey, girl." Her voice sounded tight and high. "So Harvard's a no-go?"

"They said the focus was too narrow."

"Their loss."

"It's not a complete fail," I said. "My counselor says there's always time to submit a new project."

"Right. That's cool, I guess. I mean, if you wanted to."

I frowned. "Is this a bad time? You sound a little distracted."

"No way, Goose, I'm here," she said louder. "So what are you up to? It's still day over there, isn't it?"

"Yeah, Weston and I are going grocery shopping."

"A hot date at the grocery store. That is so you."

My cheeks warmed. "Not a date. We're only friends."

"So you keep telling me."

"Because it's true."

"Uh huh. You've been spending a lot of time with Mr. Turner. Anything interesting happening I should know about?"

"In the six seconds since I told you we're just friends? No. My status has not changed."

"Too bad. *It's complicated* is way more fun."

"I'm sticking to my vows to stay focused on my work, and he's still learning to cope with his new life. Neither of us is looking for more."

"Sounds practical, safe and more boring than corn gasoline," Ruby said. "How's Wes doing, anyway?"

"He's fine. Definitely much better than the last time you saw him. He's getting through his econ major and rehab and he seems to be adjusting better and better every day."

"Good. That's good. Glad to hear it."

The distraction was back in her voice. "Ruby, what—?"

"So listen, I gotta run. Have fun at the grocery store, you two crazy kids," she added with a laugh that sounded forced.

"Okay," I said. "Talk to you soon?"

"Very soon," Ruby said. "And Auts?"

"Yeah?"

A short pause.

"I'm sorry about your Harvard thing falling through. I'm really am."

"Okay. Thanks, Rube."

"Love you."

"Love you too."

I hung up, pursing my lips at my phone and making excuses. Ruby was plenty busy herself. She gave off a YOLO vibe but she was super smart and worked her ass off, which is how she was granted the year abroad in the first place.

I checked my texts again. Nothing from Weston. He should've been done with his rehab by now, and lately we'd been answering each other's texts within minutes.

Because that's what friends do. Nothing complicated about it.

Snow was falling as I walked briskly from my apartment on Rhodes to Weston's luxury condo on the outskirts of the campus. Christmas lights wrapped around lampposts added spirals of gold to the gray afternoon.

My breath plumed in front of me, and I couldn't keep a smile from my lips. I was looking forward to grocery shopping with Weston a lot more than I'd admitted to Ruby.

I knocked on his condo door. Then rang the bell. Faintly, I heard a dull, lifeless "Yeah."

Weston, sounding like he was reluctantly answering roll call. *I'm still here.*

He always left the door unlocked for me; I went inside and found him in the kitchen, hunched over in his wheelchair, staring at a spray of shattered glass around the wheels. It crunched under my shoes as I moved to him.

"Holy shit, what happened? Are you okay?"

He raised his head, his blue-green eyes like a sea, stormy and turbulent. "I was getting a glass of water," he said. "I dropped the glass and heard the gunshots."

Panic lit up my veins for a split second until I realized he was speaking of the past. His deployment. The war.

"You're okay," I said. "It's over."

"Doesn't feel over," he said. "I wasn't hearing the shots that hit me. It was the shots I fired." He fixed his red-rimmed eyes on me, anger burning behind his words. "I killed six people, Autumn. Maybe more. Maybe a lot more."

"You did what you were sent to do. You defended your unit. You saved Connor's life."

"I haven't felt this shitty in a long time. Like I'm underwater." He winced suddenly and reached for his right calf. "And these fucking muscle spasms..."

"Let me." I nudged aside glass with my foot, then crouched on my heels and began rubbing his leg through the course material of his jeans. I noticed his wrists were smudged with black, the palms red with blisters.

"Didn't you tell me your psychologist said the grief comes in waves?" I asked.

"Yeah."

"This is a wave. You're underwater but it'll pass." I kneaded his calf muscle.

Weston stared down at my hands on his leg, longing and regret etched across his downturned mouth and heavy eyes. I was suddenly acutely conscious of him under my fingers; innocently touching him over his jeans but touching him. And touching his legs now wasn't the same as before his injury.

"I'm sorry," I said, snatching my hands back. "I just wanted to help."

"You helped," he said. "But I get it, it's repulsive."

"Repulsive? Why would you say that?"

"Because they're dead."

"They're not," I said. "You can feel pressure and you have spasms, which means they're alive." I took his blistered, dirty hand in mine. "Nothing is repulsive about you, Weston. You're…"

Magnificent.

We locked eyes, and the air between us thickened. The mix of longing and regret in his eyes intensified and for a split second, I saw our night together on the couch reflected in them.

I want to be there again…

I jumped to my feet and went into the pantry to grab the broom and dustpan, my heart pounding.

"You don't have to do that," Weston said as I began sweeping the glass.

"I'm already doing it," I said. I dumped the mess into the trash. "Forget grocery shopping today. I'll make us dinner or we can order in. Or I can go if you want to be alone—"

"*No,*" he said, then gentler. "No. Please stay."

Our eyes locked again. "Okay," I said softly. He was so beautiful. He was wearing a gray, V-neck T-shirt. Was it the same shirt I'd mistakenly put on after I spent the night with Connor, thinking it was his?

Except it was Weston's and I'd never been so turned on by a man's shirt before in my life.

Desperate for a distraction, my eyes fell on a brochure left on the kitchen counter. "What's this?" I flipped through it. "Wheelchair racing, wheelchair basketball, polo…"

"It's nothing. Something Frank, my rehab therapist, gave me. Stupid."

"It sounds great. So many sports you can do. Look, here's *racing*—"

"I don't want to talk about it, okay? I don't want to talk about anything that has to do with me. I'm sick of the subject of *me.*"

He sat still, stiff, bracing himself for me to insist that he talk, that he feel better so that *I* would feel better.

"You don't have to," I said. *Not with me.* "Let's find a silly movie to watch and eat pizza."

He eased a sigh of relief that looked like it began in his bones. "Sounds good."

"I'm on it."

"Autumn." He caught my wrist as I went to get my phone out of my purse.

"Yes, Weston?"

L O N G L I V E the Beautiful Hearts

He looked at my hand in his scarred one and let go. "Thank you."

"Of course," I said, my voice thick.

That's what friends are for.

We ordered pizza and put on *Groundhog Day*. Weston sat on the couch while I sat on the floor in front of it. He didn't laugh once, and toward the end of the movie, he fell into an exhausted sleep.

I shut off the TV and gently eased him to lie down. Carefully, I lifted one of his legs at a time, then went to get the high-tech blanket he wore to improve circulation. I guess it was working because his calf muscle under my hand still felt strong and whole.

"You are strong and whole," I whispered, covering him up. "More than you think."

Even in sleep, his brows were furrowed. I stroked his head until they smoothed out, thinking of a different couch. Weston and I kissing and touching, his body strong and powerful over mine. The strength in how he moved, and the power in his gaze. It stirred my blood. Even after all this time, my mouth could still taste his kiss and my ears remembered the way he said my name as if it were a wish or a prayer.

I pushed down a jagged lump of *complicated* emotions, shouldered my purse, and quietly went out.

CHAPTER
Eighteen

Weston

Ten days before Christmas, Autumn knocked on my condo door.

"It's open," I called.

She came in smelling like clean winter snow and cold, her coat's fur-trimmed hood framing her oval face like a picture.

"Ready for our oft-postponed grocery shopping?" She checked her watch. "I have T-minus four hours to Amtrak."

She was catching the train to Boston, then a flight to Nebraska, but willing to spend her last few hours braving holiday grocery store crowds for me. Food shopping was one of my rehab therapist's assignments. It kept me from relying on take-out food or living off of Amazon.

"Almost ready," I said, tying my laces. "Tell me again why I bother with shoes? Who am I trying to fool?"

"It's so your feet don't freeze," she said. Then she handed me a box wrapped in shiny green paper and tied with a bow. "Merry Christmas."

I scowled at her smug expression. "We swore an oath we wouldn't get each other anything for Christmas, remember?" I said. "An *oath*."

"I'm terrible at remembering oaths." Her smug grin turned shy.

"Besides, it's nothing… It's just a thing. Open it."

Inside the box were two pairs of fingerless gloves made of high-tech nylon. Weatherproof and durable on the outside, soft on the inside.

"I did some research and these are supposed to be the best," she said. "You can still grip the hand rims but they should protect against blisters and help keep your wrists from getting dirty."

"They're perfect." I turned them over in my hands, shocked at how much a pair of gloves affected me. I looked up at her. "Thank you."

"I'm kind of surprised your therapist didn't mention them sooner."

"I'm sure he did, but I wasn't listening."

"I'm sure you didn't even show him your blisters."

"I thought they'd heal eventually," I said. "And no one likes a complainer."

She stared down at me with soft eyes.

"What?"

"Nothing," she said, giving her head a little shake. "Let's go take your gloves out for a spin. Literally."

Outside, snow was piled high in the gutters and the air tasted of ice.

"Walk or ride?" she asked. She wagged her eyebrows. "Or walk and roll? Get it? Walk n'roll?"

I groaned. "That's terrible."

"Isn't it?" she said, laughing.

"Walk," I said. "Ride back." I wanted to spend as much time with her as I could before she got on that plane today.

The sidewalks were clear of snow, though twice I was jolted forward trying to get over a crack.

"You'd think the town would take care of those things," Autumn said. "Simple courtesy to wheelchair users. And anyone who doesn't want to trip and fall on their faces."

"You'd think," I said. I had a list a mile long about how things could be made easier for wheelchair users but saw no sense in getting Autumn riled up about it.

At the grocery store, she grabbed a cart, but I shooed her away.

"I'm supposed to practice," I said, "or I'll never be able to do it alone."

"I'd have to come with you every time."

If only.

"Where to first?"

"Anywhere," I said. "I need three days' worth of food. Nothing frozen. One of my other rehab assignments is to cook a meal."

"Easy enough," Autumn said.

I snorted. "I couldn't cook *before* I was paralyzed. If I don't burn the condo down, it'll be a miracle."

We headed to the produce section—food I could reach on my own.

"Did Connor do the cooking for you guys?" Autumn asked. "I can't imagine he did."

"No. We were a pizza, sandwich, and hot wings household," I said, watching her face.

Does she miss him? Does she wish she were spending her last hours before Christmas break with him instead of me?

"I miss him," she said.

That would be a yes, Sock Boy.

"Me too," I said. A sudden rush of grief welled up from my gut. I breathed through it, instead of fighting it, and let it pass through me. Another strategy from my therapist.

Autumn's smile was sad. "I just want him to be okay."

"His mother tells me he is. She hears from him now and again."

"Does he still not tell her where he is?"

"Nope."

"He's not coming back for Christmas?"

I shook my head and struggled to round a table full of melons with my chair and the shopping cart.

"That's too bad." She picked up a lemon to squeeze. "I hope he's with people who care about him."

"Do you still care about him?" I asked. I didn't want to know, but I had to know.

She glanced at me, then looked away. "I'll always care about him. He's part of my history. But I don't miss *us*, necessarily. Parts of us, maybe. His laugh and his generous heart, mostly."

Not his words?

We circled the produce stands, Autumn picking fruit—keeping or discarding as she spoke—while I followed behind, listening.

LONG LIVE the Beautiful Hearts

"You know, when Connor broke up with me, I made these vows to myself. About not living my life by what my heart dictates. To not let my romantic ideas and hopes make decisions for me, because it only brought me a lot of hurt. First with Mark, then Connor."

And me.

"I vowed not to love again until I knew it was real and true, and wouldn't leave me second-guessing or wondering where I stood."

I nodded, anger burning in my heart for my role in these drastic vows. I took someone as vibrant and full of love as Autumn Caldwell and made her cut herself off from it.

"But you know what vow I forgot to make? To love and trust myself. I might fail, but I'm not a failure. When we stumble and fall, we pour so much energy and attention into the fact that we fell, and less on how we get back up again. Don't you think?"

I nodded my head slowly. *The Once Born and the Twice Born,* I thought and the image of my dad's car speeding away rose in me.

You fall but you get back up.

You keep going, but you stop running.

"I'm starting to think my father was right," Autumn said. "The love I have to give isn't my weakness but my strength."

"He is right," I said. "He's one hundred percent right."

She smiled and flapped her hand. "Apples?"

"Sure."

Autumn set a bag in my cart. "Anyway, what happened between Connor and me hurts. I miss him, but I think it all happened for a reason. And all paths converge right here, to this moment. In a grocery store with you."

She went to get a twist-tie for the plastic bag and didn't see my reaction. God knows how unguarded I must've looked. My heart pounded against my ribs and I sucked in deep breaths to compose myself before she came back. We continued through the store, picking up chicken, rice, and potatoes, then to the soup aisle.

"Which one?" Autumn asked.

"Tomato. The one on the top shelf, of course."

She started to reach for it. "Wait. Am I allowed to help now? What's your therapist say about that?"

"*It's imperative I ask for help instead of going without the items I want or need,*" I recited.

Autumn nodded, stood on her tiptoes and plucked the can off

the shelf. "Do you find people helpful?"

"Most are. Others not so much."

"But you don't let that stop you."

"You haven't heard my new nickname around campus?"

She chucked the soup can into the cart. "Better than Amherst Asshole, I hope."

"Weston 'can you reach that for me?' Turner."

She snickered.

"I'll also answer to 'I'm down here, dumbass,' and 'I can hear just fine, it's my legs that don't work.'"

Autumn frowned. "What about your hearing?"

"Some people talk to me like I'm deaf." I moved down the aisle, rolling my chair with one hand and pushing the cart with the other. "Or like I'm mentally challenged."

"This happens a lot?"

I shrugged. "More than once."

"People should talk to people like they're…people," she said. "Not assume anything until the person tells them what they need. If anything at all."

"That kind of thinking is why you're going to save the world, starting with our nation's farmland." I held up a can of corn. "Gasoline is cheap these days."

"Oh my God, I never told you," she said. "Harvard rejected my project."

"No shit? Damn, I'm sorry." I gave my head a shake. "Wait, no I'm not. You hated the biofuels thing."

"I know, but I feel like I let my family down. And what am I going to do instead? It took me ages to come up with biofuels." She sighed and leaned her arms on the grocery cart handle. "Maybe I should pick a different major."

"Your whole thing is helping people."

"But where to start?"

I shrugged. "Whatever your heart tells you. Whatever feels right."

She put her chin on her hand. "Wise man once told me, 'Feelings…are like tonsils.'"

"He wasn't wise, he was an idiot to say something like that to a girl like you."

"A girl like me?"

LONG LIVE the Beautiful Hearts

I looked away, shoved the cart forward. *Not going there.* "These gloves you got me are a fucking miracle."

She smiled. "I'm glad. Let's get out of here. Get some hot chocolate at the Panache. I need to say goodbye to Edmond before I catch the train."

At the cash register, the woman rang up my purchases.

"Paper or plastic?" the bagger asked Autumn.

"Plastic," I said. "It's damp out."

"That'll be thirty-three, fifteen," the cashier said to Autumn.

"I got it," I said, and fed my bankcard into the machine.

Autumn's arms were crossed, expression narrowed as she watched this play out. When the cashier went to hand her the receipt, she was done.

"It's *his*," she said, and folded her arms into her coat. "Jesus, he's right here."

I smiled thinly at the woman and took the receipt. "Have a nice day."

Outside, Autumn's breath plumed in indignant puffs. "What is *wrong* with people? Does *that* happen a lot?"

"It happens enough," I said.

Another puff of sighed air and her eyes circled the sky. "Seriously? I don't want to make a scene or embarrass you, but that's just tacky."

I shrugged while I crammed the grocery bag into the backpack hanging on the back of my wheelchair. "I'm used to it."

"You are?"

"No," I admitted. "But what am I going to do?"

Autumn worried her lower lip between her teeth, thinking. I couldn't help but smile at this girl.

And what are you going to do, Autumn?

"Mon homme tranquille and my thoughtful girl," Edmond said at Panache Blanc, setting down cups of hot chocolate. "This, I like."

He began a Puccini aria, and went to the back to get a cranberry scone for us to share. Autumn tried to wave it away, but he plunked the plate down, without missing a note of his song, and swept away again, but not before shooting me a knowing look and a wink.

Autumn pulled the scone apart. In that moment she was impossibly beautiful. Red velvet hair and pearl skin against the winter window of snow and gray.

A long time ago, in another life, Edmond once said in French: "The heart hides itself behind the mind."

But what if the heart has to hide to keep from hurting the one it loves?

"Weston?" Autumn asked. "Hungry?"

I blinked and focused. "Yeah, looks pretty good," I said for lack of something better. "You going to have some?"

Autumn gave me a smile I couldn't decipher, soft and almost nervous.

"I guess a few bites can't hurt."

We headed back to Autumn's place to get her suitcase, then took an Uber to the train station. It was bustling with holiday travelers heading to Boston. We found her platform ten minutes before boarding. Autumn sat at the end of a crowded bench and I parked my chair beside her.

"Will you be okay in Boston for the holiday?" she asked.

"I'll survive."

She nodded, huddled deeper into her coat. "I wish..."

"What's that?"

She smiled and shook her head. "Nothing."

Time was ticking down. I wished the people sharing her bench would scram, but it was now or never. I reached under my chair, to the small net beneath the seat, and pulled out a gift wrapped in white paper with a red bow.

Autumn's eyes widened. "An oath, Weston Turner. We took an *oath.*"

"You're one to talk," I said, flashing her my gloves. "Oathbreaker."

"That's not the point." She huffed a sigh and surreptitiously wiped the corner of her eye.

"You haven't even seen what it is," I teased her. "It could be a calendar of World's Best Outhouses."

She nudged me with her arm. "Shut up, the wrapping is beautiful."

The paper fell away to reveal a hardbound journal. A field of puffy white dandelions reached towards a pink and gold sunrise, and gave their feathery seeds to the wind

"Weston, this is beautiful." Autumn trailed her fingers over the cover.

"I figure you can write down your brilliant ideas for saving the world," I said. "Maybe it'll help pick one you truly care about."

She nodded, her gaze on the book, tracing round circles over a flower. "I love dandelions. We have these all over our farm in spring. Mom calls them weeds, but Dad taught us they're for making wishes. I must've made hundreds of wishes on dandelions when I was a kid."

I could see it so easily: a little girl with red braids squeezing her eyes shut as she blew her wishes into the universe. Wishes that she could help make things better, help her family. Before my eyes the little girl morphed into a woman, her poetic heart wishing for someone to share her life with.

Someone worthy of her.

"Thank you," she said.

"You're welcome."

She set the journal down and stood up. She bent at the waist, trying to hug me, but the wheelchair footrests kept her at a distance. I wanted to feel her against me, our arms wrapped tightly around one another. I wanted to *hold* her.

Autumn gripped my shoulders as best she could, then stood back. "Sorry, this isn't going to work."

And before I could even process that, she sat in my lap.

She sat sideways, her hip against mine, and I felt the faint pressure of her weight on my thighs. Our faces were level, inches apart.

"Better?" she asked, her words whispering sweetly across my face.

"Yeah." I swallowed hard. "Better."

She leaned and wrapped her arms around my neck. Mine went around her body, crossing over her slender back and pulling her in close. Her small breasts pressed to my chest, one heart beating against the other. We hugged like kissing, slow and languid, and I breathed into it. Into her. Her lungs expanded under my hands and the heat of her exhale wafted over my neck. I nearly pulled off the gloves she gave me, nearly slipped my hands under her coat, wanting to feel the smoothness of her dress on my palms, the warmth of her skin beneath.

To touch her naked back, to skim my hands over her silken skin, and not stop this time. Nobody in the next room. Nowhere to go the next day.

I had her now though. Right here, right now, I held Autumn and she held me, and it was enough. It was perfect.

"Merry Christmas, Weston," she whispered against my ear.

"Merry Christmas, Autumn," I said hoarsely.

She got up from my lap and went to sit on the bench again, not looking at me. I couldn't stop looking. Holy God, she was radiant. Her cheeks flushed pink and her eyes were dark and deep with…longing? Couldn't be. My body was broken. I had nothing to give her, and yet those eyes of hers wept over me—all of me, head to wheels, while her bottom lip slowly inched back under her teeth.

As if she wanted to kiss me.

The PA loudspeakers split the moment open, announcing her train. She picked up the journal, took the handle of her suitcase and gave me a little wave. "I'll see you soon."

I nodded, cold in my skin now, warmth and hope rising in me, melting the ice and despair and anguish of my new life. But time and distance would kill this moment, like it killed our night on the couch. She'd come back to Amherst having reaffirmed her vows to keep her heart protected.

And she should.

I watched until she made it safely onto the train and I didn't move from my spot until it left the station.

Three days later, at my place, I packed for what was sure to be a Christmas from hell. Ma's old house was probably built before the wheelchair was invented. Navigating it was a bitch. I set one pair of gloves on top of my clothes in the luggage and kept the other on. Because they were so good at relieving the pain.

Driving east in Paul's silver sedan, I stared out the passenger window while Paul tapped the wheel and whistled along to Steely Dan on the radio.

LONG LIVE the Beautiful Hearts

"Autumn heading to Nebraska?" he asked.

"Yep."

"How's she doing?"

"Fine." I hid a smile.

She's bringing me back to life.

CHAPTER
Nineteen

Autumn

January 17, 20—

Weston gave me this journal to write down ideas or concepts for my 'save the world' Harvard project. But I think I'm going to use it as a regular old journal instead, to write down thoughts and feelings. I need the outlet. Ruby hardly talks to me anymore. She rarely texts and our phone conversations are short. When we do talk at length, she still sounds distracted. I know she's busy and living it up in Italy, but I miss her. I've hung out with Julie and Deb down the hall a couple times, but mostly I just like to be with Weston.

We've been hanging out a lot since I came back from Christmas in Nebraska. Almost every day and talking on the phone almost every night. Sometimes for hours. It's so easy to be with him. I don't have to make small talk, he hates gossip as much as I do, and he has no patience for trivial things. Being with him is like being with a mirror. I see my reflection in his eyes and I'm beginning to really like the girl I see. I hope our time together is half as valuable to him as it is to me.

He's so close to his economics degree and I know it gives him no joy. Something inside Weston is begging to come out. I don't know what, but it's something deeper than numbers. Maybe whatever it is inside him was buried in the sands of Syria.

The Sands of Syria. Sounds like a made-for-TV movie.

Weston has so much more to give than he knows. I think once he's adjusted to his new life a little more, he'll find that something and break free of whatever's holding him down. It's not the paralysis that's keeping him trapped, but something intangible. I can't quite put my finger on it, but I know he'll be magnificent one day.

I notice I use "magnificent" a lot when it comes to Weston.

Yes, I remember my vows and I am sticking to them. I told Weston about them at the grocery store—because all deep and meaningful conversations happen in the produce section, don't they? I still have to work on myself. But myself is someone I'm trusting more and more.

I trust Weston more and more.

I'm staring at those words and I don't even know what they mean. Trust him with what? I'm thinking about that night we kissed on the couch almost a year ago. I think about that a lot. Almost every day if I'm being really honest (and where else can I be honest, if not in my own diary?). I wonder if he thinks about it too. Probably not. Or if he does, it's just something that happened in his 'other life.' I suspect he thinks his body is too damaged to be sexy or sexual. Neither is true, in my humble opinion. For his sake, I hope his doctor's appointment will bear that out this weekend.

We're going on a mini-vacation to Boston for three days. Weston has his annual major physical and check-up. We'll stay in a hotel (separate rooms TYVM) and after his appointment, go to dinner. Maybe we'll do something touristy in Boston, or have dinner with Paul and his mother... Actually I don't care what we do.

I just want to be with him.

Is that wrong? He's Connor's best friend. But Connor left and took his words with him. I'm starting to wonder if it was meant to happen. To show me what I've believed all along—that pretty words don't mean anything if there isn't something real behind them. I loved those letters and poems and Connor knew that. But I'm realizing he shut them on and off like a tap. I agonized time and again, how he could write so deeply, drawing me to him enough to keep me. To use them when he needed them.

I don't think he meant to hurt me—I know he struggled to find

147

his true self under his parents' pressure. But the fact is, he manipulated my feelings instead of honoring them.

And speaking of facts,_I didn't honor my feelings either. I wanted the relationship he crafted in those words so badly that I lost myself. Gave myself up to it, over and over. I need to honor my feelings and right now, they're all for Weston.

And it doesn't feel wrong at all.

CHAPTER Twenty

Weston

"The Ritz-Carlton?" Autumn asked incredulously. She stared out the window as our Uber pulled into the front of the hotel and then whacked my arm lightly. "You said we were staying at a nice hotel."

"The Ritz is a nice hotel," I said.

"It's a five-star luxury hotel," she said. "Little more than *nice*, pal."

The Uber driver brought around my wheelchair. I transitioned into it and Autumn rolled both of our suitcases behind her as a bellhop approached.

"I've never stayed at a luxury hotel before," I said. "Have you?"

"No, never," she said. "This is a first."

We exchanged knowing looks. Two scholarship kids indulging a little. I mentally high-fived myself for being able to give this to her.

While I checked us in, Autumn gaped at the elegant lobby, with its gleaming, marble floors, delicate light fixtures and rich furniture.

"This is crazy," she said. "Is it tacky to ask if you can afford this from Connor's going-away money you told me about?"

"You can ask me anything," I said. "And no, it's not his. I've been living like a miser on that money. I hate it, and yet..."

"I know you do," she said, as we headed to the elevators. "You hate it, but you sort of need it."

"For now, I do. But this trip is courtesy of a little bonus check from Uncle Sam. Some kind of pension adjustment. This felt like the right time and place to spend it."

And the exact right person to spend it on.

She smiled down at me, her eyes shining. "Thank you, Weston. It's a lovely surprise."

"Don't start crying on me already, we've only seen the elevators."

"Then stop doing nice things for me," she said with a laugh and a sniff.

"It's payback for you coming with me to my doctor's appointment," I said as the elevator opened on our floor.

I had Amherst pretty well mapped out as far as where I could and couldn't go in a wheelchair, but Boston was an old, colonial city. The brick sidewalks alone could spell trouble and I didn't want to risk the humiliation of being stuck somewhere without backup.

Cute story, Sock Boy. Having Autumn sleeping one room over has nothing to do with it, I'm sure.

We had adjoining rooms overlooking Boston Common and the Public Gardens. I hadn't been inside mine a minute when Autumn burst through the connecting door.

"This is stunning. Did you see your bathroom? You need to see the bathroom."

The counters and shower were gray marble, the aisle wide enough for my chair to fit with room left over, and it had a soaker tub with a bar.

"It's all accessible, isn't it?" she said.

"And then some."

"Thank God. You know, I've been researching where we can go sightseeing this weekend and it's pissing me off how many places are either impossible for you to go to, or very difficult."

"I take it a Hop On and Off bus tour is out of the question?"

"*Yes,*" she said pointedly. "So are harbor cruises and ninety percent of the Freedom Trail."

"Boston is old. I expected it."

"It doesn't bother you?" she asked. "It bothers the hell out of me."

"I noticed." I glanced around. "Can we continue this conversation somewhere that's *not* a bathroom?"

Autumn's smile returned. "All the best convos happen in bathrooms and produce sections."

She bent and pecked a kiss on my cheek. As we returned to the main room, I resisted the urge to touch my skin where her lips had been.

Both of our rooms had a desk by the window, a king-sized bed and a huge flat screen TV mounted on the wall opposite.

"This is a pretty swanky joint, Weston," Autumn said, parting the window drapes and taking in the wide expanse of the Common. "Maybe too fancy for my blood."

"Nope. You fit right in."

Her smile was beautiful and a little shy. "I'm going to freshen up and then we can head to your doc. Dinner after?"

"Yep."

"Where're we going?"

I grinned. "Someplace nice."

We took a cab to Boston Medical Center and were directed toward the Orthopedics and Spine Specialists department, fifth floor.

"You sure you don't want to go out to a coffee shop or sight see?" I asked after I checked in. "This appointment is going to take a while."

"Nope, I'm fine," Autumn said from behind a brochure on muscle spasticity. "Plenty of reading material to keep me busy."

"A riveting subject," I muttered.

She put her hand on my arm, looking stunning in a blue turtleneck sweater, long black skirt and boots. "You okay?"

"Sure."

"I mean, are you nervous?"

"Not really," I said. "I know they're going to tell me I've plateaued. Back at Walter Reed, they said any progress I'd have would manifest within six months of the injury. I'm closing in on nine months."

"I'm sorry for that, Weston."

I shrugged. "I just want to stand up. Just once."

She gave my arm a squeeze. "I know you do."

I eased a sigh. Autumn never told me a bunch of bullshit to make me feel better, or that I was 'an inspiration' for trudging through a life no one else wanted—one that I never asked for. She let me feel shitty about something if I needed to feel shitty about it.

And the irony is that I feel less and less shitty when I'm around her.

"But for real, it could be two hours or more," I said. "Two different doctors are going to take their shot at me."

"I'm *fine*," she said. "I saw a Starbucks kiosk downstairs. I'll grab a coffee and get cozy."

I didn't push it, relieved she didn't ask me about the second doctor—a urologist who'd discuss with me all the ways I wasn't ever going to have sex again.

A nurse at the door to the exam rooms glanced at her clipboard. "Weston Turner?"

"Give 'em hell," Autumn said, and chucked me on the shoulder.

I was directed to a room and instructed to change into a hospital gown. A few minutes later, Dr. Cerenak arrived. He was a younger man with a bald head and friendly demeanor who liked to ask and answer his own questions as a means of relaying information. He examined me thoroughly, then asked about wheelchair adaptation, pressure sores, and muscles spasms.

"They suck and they're frequent," I said about the spasms. "Why I can't feel pain in my legs but can feel those fucking spasms is beyond me."

"I'll give you a prescription," Dr. C said. "But massage and acupuncture can help too."

"More needles," I muttered. "Awesome."

Dr. C palpated around my replaced hip, which only registered as faint pressure. Then he moved to examine my back, his fingers pressing over the scars where I'd been shot in the spine.

"Holy shit," I said, as an icy-hot sensation flared at the wound site. "What did you just do?"

"Is this painful?"

LONG LIVE the Beautiful Hearts

"No," I said. "It's just hot...and cold and tingling. Lots of sensation and it's moving. I mean I can feel it in my upper back and my chest. What is it?"

"Referred sensation," Dr. C said. "It's a reorganization of your sensory pathways, converging at the place where your healthy spinal cord ends and the damage begins." He continued his exam. "Some SCI patients report that it can be pleasurable to have that area stimulated."

"I've touched it a hundred times and it's never felt like that before. Does it mean I'm getting feeling back?"

"The pathways can take months to reorganize. Is that progress? Not necessarily. After the exam is complete, I'll tell you where we stand."

You mean, sit.

Dr. C poked my legs with six-inch needles to assess pain and pressure. I held my breath, my heart pounding and willing my brain to acknowledge pain. Nothing. Pressure but not pain. I knew before Dr. C spoke what the verdict would be.

"I think it's safe to say your incomplete SCI has stabilized," he said. "What does this mean for you? Probably that you won't see any significant change as far as sensory or motor function from here on out."

"This is it, you mean," I said.

He nodded. "This is it. But there are tremendous advances in the field of robotics. Your muscle tone is good; you're keeping yourself fit. If you're interested, I'll put you on the list for a new trial starting this summer."

"A trial for what?" I asked dully, while *this is it* played over and over in my head.

"New tech that allows a paraplegic to walk with the use of a robotic exoskeleton that fits around the waist, legs and feet. I think you'd make a great candidate."

"Walk," I murmured. "If I could just stand up," I said. "I want to *stand up* out of that goddamn chair. And not on the bars at rehab. Somewhere real."

With Autumn.

"The trial might be just right for you. It's being offered to military veterans first." Dr. C clapped his hand on my shoulder. "I'm putting your name on the list."

Twenty minutes later, Dr. Rinsky took Dr. C's place. The

urologist was an older man with graying hair, a kind smile, and an extremely blunt manner. He asked me another thousand questions about bowel movements, catheterization, and digestion.

"And what about erections?"

"What about them?"

"Are you achieving any?"

"I haven't tried."

Dr. Rinsky looked up from his notes. "You haven't tried?"

"Okay, so I've tried, and it takes forever and I can't finish. I know what that means. It means I won't ever have a normal life."

Because this is it.

"Not necessarily," Dr. R said. "Given the right circumstances, with the right partner and plenty of communication, it's more than possible for you to have a normal life."

I ground my teeth. "It's humiliating and wrong to expect a woman to put up with this." I indicated everything from my waist down.

"Someone who cares about you wouldn't consider it embarrassing or 'putting up with you.' Rather she'd understand it's a part of what it means to be with you."

"Yeah, okay, can I get dressed now?"

Dr. R took off his glasses and folded his hands. "Do you have anyone outside the medical profession you can talk to about this? A good friend, perhaps, or your father—?"

"Nope," I said. "I'm fresh out of friends and fathers."

He handed me a pamphlet from a rack on the wall: *Spinal Cord Injury and Sexuality.* "Give this a read, at least."

I took the pamphlet to humor him. There was a reason it was a pamphlet and not a book; sex after a SCI could be summed up in a few folded pages.

"And Weston," Dr. Rinsky said, "your body isn't what it was, but it can be more than what it is. Like everything else for you now, you might have to work harder. Including finding a woman who won't mind that things are a little different for you. And I assure you that kind of woman does exist."

He gave me a parting smile and shut the door behind him.

Autumn exists.

There was no other woman on the planet I wanted to be with, and if anyone could overlook my limitations it was her. But even if she

LONG LIVE **the Beautiful Hearts**

wanted something with me, how long would it take before she realized she needed more? Months? Years? She deserved a full life. She deserved having children without needing a laboratory to conceive them. Hell, she should be able to go anywhere she wanted without having to check if there were stairs first.

And there's the small matter of how you manipulated her and lied to her face for months.

I finished getting dressed and chucked the pamphlet in the trash.

Autumn's face lit up to see me and then fell when I joined her in the waiting area. "Bad news?"

"It's what I expected. I'm not going to get any better than this," I said. "I'm never going to walk. Not without them turning me into a robot."

"I'm sorry," she said. "Do you want to go back to the hotel? Let's forget about going out. We can order room service—"

"No, I want to go out. I want to take you out to dinner. I promised."

"Yeah, but if you're not up for it—"

"I'm okay. Really."

I need to see you across a candlelit table and watch the flame illuminate the gold flecks in your eyes.

The faint poetry in the thought caught me by surprise, and by the time we left the Medical Center my foul mood was lighter.

That night, after a shower that took thirty minutes when it once took ten—I changed into a dark gray suit, white dress shirt, and maroon tie. I'd made reservations at the Artisan Bistro downstairs. We met in the hallway outside our rooms, and my breath caught to see her. She wore a white dress with black flowers and vines over the flared skirt. Black heels and a black clutch purse. She wore very little makeup but for her lips that were ruby red.

Because she wants to draw attention to her mouth. She wants to be kissed...

My thoughts about Autumn were spiraling out of control lately, and I fought for composure, finally noticing she was staring just as unabashedly at me.

"You look dangerously handsome," she said. A pink blush spread across her cheeks.

My throat went dry. "Dangerously?"

"Yes," she said. "The kind of handsome that makes girls do stupid things."

Like what?

I was desperate to ask but couldn't. Nothing was dangerous about me. Not anymore. Not in this chair.

But she's not looking at me in the chair. She's just looking at me. Because women like her do exist.

"My turn," I said when the moment grew too long and quiet. "You look..."

Beautiful. Stunning. Incredible. All true but boring. Trite. My mind took off like it hadn't in almost a year, composing a better compliment that no 'friend' would ever say to a friend.

You are exquisite. There is poetry in the line of your neck, in the curve of your breasts, and the bow of your lips. The composition of you is perfection and I want to know every verse...

"Weston?"

I blinked. "What?"

She laughed. "I think you're staring at me."

"Am I? Sorry..."

"It's okay," she said. "Stunned silence is a lovely compliment."

It wasn't enough. Not nearly enough for a woman who'd stripped me down in a few sentences, laid my heart bare, naked and pulsing, and full of words. Words I thought were dead and gone but were still there.

Buried and faint, but still there.

CHAPTER
Twenty-One

Autumn

We sat at a little table in the hotel bistro, a candle burning between us. Dressed up and surrounded by romantic ambiance. We'd hung out together a hundred times, but this was the first time it felt like a date.

Did Weston plan it that way?

I couldn't keep my eyes off of him, and no way his sharp-as-a-diamond mind didn't know it. If he asked, I didn't know what I'd say. Except that Weston in a suit should be illegal; that he was too beautiful, and that being with him made me happy.

God, that makes this a date. Right?

All through dinner, Weston struggled to make conversation. More than once, he looked on the verge of saying something, then changed his mind and went back to pushing his food around. I gave him space. After all, he'd heard bad news today, whether he expected it or not. He needed a friend, not someone who was undressing him with her eyes every other second.

The dinner was lovely and Weston made light conversation but wasn't his usual self. Back upstairs, outside our doors, we lingered in a tense silence. Again, Weston looking about to say something and me feeling I should back off, though it felt wrong to leave him alone to cope.

"I had all that coffee at dessert," I finally said. "I'm not tired at all. Do you want to watch a movie or something?"

"I don't know…" A grimace twisted his face as he bent and seized his right calf. "Goddamn spasms."

"You know, I bought something today that might help those.

Let me get it and change. See you in twenty?"

He hesitated, then nodded. "Okay."

As I changed into pajama pants and a shirt with buttons down the front, I eyed the gift bag on my bed. In the waiting room at the doctor's office, I'd read a pamphlet about the benefits of massage for people with SCI's to keep their nerves stimulated. Before dinner, I went to the hotel spa and bought a bottle of massage oil.

I knocked gently on the dividing door to our rooms.

"Yeah," he said.

He sat on the bed, propped against the headboard with a pillow, wearing a T-shirt and sleep pants. Looking just as devastating as he had in a suit. Suddenly my innocent notion of giving him a massage didn't feel so innocent. Putting my hands on his bare skin felt more for my benefit than his.

"My waiting room pamphlet-reading paid off," I said. "I read that massage can relieve a lot of pain and stress. I was thinking I could...rub your back? If you want. You're overdue, actually. You should be getting massages a few times a month, from trained professionals. Maybe I could book you an appointment at the spa tomorrow?"

I was conscious that I was babbling. I never babbled around Weston.

You can be an adult about this. He's your friend.

He shook his head. "I don't know."

"It's okay," I said. "We don't have to. I just wanted to help."

"I know you do."

He held my gaze a long moment and I moved closer to the bed. "Are you in pain? Tell me the truth."

"The truth," he muttered with a small, bitter laugh.

"Weston—"

"You really want to touch me?"

He struggled so badly with his self-perception, while I struggled with how to tell him he was perfect. Meanwhile, my hands longed to hurry up and get to the part where I could touch him.

"I think it would help," I said, my heart pounding against my chest. "But only if you're comfortable."

He was silent a moment, his sharp expression melted into nervousness. He nodded, then stripped out of his T-shirt.

The bottle of oil nearly slipped out of my hands. The night on

158

the couch came roaring in on a tide of heated blood. The body I'd felt above me and on top of me finally revealed, and every inch as hard and defined as I remembered. His chest was a smooth plane of pecs that tapered into a V where his ab muscles were stark and hard. But his arms...

Months of pushing a chair had turned Weston's arms into works of art. I had to drag my gaze from his biceps, shoulders, and even his forearms—especially his forearms—defined and cut under tanned, smooth skin.

"Should I lie on my stomach?" he asked.

"Uh, yes. Please."

He scooted down on the bed and turned his torso to the side, pulling one leg with him. He stretched out on his stomach, his face turned on the pillow.

I poured a few droplets of the champagne-colored oil on his back, which was just as defined as his front. All hard muscles under warm skin. I rubbed the oil over the smooth perfection of his shoulder blades, and the valley between them.

"Is this okay?"

He nodded against the pillow, his voice already slurry. "It's perfect."

"I thought so," I said with a sigh of relief. "The pamphlet said it's important to keep your body stimulated."

I worked my hands down his back, kneading tight knots, and pressing my fingertips along the contours of his perfectly sculpted back, lower and lower—

"*Shit,*" Weston cried, his torso suddenly writhing under my hands.

I snatched them away. "What? I'm sorry. Did I hurt you?"

"No, no, it's the scar. Where I was shot. Touching it sets off this weird reaction." He settled back onto the bed. "The doc told me about it today. Sorry, I should have warned you."

My gaze dropped to the waistband of his pants where the white seam of a scar peeked out and ran along his spine.

"What does it feel like?" I asked.

"A jolt of something all through my chest. Cold, hot, tingling."

"Good or bad?"

He was quiet for a moment. "Good," he said finally. "It felt...good."

159

"Should I keep going? Gently?"

He nodded against the pillow. "Yeah. Keep going."

I moved my hands around either side of his waist, then skimmed them across his lower back again. He drew in a sharp breath and his back muscles tightened in a delicious play of power and strength.

"I should stop," I said. *For a lot of reasons.* "It seems like it's hurting you."

He didn't answer that but said, "We can stop. I feel better. Thank you."

When he didn't move, I got the impression he was waiting for me to do something.

"I'll just go wash the oil off my hands."

"Cool," he said.

I went to the bathroom and ran soap and water over my hands. The oil rinsed away but I couldn't get the sense memory of his skin off my palms. The girl in the mirror had a flushed face, her eyes bright and her pulse pounding.

What just happened?

I peeked back into the room. Weston had put his shirt back on, and was sitting up again, one pillow against the headboard, one across his lap. He had the remote in his hand, flipping through the TV channels. His entire demeanor and expression looked conflicted, his mouth drawn down but his eyes lit up.

What the hell was I thinking? I'd made him uncomfortable and now the equilibrium between us was off. He didn't want anything intimate right now. Maybe never. And not with me.

Maybe it's better. I have my vows. He's my best friend. I'm not going to ruin that.

I turned off the bathroom light and stepped into the room.

"*Pulp Fiction* is on," Weston said, his eyes on the TV. "Seems like our best bet."

"A classic," I said. "Can I sit?"

I indicated joining him on the bed, on one side of the giant king. Because we were friends; we'd sat together plenty of times, and it would be even more awkward and obvious if I suddenly insisted on sitting on a chair beside him.

He nodded, and I climbed up and stacked some pillows against the headboard. We watched the movie, and despite the tumult of emotions I'd been battling all night—or maybe because of them—my eyes started to droop around the time Bruce Willis had to go back for his watch. I slipped under completely sometime after that scene and came half-awake what felt like hours later.

The lights were off.

An arm was around me.

Instinctively, I curled into it. Into him. Into his warm, strong body and a place where tumult and disequilibrium didn't exist. Only peace. His arm around me tightened. His chest rose and fell under my cheek in a deep sigh.

One last thought slipped across the darkness behind my eyes before I slept again.

This is where I'm supposed to be.

CHAPTER
Twenty-Two

Weston

She slept in my arms, her body melting against mine like butter. I held her as close as I dared, inhaling the apple cinnamon scent of her hair. It mixed with the fainter scent of the massage oil still lingering on my back.

Months of fantasizing were nothing compared to the feel of her hands on my skin. When she touched the sensitive knot of nerve-endings at the base of my spine, I got hard. I'd felt the subtle stirring while she touched me and rolled over to see there was nothing subtle about it. I concealed it with a pillow, but holy *fuck*.

And Autumn's hands woke up more than just lust and need. They broke down the walls that had locked away my words, and suddenly, I wanted to write. *Needed* to write.

I waited, sleepless, until the dead of night, then carefully extricated myself from her. I transitioned into my chair and wheeled over to the desk by the window. By the light of the moon, I took up the hotel stationary and began to write.

My pen never stopped, and out of it poured the hopeless, desperate desire to touch her with hands scarred and calloused, dirty with grime and guilt.

When the poem was finished, I tucked the paper into my

LONG LIVE the Beautiful Hearts

suitcase and returned to bed. I didn't reach for Autumn again. I lay flat on my side of the bed, staring at the ceiling while inescapable truths blared across the dark landscape of my mind.

You love her. Your words are back. You have no choice but to tell her the truth now.

Dirty Hands

How can I look at you
When my eyes reflect
Memories we can't speak of?
I see you becoming
Naked under me
I hear your breath
Catch
before I steal it
With a kiss that isn't mine
To take

How can I speak your name
When every word that follows
Should be a truth
That destroys your happiness?
Words are my undoing
You bring them back
To life
From out of the dead garden
Where I thought only
the bones of my legs
And the echoes of a car's engine
remained

How can I touch you
With these dirty hands
Lined with grime and guilt
Pushing my broken body?
Through life that doesn't feel so broken
Hour by hour
Minute by minute

Emma Scott

The scaffolding around me
falling away

I am born for the second time
Emerging from the darkest night
Into the light where you are
Waiting
If only I could see you with these eyes
And speak the truth with this breath
And touch you with something more
real and good than these
dirty hands

PART V

February

CHAPTER
Twenty-Three

Weston

I wheeled out from the parking lot to the racing track. It was older than my Amherst track, a few miles south, and down by the golf club. Men and women raced in triangular-shaped chairs with three wheels—two in the back, one mounted out front, on the point of an extended frame. The racers' legs were tucked under instead of bent in front of them.

An older man, maybe in his late fifties with a windbreaker over his paunch, broke from a small crowd to walk over to me.

"Wes Turner?"

"That's me," I said. "Ian Brown?"

"Call me Coach." He shook my hand. "Frank says you're interested in racing?"

I shrugged. "Maybe." I watched a pair of racers tear around a curve, easily doing thirty miles an hour. "I used to run track and field," I said, deciding it wouldn't kill me to be honest. "I miss being fast."

Ian grinned. "I don't doubt it. Want to check out a chair?"

"Sure."

As I followed him to one of the modified chairs, racers and coaches of various local teams nodded at me. I nodded back.

"This is your standard racer," Coach said, indicating a blue-framed model. Judging by the peeling paint and worn out seat

LONG LIVE **the Beautiful Hearts**

apparatus, it wasn't new. "To transfer from your chair, you'll have to perch on this side bar while you tuck your legs into the seat here. Your butt goes here and you kneel down. That puts your arms right over the big wheels."

Feeling like the greater state of Massachusetts was watching, I parked my chair next to the racer and did as Coach instructed. I nearly toppled on my ass but managed to get my legs tucked under me. It put my chest flush with a strip of worn leather and gave my hands easy access to the wheels.

"How do you steer?"

Coach showed me a spring mechanism between me and the front wheel called a track compensator.

"When the track curves left, you give it a whack to the left. When the track straightens out, you whack it right. Hand break is here."

"Okay, let's go."

Coach chuckled. "Let's go, he says." He plonked a helmet on my head and handed me special, cushioned gloves, vital to protect a racer's hands as they madly spun the wheels.

"Take it easy to start," he said. "Just get a feel for it."

"Sure thing," I said. "Nice and easy." I put my earbuds in from the iPod in my sleeve—the one I used to wear when running.

I put on "Natural" by Imagine Dragons and navigated the racer onto the inside lane of the track. I quickly felt the balance of it, how much quicker it was to get it moving than my regular wheelchair. It took some fits and starts, learning to whack the track compensator, but then I hit the straightaway and spun the wheels faster and faster.

Somewhere behind me, Coach hollered to slow down.

Fuck that.

I cranked the music up higher.

The track sped beneath my wheels, faster than it ever felt when I was a runner. My arms were screaming and adrenaline coursed through my veins, carrying a tide of racing memories with it. Grief, exhilaration, nostalgia for what had been, and possibility for what lay ahead.

The song pounded in my ears. An anthem of Fuck You.

That's right, motherfuckers, I thought. *I'm on the edge but I'm still face up.*

I pushed my arms faster and faster, gave the track compensator a whack to keep to the curve. My timing was rocky—I nearly spilled into the grass and had to give another whack to right myself. I overshot *that* and crossed into another lane, which would probably cause a pile-up in a real race.

But I was fast. Holy shit, I was fast.

I came around the final stretch and Coach was standing in the middle of the track, waving his arms. I used the hand break to slow myself to a stop and pulled off my helmet. I shut off the music, which was replaced by the other racers and spectators clapping for me.

Coach Ian approached, and at first, I thought his grimace meant he was pissed, but he was laughing his ass off.

"Oh lord, we got a live one, folks." He clapped me on the shoulder. "You are one crazy bastard."

"You got room on your team for a crazy bastard?" I asked. The fact I was winded concealed the naked hope in my voice.

"As a matter of fact, I do."

Later that afternoon, I careened my wheelchair down the hallways of Amherst's Creative Arts Building to Professor Ondiwuje's office. I rolled through the door without knocking, but the professor looked up from his work unrattled, his expression one of amused surprise.

I slammed "Dirty Hands" palm down on his desk, breathing hard. "I'm completely fucked."

"Wonderful to see you too, Mr. Turner," Professor O said, taking the paper off his desk. A slow smile spread over his face as his eyes scanned it. "This is a poem you wrote?"

"Yeah, it is. And do you know where I was just now? At a track, racing a fucking wheelchair."

He held up a hand. "Shh. I'm reading."

I kicked up my chair to rock on the back wheels while he read, focusing my nerves and frustration on keeping my balance. Finally, Professor O sat back in his chair, still holding the poem, the other hand pressed to his mouth.

"Well?" I asked, slamming back down to four wheels.

"As far as poems go, I wouldn't say it warrants a 'completely fucked.'"

"It's not about how much it sucks or not; it's the fact that I *wrote* it. I'm *writing*. I want to write. Looking at my econ texts makes me physically ill. And did I mention I just joined a fucking racing team?"

"It sounds to me, my friend—as your own poem states—you're emerging from the dark forest of your trauma into the new light of day. The question is, why aren't you celebrating? Why aren't you proud of yourself?" He waved the poem in the air between us. "Weston Turner, take one minute of your life to be proud of your triumphs."

I sagged in my chair. "I would, except *she's* brought me back to life and I can't celebrate that with her."

Professor O set the paper down and laced his fingers together. "You haven't told her the truth."

"No. And now that I can write again, I have to tell her. Hence, completely fucked." I scrubbed my hands over my face, the nylon of the fingerless gloves she'd given me rough on my skin. "Christ, I can't have anything good without sabotaging it."

"What keeps you from telling her the truth?"

"Aside from losing her? Aside from how she's been the first true happiness I've ever had?"

"Is there more than that?"

"I lied to her. Right to her face. I manipulated her feelings…" I shook my head, disgusted with myself. "She's finally built up trust in herself and trust in me. I'm going to tear it all down and it's going to *kill* her."

Professor O nodded. "Yet you can't keep going as you are, can you?" he asked gently. "Because you love her, and she loves you."

His words whipped my heart and I squeezed my eyes shut. "God, maybe. I don't know."

But a movie reel started playing through my head, highlights of my time with Autumn. Long talks and laughter. Her calling me on my shit and me teasing her for being sentimental. Her hug at Christmas, which was better than any sex I'd had in my life. How she looked at me at the Ritz, seeing me and not the chair. Never the chair.

"She's in love with my soul," Connor said. *"And my soul is you…"*

I heard his chair creak and then Prof Ondiwuje sat on the edge of his desk and laid his hand on my shoulder, like a benediction.

"If there is love, there is hope for forgiveness."

"I don't want her forgiveness," I whispered. "I want to keep from hurting her."

"That might be impossible. But you must know you are worthy of forgiveness, no matter the pain you cause her. In my mind, Wes, that has always been the fault of your armor; you have built it so strong that it doesn't protect you so much as it hurts you to carry its impossible weight."

He went back behind the desk, reached into a drawer, and slid a form across the mahogany top. "That's a class auditing form. Fill it out. Type up your poem and be ready to hand it in. I expect to see you first thing Monday morning. No exceptions."

I reached for the paper like it was a lifeline. "I'll be there."

I turned to go and Prof O called after me. "Wes, one more thing."

"Yeah?"

"Forgive yourself for deceiving her. Let it go. Pledge to start over again and this time, never give her anything but the truest words of your heart. Because you *both* deserve that."

CHAPTER

Twenty-Four

Autumn

Panache Blanc was nearly empty on this cold, gray afternoon. Weston and I were set up at a table near the back, our study materials strewn all over. I bent over my work, while Weston hardly touched his econ texts. He kept rocking on the back wheels of his chair, keeping his balance by moving the rims back and forth with his hands.

"Stop doing that," I said. "You're giving me a complex."

He dropped down to four wheels. "You want a coffee?"

"Sure—"

He was gone before I could get the word out. Fast and confident, he maneuvered through the bakery, weaving his chair through tables to the counter. He came back just as smoothly, moving the cup from one hand to the other when he needed to steer. He set the coffee on the table beside my research materials, then tilted his chair back again

"I'm serious, Weston," I said. "That makes me so nervous."

"Mind your business and get back to work, Caldwell."

I balled up a napkin and tossed it at him. Still perched on his rear wheels, he deflected it easily, looking vibrant and alive. Joining the racing team had done wonders for him; he practiced with a new crew three times a week now, and seemed happy. Happier, even, than when he was running for Amherst.

But I couldn't figure out today's restlessness. I frequently caught him looking at me with a torn expression, his eyes full of thoughts.

Something is happening...

I couldn't deny it any longer. I was standing at the edge, ready to jump, and savoring the moment. Relishing anticipation's potent mix of exhilaration and fear. Waiting for the *thing*—the moment, the event, the word—that would push me over. It was coming. I could feel it. I could see it in his eyes.

"Don't you have work to do?" I asked when I caught him looking at me again. "I thought we came here to study."

"I'm done."

"Don't you have a big exam coming up?"

He tipped back in his chair, shrugging. "Yep."

"And?"

"I got it covered."

I went back to my classwork, still aiming to graduate Amherst with honors so that when and if I came up with a Harvard project, I'd still be a viable candidate. But my concentration wavered at an idea that had taken hold and not let go.

"So, Weston."

"So, Autumn." He was back on two wheels and wearing a dry grin, trying to get a rise out of me.

"I have a proposal for you."

"Shoot."

"We have a three-day weekend coming up and I was thinking about flying out to Nebraska. Want to come with me?"

"Me?" He dropped back down to four wheels with a thud. "You mean, meet your family?"

"Well, yeah." I tucked a lock of hair behind my ear. "And to see the farm. I think you'll like it. The sunrises are beautiful and it'll be a nice change of scenery."

Weston's expression divided into the familiar wrestling match of pain and longing.

"You can say no," I said gently.

"I'll go," he said.

"You will?"

"Yeah, sounds good. I'd like that a lot." He cleared his throat.

172

LONG LIVE the Beautiful Hearts

"I've never been on a farm before."

"Great," I said. A wide smile spread over my lips and warmth bloomed in my chest. "I'll let them know you're coming."

The Friday morning we left for Nebraska, Weston met me outside my place. He wore an expression so dark and moody, I was certain he'd changed his mind.

"What's up?" I asked.

"I can't find my backpack. Have you seen it?"

"No. When did you have it last?"

"Not sure," he said. "Couple of days ago? It wasn't until I was packing last night that I realized it was gone."

"Oh shit, did it have your wallet?"

"No, just schoolwork and some…papers."

"Maybe it's at the bakery. I'll call Edmond."

Weston watched me make the call, a stiff expression on his face.

"Okay, thanks anyway, Edmond," I said and hung up. "He says he hasn't seen it."

Weston nodded.

"I'm sorry," I said. "Hopefully it'll turn up."

"Yeah." He smiled tightly. "Hopefully."

We took a train to Boston and a cab to Logan International. We had no baggage to check, but airlines required Weston to check his wheelchair. We had to wait twenty minutes while they brought an airport wheelchair to take him to the gate.

"This thing weighs a ton," Weston said, shoving the wheels around.

"I don't see why you can't keep your own chair," I said. "It's like forcing someone to take off a prosthetic leg and use the airport's

173

generic model."

Weston shrugged. "It is what it is."

We joined the crowds waiting to pass through security. When it was our turn, Weston rolled through the screening gate and the red lights went off.

"This way," a TSA agent said, waving him to a side area. "If you can't walk through the detector, you get the wand and a pat-down."

Not liking the agent's callous tone, I passed through the detector and put my shoes back on, watching the agent wave a wand over Weston. It beeped over his left hip.

"What's going on there?" the agent asked.

"Titanium hip replacement, plus I've got metal plates in my spine," Weston said. "Lotta hardware in here."

The agent frowned. "Hold on." He went to confer with another agent and returned. "Sir, we're going to need a more thorough screening." He indicated a curtained partition where they did private pat-downs.

"Is that really necessary?" I asked. "He's a veteran of the U.S. Army."

The man held up his hand to me. "Ma'am, you need to step back. Right now."

"It's okay," Weston told me. "It'll be fine."

I bit my lip as he was taken to the private screening area. He came out a few minutes later with the go-ahead to proceed to our gate.

"I can't believe you had to go through that," I said.

"Right?" Weston said, pushing the borrowed chair beside me. "He should've at least bought me dinner first."

"I'm serious. Seems excessive."

"They're just doing their job." His voice lowered. "But…thank you."

Being in the pre-board group let us take our seats before anyone else. An airline attendant wheeled Weston down the jetway and to his aisle seat at the front of the plane.

"They'll bring your own chair to you here after the flight," she said as Weston transitioned.

I watched her go and frowned. "What happens if there's an emergency? How would you get off the plane?"

Weston shrugged. "I'm sure they have protocol. But yeah, it

feels weird to be without wheels. Trapped." He gave a little laugh. "Funny, when I sat in a wheelchair for the first time, it was like a piece of myself died. But now…I almost don't even think about it."

I pulled a little notepad and pen and started jotting down my impressions from drop-off to boarding. A seed of an idea struggling to take hold in me.

Weston chuckled. "Are you writing a strongly-worded letter to the FAA?"

"Maybe," I said. "Some of these things are bullshit. What about using the bathroom? Our flight is short, but what if we were going to Australia or Japan?"

I realized I'd said 'we' not 'you'; my train of thought had derailed at the idea of traveling somewhere exotic with him. Being on a beach with him in Cairns, or under the cherry blossom trees in Tokyo.

I avoided Weston's gaze and scribbled furiously in my notebook.

Damn, girl. My inner Ruby rolled her eyes. *You are such a goner.*

When we landed in Omaha, we had to wait while the rest of the plane disembarked. We sat alone on the empty plane for ten minutes before a crewmember came by.

"Sorry for the delay," she said. "We're just waiting for the grounds crew to locate your wheelchair and bring it up."

"Sure, no problem," Weston said, his tense face and tightly-laced hands indicating the exact opposite.

Twenty minutes passed.

"This is ridiculous," I muttered. "Excuse me," I asked an attendant who was going through the aisle collecting trash. "Where is his chair?" I kept my tone even, but I was seething now.

The attendant spoke with some crewmembers and came back to us with an apologetic look. "They're still looking, but we have a chair you can use to disembark."

"How can you lose his chair?"

"It's not lost. It's with the rest of the luggage—"

"It's not *luggage*," I said. "It's his mobility. You shouldn't treat it so carelessly."

"Autumn." Weston shook his head. "It's okay."

"It's not okay," I said. "You shouldn't have to put up with this.

175

You should be able to stay with your chair at all times."

The flight attendant smiled tightly. "Be that as it may, we really need to prepare for the next flight, so I'll tell the crew to bring the—"

"No, thanks," Weston said. "I'll wait right here."

The attendant gave an irritable sigh and left us alone.

"Utterly ridiculous," I muttered, texting my brother who was at the curb outside and wondering where the heck we were.

Another twenty minutes passed before they brought up Weston's wheelchair.

"I'm so sorry you had to go through that," I said, once we were on our way down the concourse.

"Not your fault," Weston said.

"I feel responsible. I mean, I asked you to come with me."

"And I agreed."

"I know. I just…"

Wanted things to be perfect.

Instead, things only got worse.

My brother met us on the curb outside with his pick-up truck. After we hugged and Travis and Weston shook hands, I realized how hard it would be for Weston to transfer from his chair to the truck's cab.

I got in first, feeling like shit as Weston first transitioned from his chair to the floor of the cab, then hauled himself onto the seat. Travis shut the door and put the wheelchair and our luggage into the truck bed.

"I am so sorry," I said.

"Don't be," Weston said. "I don't want to be anywhere else."

I looked over at him, a sudden deep swell of emotion in my chest. It crashed in waves in my heart as he looked back at me for one fragile and delicate moment. Then Travis climbed behind the wheel like a bull crashing into a library.

"Y'all ready to roll?" he said, cranking up the radio.

Weston smiled. "Always."

We drove into the small town of Lincoln, with Travis playing tour guide.

"See that *Lucky Billiards*? That's where Dad taught sis and me to shoot pool. And that right there?" His arm came across us to point at something on Weston's side. "Lucy's Diner? That's where Auts had her first date."

"Oh yeah?" Weston said. "Tell me more."

I whacked my brother's arm. "*Do not* tell him more."

"Brad Miller, right, Auts? Good old Brad with the braces and who never changed his clothes after working in the stables all day."

"I was fourteen," I said. "I can't be held responsible for my choices."

"She came back with a little bit of the Miller magic wafting off of her," Travis said, cackling gleefully.

"Oh my God, *shut up*."

"What's that mean?" Weston asked.

I gritted my teeth. "He was my first kiss. *And* he was a total gentleman," I added, elbowing Travis hard. "Anyway, afterward he put his jacket around me and I came home smelling like hay."

"Hay that's seen the business end of a horse's ass."

"I'm going to kill you in your sleep," I promised my brother.

Weston laughed. "He was your first kiss?"

"Yep," Travis said. "Right on the sidewalk in front of Lucy's."

I rolled my eyes and crossed my arms. "So what? It was sweet; it was a romantic moment and I don't regret it at all."

"That's my big sister in a nutshell," Travis said, driving us out of town and onto the more rural roads. "What's the phrase? Incurable romantic. She wore out our TV watching *Titanic* and cried every time Leo DiCaprio croaked. Every. Time."

"The door had room for two people, that's all I'm saying." I looked at Weston. "Are your sisters this obnoxious when it comes to childhood's most embarrassing moments?"

Weston shook his head, a small smile over his lips. "I could listen to him talk about you all day."

The blue-green of his eyes seemed miles deep. Wedged this close together in the cab, it'd take nothing for our lips to brush. One good jostle of the truck...

"Here we are," Travis announced.

We pulled up in front of our farmhouse. "God, how bad were the rains?" I asked when I saw the field of mud puddles along the side of the house.

"Bad."

I shuddered to think what the dirt paths to the barn and corrals might look like. "Is the whole yard this muddy?"

"Pretty much," Travis said. "Why? Oh." He glanced back at the wheelchair. Weston wouldn't be able to go anywhere if the paths were choked with mud.

Travis smiled brightly. "Well, hopefully it'll dry up some by tomorrow."

Weston transferred from the seat to the floor and down to the chair. Then we headed toward the front door.

The porch had three steps and I grabbed my brother's arm. "You said you'd take care of those," I hissed.

"I did." Travis went around the side of the house and came back with a square sheet of plywood to make a ramp.

"That works," Weston said and pushed up the incline. It was too steep and bowed in the middle, but he made it. My stomach burned at how hard this trip had been.

"Mom's at the grocery store," Travis said, holding the door open. "Getting a few things for dinner and Dad's probably out in the barn."

My beloved house suddenly looked small and cramped in my eyes. The interior of the house was a minefield of furniture packed too closely together and narrow hallways. I wanted Weston to see the fields, but I'd forgotten about the step from the kitchen door to the back porch. He handled it easily and rolled his chair to the edge. The sun was setting behind our fields of corn, casting an amber glow over the damp, papery stalks.

Weston was quiet as he watched the play of light across the field.

"I'm sorry," I said. "I didn't plan this well and everything's just been—"

"Perfect," he said, his voice low. "It's perfect."

CHAPTER
Twenty-Five

Weston

The Caldwells set me up in the den on the first floor. It wasn't truly a guest room—instead of a bed, I slept on the couch. But the den had its own bathroom, and with some creative maneuvering, the door was just wide enough to navigate my chair through.

Autumn was distraught about the accommodations and upset that the paths around the farm were too muddy for me to navigate. I didn't venture off the porch much, but I didn't care. Not about the mud or the couch or the inconveniences or any of it. I just liked being in the place where Autumn began. Being in the house where she grew up and meeting the people she loved best felt like a privilege.

Henry Caldwell was only fifty-eight but he looked older. His recent heart attack had drained away much of his vitality. He was a deep-talker, and I could see Autumn got her sensitive heart from him. Lydia Caldwell reminded me of Drill Sergeant Denroy from Boot Camp, minus the short temper and profanity. The sun rose and set because she permitted it to. She was less warm than Henry, rather her love for her family was embedded in everything she did.

Travis was a happy guy with an easy smile. He seemed perpetually content, as if nothing could rattle him for long.

He reminded me of Connor.

In the twilight hours of my second day at the farm, I hung out with Henry on the porch, while Autumn strolled the yard among the dandelions.

"So, tell me, Wes," Henry said. "What do you think of Nebraska?"

Autumn wore a cotton dress, galoshes, a coat and scarf. The falling light caught in her hair and turned the red to a molten copper.

"I love it," I said. "It's beautiful."

"Isn't it? More beautiful in my eyes than it has ever been. And precious."

She's precious to me too. I don't want to hurt her.

"Everything changed when I had my heart attack," Henry said. "I think you know something of that, eh? To get that close to the veil between life and death."

I nodded.

"It makes you realize some things. That it's right there, all the time. Once you've been to that edge, you see what's really important. And it's only one thing."

I tore my gaze from Autumn. "What's that?"

"How much love you got in your life." He chuckled and sat back in the swing. "Oh, if Lydia heard me now. She's sick of this sort of talk. But I learned a thing or two in the hospital. Things happen for a reason. All things. Even the terrible ones." He rocked back and forth in the swing, his legs covered by an afghan. "Wait long enough, you'll see the reason. And if you stop pushing back at it, you don't have to wait long at all."

Autumn bounded up on the porch, her cheeks pink from the cold. "Daddy giving you his new life philosophies?" She planted a kiss on Henry's head.

"I'm not telling him anything he don't already know. Am I, Wes?"

I nodded for his sake. "That's right, sir."

I didn't know how to do anything *but* push back. My entire life was fighting back, starting when Dad abandoned us. I fought back so hard, I nearly destroyed myself.

Professor O was right, I thought. *My armor is too heavy to carry, and it never protected me at all.*

The kitchen door opened, releasing a warm, brown scent of baked chicken and bread.

LONG LIVE the Beautiful Hearts

"Dinner's almost ready," Lydia called. "Travis, Autumn, Weston, come set the table."

Henry shot me a wink. It reminded me so much of Paul, I nearly did a double take, unsettled by how much I liked the comparison.

I kicked up my chair over the one step, entering the kitchen like boarding a ship, and Lydia was the captain. Travis joined us, her crew.

"Autumn, glasses," she said. "Travis, silverware. And here, Weston." She set a stack of plates in my lap. "Take these in the dining room."

Autumn shot me an apologetic glance. "Typically, she doesn't make guests do any chores."

"It's how she shows she likes you," Travis said, his hands full of forks, knives and spoons. "She puts you to work."

We took our places around the polished wood table, Henry and Lydia at the ends, Travis on one side, Autumn and I on the other. The antique-looking light above the table cast an amber glow. Framed photos of the Caldwell family looked down on us from every wall. The meal Lydia prepared wasn't fancy, but it was better than anything I'd ever eaten, including the dinner at the Ritz. Baked chicken, green beans from her garden, salad and rolls. We didn't have too many sit-down dinners when I was growing up. Lots of pizza, take-out, and whatever my mother scrounged up when she wasn't drinking.

It occurred to me I couldn't remember the last time I'd seen her with so much as a beer.

Not since Paul came around.

"Where are you two headed tonight?" Henry asked, his fork going between Autumn and me.

"I was thinking I'd show Weston the tables at Lucky's," Autumn said.

"Ah. Going to shoot some pool?" Henry winked at his daughter. "Show 'em who's boss."

She smiled. "I just might."

"You a pool player, Wes?" Henry asked.

"Better at darts."

Travis perked up. "Hey, I'm pretty good at darts. Haven't played in ages. I'll come with—"

"Yes, you're quite good at darts," Lydia said, without looking up from cutting her chicken. "It's a shame you promised to fix the newel post. It's been wobbling something fierce."

Travis's face scrunched up. "Now? It's Saturday night."

Autumn was glaring at him from across the table, while Henry chuckled into his water glass.

"A promise is a promise," Lydia said. She forked a bite of food and raised her eyes. "Isn't it?"

Travis slumped back in his chair. "Yes, ma'am."

Autumn turned to me, looking up through lowered lashes. "Just you and me, then."

"Yep," I said. "You and me."

It's a date.

After dinner, Autumn went upstairs to change. I rummaged through my luggage for the one and only dress shirt I'd brought just in case—black and expensive and probably too much for a pool hall.

Autumn came down in a white dress with hundreds of little pink flowers all over it, her hair brushed out around her shoulders.

"You're going to Lucky's in *that*?" Travis snorted. "Overdress much?"

"You hush," Lydia told her son. The entire damn family was gathered in the foyer, seeing us off.

Because it's a real date.

"You look nice," Autumn said.

"So do you," I said.

We could've shaken hands on it; it was such a dry, formal moment, but I was acutely conscious of her dad watching me. Sentimental or not, he probably wouldn't hesitate to put my balls in a sling if I hurt his little girl.

"Bring coats," Lydia said. "They're predicting more rain."

"Have fun," Henry said. "But not too much."

"*Okay*," Autumn said, grabbing our coats off the rack. Once outside, she shook her head. "Sorry, my family is so involved."

"I'm glad," I said. I took her hand before she could take another step. "And you're not overdressed. You're stunning."

LONG LIVE the Beautiful Hearts

Her fingers squeezed. "Thank you."

The moment caught and held. I felt both of us poised on either side of it, longing to talk. To confess. If she said what I thought she'd say, it would be the most perfect moment of my life.

But what I had to tell her would likely destroy us.

The silence stretched and broke.

"Should we go?" Autumn asked, a breathlessness in her voice.

I nodded, as everything I wanted to tell her reduced down to my usual ineloquence.

"Yep."

Autumn drove us to downtown Lincoln in her mom's Camry, and we parked in front of *Lucky's Billiards*. She killed the engine and we both sat staring at the blinking neon light.

"This place reminds me of Yancy's," she said quietly.

"Me too," I said. "I don't think I'm up for pool. I thought I was but... I can't."

"Not without Connor?"

"Yeah," I said. "Exactly."

She looked at me. "Do you miss him?"

"Every day. Like I lost another part of myself." I drummed my fingers on my unfeeling thigh. "Do you?"

She turned to face forward again, the neon lights dashing her skin with red and gold. "I miss him when he was his happiest. But I don't miss how I felt when I was second-guessing how he felt about me. His letters undressed me, but his silence left me naked. Exposed. Does that make sense?"

"Yeah," I said slowly. "It makes perfect sense."

"I don't know why I told you that except... I feel like I can. I can tell you anything."

God, Autumn.

She started the car. "We'll go to Lucy's Diner. They have killer milkshakes."

"Isn't Lucy's the scene of your infamous first kiss?"

I expected a swat on the arm. Instead her chin tilted and her smile curved thoughtfully. "It sure is."

I expected Lucy's to be the quintessential small-town diner with a 1950's vibe. Bright lights, red vinyl seats, and chrome fixtures. Instead, it was dim and cluttered with musical memorabilia. The walls were papered floor to ceiling with playbills, posters, concert announcements and album covers. Beatles next to the Foo Fighters; Roy Orbison next to Beck; Patsy Cline beside Alanis Morissette.

"Cool, right?" Autumn said. "This is where I discovered alternative music. Someone keeps the jukebox stocked with more than country or blues."

Only a few tables were occupied. The scents of grease and apple pie hung in the air. We situated ourselves at a table and ordered milkshakes—chocolate for me, strawberry for her.

"So, what's the verdict?" Autumn asked.

"On?"

"Casa de Caldwell."

"Yours is the kind of family I thought only existed in TV shows."

"Is that good or bad?"

"Good. I've never met anyone like your parents. They're like planets in the same solar system, revolving around you and Travis. Never colliding but staying on their steady courses, in perfect sync. You can tell they've been that way for years and they'll continue for years to come."

"Wow," Autumn said softly. "That's a beautiful way to describe them, Weston."

I looked away from her soft gaze.

"So, I wanted to talk to you about a couple of things," she said.

"Me too," I said, forcing the words past my teeth. "I need to tell you something."

"Oh?" She sat back. "Sounds serious."

I hesitated. Christ, she was too beautiful. Too vibrant and full of light and surrounded by memories of her best times. Her childhood happiness, first kisses, and safety. Lincoln, Nebraska was her *home*, and I wasn't going to piss on it. Not tonight.

"Nah. No big deal. You go ahead."

Autumn toyed with her spoon. "These last couple of days I've been doing a lot of thinking and I know what my Harvard project should be."

"Oh yeah? What?"

"You."

"I'm your project?"

"In a matter of speaking." She folded her arms on the table and leaned in. "I've seen how hard things are for you. Simple things the rest of us take for granted. And I'm not just talking about better bathrooms or more ramps."

"No?" I asked, but I'd seen her passion ignited in the plane seat beside me. I knew what she was going to say; that she would devote her entire life to something that would help me live a better one. And my undeserving heart ached for it.

Autumn went on. "After seeing how Connor's parents think PTSD isn't a real wound because they can't see it and put a band aid on it… And experiencing what you contend with as a wheelchair user. Well, a lot of puzzle pieces fell into place. I want to work on a project that helps disabled people—veterans especially—to move more easily through the world. Make it easier to just *be*. Not feel invisible or pitied, not be treated any differently than their disability requires. I don't have all the details worked out yet, but that's my initial idea." She bit her lip. "What do you think?"

"I see how it is," I said with a small smile. "You're using me to get into Harvard."

Autumn laughed. "Exactly." She propped her elbow on the table and rested her cheek on the back of her hand. "But seriously, it's what I want to do. It feels right in a way the biofuels project never did."

"But what if…?"

"What if what?"

"I don't know. What if there comes a time when…we're not friends?" I cleared my throat. "Let's say someday you hate me? Your project will be connected to me forever and you'll end up hating it too."

"Why would I hate you?" She sniffed and waved the notion aside. "Anyway the idea of working with disability rights isn't new to me. It was on my shortlist last year too. But now my focus is so much clearer." She leaned forward. "This is what I want to do and it feels right. It feels exactly right."

I stared, a thousand thoughts warring in my head, a thousand words tangled and unable to come out.

Her smile faded and the light in her eyes dimmed a little. "Did I offend you?"

"No, not at all," I said gruffly. "I think it's an incredible idea. I'm honored, actually."

Her relief was beautiful, her happiness blinding.

"I'm so glad."

We finished our shakes and I paid the bill. Outside it was raining and we stood on the front stoop of the diner. Weezer's cover of the Toto song, "Africa," played over the outdoor speakers, filling the silence between us.

We took a step out from under the awning and the rain came down in earnest, drenching us. It streamed down Autumn's porcelain face and darkened her hair so only the light above revealed the crimson and gold. She turned her face up to it, and my heart was full; fucking bursting with how much I loved her.

Hurry boy, she's waiting there for you…

Before I could stop myself, my hand snaked out and caught hers. I pulled her sideways onto my lap, buried my hands in her hair and kissed her.

I kissed her hard. My mouth filled with rainwater, the warmth of her lips, the strawberry from her shake, and it still wasn't enough. I needed more. So much more. Everything. All of her.

She gasped in surprise, then melted against me. Her mouth parted to take my kiss as deep as I wanted, tilting her head so I could explore every bit of her, my tongue sliding along hers, sucking and pulling and wanting.

Her fingers slid into my damp hair as rain streamed down our faces and into our mouths that moved with a desperate thirst. I tasted cool water over her warm tongue, felt her hot breath defeat the chilled air. My ears filled with the breathy little sounds of want in her throat.

She was on me, her body pressed to mine, and her kiss… God, kissing Autumn again erased the agony of war and hospitals and rehab.

It's like coming home.

Time vanished. Only a couple of snickering guys passing by

finally broke us apart, our breaths coming hard.

"You're shivering," I said.

"Not from the cold." She slipped off my lap with a little laugh. "And I hope you're happy, Weston Turner. You completely obliterated my first kiss with…what's-his-name."

We got in the car, water dripping from our hair and wet clothes soaking the seats. We watched the rain come down over the windshield for a quiet moment, the air vibrating between us. She looked to me, and I looked to her, and we reached for each other again.

We kissed, needy and frustrated. Too much clothing, too little space, too much *want* that couldn't be satisfied quickly enough. Without breaking our kiss, she wrestled out of her coat and I stripped out of my jacket, both of us flinging them over my wheelchair in the back seat.

Her dress clung to her body, her nipples hard and straining against the material, begging for my mouth. My hand cupped her cheek, trying to pull her closer but the lower half of my body anchored me down.

Autumn was petite; she climbed easily over the middle console to straddle me, and I reclined my seat to have her on top of me, to feel her breasts against my chest. Both my hands surged up to make fists in her hair. She moaned, her hips grinding against mine. The pressure was faint, but in this small space, with her body pressed to mine, I was suffused with the warm scent of her skin, clean and sweet with rain.

I trailed kisses down her neck and let one hand follow, cupping her breast and pinching the nipple, while the other hand slid up the smooth silk of her thigh.

"Weston…"

"Don't speak," I said. gruffly, defiant against the wrongness of touching her without her knowing the truth. "I'm going to make you come and that's all I want to hear. The sounds of you coming. Not a damn thing else."

She stared, her pulse pounding in the hollow of her throat, desire turning her eyes dark. I grabbed her and crushed her mouth to mine. I bit and sucked, drank the rainwater off her skin, while my hands skimmed down the slender smoothness of her back and under her dress. They slid up her thighs and gripped her ass, grinding her into me.

Autumn's kiss went ragged and broken as I turned my palm up

and skimmed one hand down her stomach, under the hem of her panties.

"*Yes*," she whimpered. "Oh God, yes…"

She was warm and wet. I rubbed the tight little knot of her most sensitive flesh before slipping two fingers inside her. I grunted at the slick tightness and my mouth on hers turned biting. My free hand snaked back into her hair, locking her into my kiss while my fingers made a beckoning motion deep inside her, over and over.

"Oh my God, Weston…"

Autumn moaned the words into my mouth, but I held her there, my tongue breaking them apart, swallowing them down as she writhed and rocked herself on my hand. Her hair fell down around us and the rain pounded on the hood of the car. I was relentless. My fingers driving her higher and higher, my kiss taking and taking.

"Give it to me," I growled into her mouth. "Give it to me now, Autumn."

Her lips parted over mine, her eyes squeezed shut, her body tensing. She gasped and I took it. A tiny agonized sound of pleasure escaped and I swallowed that too. I felt the orgasm rise in her higher and I pressed the softness inside her, held my fingers to the spot. One second. Two. And then she shuddered, her back arching, a cry of purest pleasure tearing through the car.

I rubbed my fingers in slow circles, coaxing her through it, wringing out every last fucking drop of ecstasy. My hand in her hair brought her mouth back to mine. I needed to suck her lips, plunge my tongue into her mouth and take the rest of her tapering moans.

Finally, she slumped against me, her breath heaving against my chest again and again.

"Jesus Christ, Weston," she said, her head tucked under my chin. "I'm dizzy." Her hand slipped down, below my waist. "And God, you're so hard. Can I—?"

"No," I said. "Not here."

Her eyes were luminous in the dark as she searched mine. I brushed the damp hair from her face, shaking my head.

"You know me better than anyone," I said, my voice soft now. I slid my hand over her cheek, back into her hair. "No one knows me like you do. No one."

"I feel the same. I can be me when I'm with you."

"I have so much to tell you," I whispered, as her lips brushed mine.

She reared back, her brows furrowed.

"What's wrong?" I said

"Nothing," she said. "I just... I had a dream a long time ago, and you said those exact words."

"It's true. Too much..."

She drew her breath in. "I know it's scary to risk our friendship like this. But what I'm feeling right now... I can't describe it except there's nowhere else we're supposed to be. Do you feel that too?"

I nodded. "Yeah, I do. Nowhere else."

"Let's just have that for a little while. Okay?" She traced the line of my jaw. "This moment is so perfect."

She kissed me, deep and slow, then tucked her head under my chin. We held each other while the rain pattered lightly in the dark night. Autumn reached a delicate arm out, and with one finger she drew a W and a heart around it in the steam we'd left on every window.

I closed my eyes and held her tighter. She was finally in my arms and I was scared to let go.

CHAPTER
Twenty-Six

Autumn

March 2, 20—

I'm in love with Weston.

Holy shit, I am so in love with him, I can feel it in every molecule of my body. I haven't just jumped off the cliff, I'm swan diving off the ledge.

There's no doubting myself. No doubting him. No mistrust. No wondering if what I feel is real, or merely the product of romantic hopes and beautiful words with no voice behind them. I <u>feel</u> us. I see us in his eyes. I hear us in the way he says my name.

I've never felt this way before. Ever. Not even when I was in the newest, deepest throes of attraction. And I can't imagine I will ever feel this way again.

For the first time in my life, I know who I am and what I want, and it's a greater joy than I thought possible. It's real, this feeling. I love him.

And I love this love because it's ours.

I kept my journal turned away from Weston, leaning against the small airline window to write. For most of the four-hour flight back to Boston, he sat with his head against the rest, eyes closed. He hadn't slept much the night before, and I suspected the trip had worn him out.

We landed and disembarked. The airline didn't lose Weston's wheelchair this time, but I still didn't like how he had to part with it in the first place. I vowed to make that one of the key focuses of my project.

God, my project. I was giddy with excitement over it. This was a purpose that stirred my heart. I glanced at Weston as we made our way down the jetway.

Because he *stirs my heart. And my body. And my soul. God...*

As we waited for the car that would take us to the train station, Weston pulled me onto his lap—a maneuver that was fast becoming one of my favorite things.

"You're so beautiful," he said, his expression almost pained. "So fucking beautiful."

I ran my fingers through his hair. "I'm so fucking happy."

He didn't answer. Something more than fatigue ringed in his ocean eyes.

"Is everything okay? I know you didn't get much sleep—"

He silenced me with a kiss. A deep, long one that stole my breath and left me feeling boneless.

"Uber's here," he said, his voice low. "Time to go."

We took the train to Amherst and went to his condo first.

"I need to go to the bakery," I said. "If I don't deposit my last paycheck, there will be trouble with a capital T. Maybe later we could..." *Do sex things.* "Hang out?"

"Yeah," Weston said in a low voice, then louder. "Yes. I want you to come over. I'll make you dinner and we can talk."

I was going to tease him if 'talk' was code for 'get naked' but wondered if the worry line etched between his brow was nervousness over what sex might be like for him now. I wanted to tell him that I didn't care what happened or how. That I just wanted to be with him, even if it meant lying in bed, skin to skin, and kissing all damn night.

But saying it out loud might make him more uncomfortable. He had a right to his feelings; I'd just have to show that I loved him in the body he had and I wanted to be with him. It didn't matter how.

I bent to kiss him. "I'll go to the bakery, then home and shower. Be back around five?"

"Sure."

"Can I bring anything?"

"No." He held my face in his hands, his thumbs stroking my cheek. His eyes were full of thoughts; it seemed as if a thousand unsaid words played on their stormy surface. "I'll see you soon."

I kissed him again. "See you soon."

On my way to Panache Blanc, I realized my phone was still on Airplane Mode. I switched it back and a text popped up from Ruby, sent hours ago.

Hey, girl. Headed back home for a short visit. See you in a bit xo

I grinned as I tucked the phone back into my bag. It had been too long since I'd seen my best friend. It had been hard living long distance; our texts and phone calls were growing non-existent.

We just need a good talk and some quality girl time to get our friendship back on track.

At the bakery, Edmond was serenading a rapt crowd of Sunday afternoon customers, while Phil rushed around behind the counter to fill orders. Watching from the door as his booming baritone filled the shop, I wondered, not for the first time, why Edmond hadn't been an opera singer instead of a baker.

The aria ended and the crowd burst into applause.

"Autumn, ma chère!" Edmond moved to me and swept me in a hug. "You are radiant. Your trip home avec mon homme tranquille was good, non?"

"Yeah, it was," I said, sure the smile on my face was on its way to becoming a permanent fixture. "It was really good."

Edmond stared at me, his large dark eyes widening to show the whites. His hands clutched his chest over his apron. "Oh my darling girl. My thoughtful girl and my quiet man? Is it true?"

I nodded and blinked hard. "Edmond, do *not* make me cry."

He picked me up and swung me around again. "This is joyous news. I am so happy for you. And for him. Come." He took me by the hand and led me to the counter. "We must celebrate. Cake, I think. Or

LONG LIVE the Beautiful Hearts

a macaroon? No, too small for such a big day."

"How about a cranberry scone?"

"Ha!" Edmond laughed. "Mais, oui. Oh, before I forget, I found Monsieur Turner's missing bag just this morning." He fixed poor Phil with a dark look. "Philippe discovered it on Thursday but didn't put it in the box of lost and found. It fell behind a sack of flour."

"That's great," I said as we headed to the back room. "Weston will be so glad to have it back. I'll bring it to him tonight."

Tonight. Oh God, the zing...

Edmond held out the dark blue backpack by the straps. "Voilà. And may I say Monsieur Turner is a beautiful poet. I had no idea."

I froze, my hand outstretched to take the bag. "What did you say?"

"I had no idea he was such a beautiful writer."

I stared at Edmond. Then at the bag in his hand. Slowly, I took it and sank down on an overturned bucket. I undid the zipper and pulled a notebook from the backpack and a sheaf of loose papers, my hands trembling.

"Forgive me," Edmond said. "I only looked to see to whom the bag belonged. I did not mean to pry."

"No, it's okay." My heart clamored in my chest as I found an Amherst audit form for a course called "Lyrical Writing and Poetry." Behind the form was a poem. Handwritten in the same jagged but neat script I recognized. The same sharp lines that had scratched words onto my heart from Boot Camp.

The poem was titled "Dirty Hands." As I read it, my heart sent a rush of blood to my ears, so loud I couldn't hear Edmond's concerned questions.

I read every word, each one striking my chest and sinking in with a familiar, painful beauty.

> *How can I speak your name*
> *When every word that follows*
> *Should be a truth*
> *That destroys your happiness?*

"Oh my God..." I let the poem fall and shuffled through the pages. I found more poems, other stanzas, words scratched in margins. Econ papers with Weston's name on them. Bits of writing on wrinkled paper. I found words I'd read before. Words that set my soul aflame.

> *Without you,*
> *The hours stretch*
> *into suffocating days;*
> *gasping through nights*
> *in sweated sheets*
> *eyes squeezed shut*
> *your name locked behind*
> *my clenched teeth…*

A sob burst out of my throat. I grabbed another paper, old and coffee-stained.

> *In the space between us*
> *A thousand unspoken words*
> *Hang*
> *A noose tightening*
> *Around my throat*
> *choking me silent*
> *Heart bleeding*
> *For autumn colors…*

Tears blurred the rest and I crumpled the paper in my hand, a low moan issuing from my heart and soul.

"Ma chère," Edmond said, his hard voice breaking through the shock. "Look at me." His tone softened as he eased his bulk on the floor beside me. "Tell me what's wrong."

"The letters Connor wrote from Boot Camp," I said. "I think that's when I knew."

"Knew what?"

"But I *asked*. I asked them both and they lied… Oh my God, they lied to me so many times …"

"Who, ma chere? Who lied to you?"

"I asked him and he said no. He didn't write. He couldn't write. And I trusted him. I believed him *because* I trusted him."

"Autumn…"

Numbness sank into my body like icy water. I dried my tears, shoved the papers back into the backpack and rose on shaking legs.

LONG LIVE the Beautiful Hearts

"Thank you, Edmond," I said, my tone even. I fought to smile or he'd never let me leave. "I'm okay. I'm sorry if I scared you. These poems are just so…" I swallowed hard. "So beautiful. But I'm okay now. I'm going to return this to Weston."

Saying his name put a crack in the ice in me—a jagged, stabbing slice in my heart—but I froze it over again. I had to get out of here.

Edmond shook his head. "Autumn, I don't know what has happened—"

"Neither do I. Or rather, I know exactly what happened. Finally." I inhaled through my nose and straightened. "I'll see you tomorrow morning."

I turned and left, my steps carrying me quickly from the warm sugary bakery into the cold. I walked the entire way from downtown to the condo complex.

Weston always left the door unlocked for me, but I knocked. My heart pounded with it, cracking the ice and letting the pain seep in, hot and oily.

The door opened.

I held out the backpack. "Found your bag."

Weston's eyes widened. His expression slapped my face. The pain in his eyes told me it was real.

All the lies were real.

CHAPTER
Twenty-Seven

Weston

It's over.

The thought slammed into me. Not, *We might have a chance,* or *I can fix this,* or even *Oh shit, you fucking idiot,* though that was a close second.

My heart sank like a rock to the bottom of my chest as I took the bag from Autumn. She stepped past me and walked into the living room, hunched over, her arms hugging herself. I turned my chair and followed her, remembering one of the first conversations we ever had. In the Amherst library. She told me how important honesty was to her. That when it came to love, she wanted something real.

"So?" She turned to face me and gestured to the backpack in my lap. "Is this what you wanted to talk about tonight?"

"Yeah." I tossed the traitorous bag on the floor. "Yeah, it is."

"What makes tonight so special?" She was striving to stay strong, but her voice wobbled at the edges. "As opposed to, say, any other night over the last *year and a half?"*

I ignored her sarcasm and told her the truth. For once in my life, out loud...and too fucking late.

"Because I love you," I said. "I'm completely fucking in love with you, and have been—"

LONG LIVE **the Beautiful Hearts**

"No." She was shaking her head, her lips pressed together. "You don't get to say things like that, Weston. Not *now*."

I moved my chair closer. "I have to. I should have… *Fuck*, I should've told you everything so many times. But I couldn't. Or thought I couldn't."

"It was you all along," she whispered. "It was you writing to me and giving Connor the credit."

I nodded.

"Why? Why would you do that to me?"

"Connor cared about you," I said, the words sounding weak and pathetic. "He truly did. But he didn't know how to talk to you."

"So it was all for him."

"At first. After a while it was for both of you. I thought… I wanted to help him make you happy because I didn't think I could."

"And I was an easy target," Autumn said. "Because I loved poetry and romance and pretty words." She crossed her arms tighter. "How did it work? You wrote the poetry and passed it to him like exam answers in high school?"

"It started with the texts," I said. "And that's all it should have been. But that first poem—"

"The one that convinced me to go to bed with him? That poem?"

"I didn't write that for him," I said. "I wrote it for me. For you. But you found it and Connor said it was his. It's no excuse or justification, but it's what happened. I swear to God. I didn't write a poem so he could use it on you. I was pissed at him for stealing it in the first pl—"

"You were pissed at him," she said. "But not enough to protect me from digging myself in deeper. Not enough to tell me the truth."

"I thought it was too late," I said. "I loved you. But I loved him too. I wanted both of you to be happy."

She stared at me a moment, arms uncrossing and hands moving to her hips. "What else?" she said. "The poems. The letters from Boot Camp and—?"

"The phone call in Nebraska."

"The *phone call*? When my father had a *heart attack*? That was *you*?"

I met her disbelieving gaze, because I had to take it. "That was me."

197

She staggered back and dropped down on the edge of the couch. "Jesus. You must think I'm an idiot."

"No, I—"

"You said you had a *cold*. And I was so scared for my dad, so exhausted I could hardly think straight and you just *used* it—"

"No, I swear it wasn't like that," I said, my hands clenching the rims of the chair. "I needed to talk to you and I wanted you to feel better. I wanted you to feel cared for and loved in a way Connor couldn't fucking show you."

She shook her head, elbows on her knees and dragging fingers through her hair. "God, when I think about the time I spent anguishing over Connor. How many sleepless nights... How many months I waited and worried and questioned *everything* about us. I had *Thanksgiving* at his house, with his parents. I made a fool out of myself mooning over those goddamn letters."

Happy, Sock Boy? Your worst fear come true.

My stomach churned. This is what I hated; how the truth made her feel as if she had made the mistakes; how *she* should be judged unfairly—even in her own eyes—when all she had done was trust us with her heart.

"You're not a fool," I said. "You trusted us and you had no reason not to."

"That's right, because I couldn't believe, for the life of me, you'd do something like that to me. And then keep it going and going. Through war. Through hospitals and rehab and months and months of you and me..."

She shook her head, tears spilling onto her lap.

"I know," I said, my chest fucking aching. "Too much time passed. It felt impossible to undo it all. Once Connor left, I thought I'd just let it go. I couldn't write a word anyway. It was dead in me. My writing was gone, you'd never see it again. I thought telling you would hurt you more."

"The whole thing hurts," she cried, whipping her head up. "There is no hurting more or less; there is just what happened and it's so wrong. You made me feel things for Connor and then he left and took all those words with him."

"You're right," I said. I ventured to take her hand. "You're right. I made a hundred mistakes and I have no more excuses. I love you—"

LONG LIVE **the Beautiful Hearts**

"Stop *saying* that." She wrenched her hand free and stood up. "You don't get to say that now."

"I have to tell you," I said, my voice rising. "I have to say the words with my own goddamn voice. These last few months have been the best of my life. You're the reason I'm surviving."

"No..."

"I swear to God, Autumn, everything I wrote and everything we've said up to this fucking moment was real."

"Real," she whispered. "The one thing I want and the one thing that keeps slipping from my fingers."

"What you had was real. It just wasn't Connor." Tears threatened in my eyes. "It was me."

Her eyes met mine and for a moment I had a sliver of hope. I saw in her eyes how badly she wanted to forgive.

"That night on the couch," she said. "God, I never wanted a man so badly in my life. I blamed tequila and loneliness, but I knew it was something more."

"It was," I said. "It was everything."

She shook her head, looked to the ceiling for a moment. "I asked you to your face if he wrote those letters, and you said yes. I asked Connor to his face if he wrote those letters, and he said yes. And I believed you both. I trusted you. But you didn't trust me with my own feelings. I slept with Connor of my own free will, but I *stayed* with him and slept with him again and again, because of the game you two were playing. Stringing me along until you deployed. And just when I thought Connor and I were done, along came the letters from Boot Camp. And God, Weston, I fell so hard then. So hard."

She's in love with my soul, and my soul is you.

"I'm sorry, Autumn," I said. "I'm so sorry."

She shook her head, her eyes on the window outside where night was falling, dark and cold. "The sad thing is, Connor's a wonderful man. Maybe we weren't written in the stars, but he didn't need to do this."

"He saw what I see in you," I said quietly. "He knew if someone had your love, they'd best do everything in their goddamn power to keep it. They'd be fools not to."

"But my love should've been for you, Weston," she said, "All of it. This entire time. Whatever you see in me wants to be with you, but now..."

"Don't tell me it's too late. Please. I can't…" My words choked off in a throat clogged with tears.

"You know," she said, her own voice watery. "I read those stunning letters from Boot Camp and I thought, *My God, these are for me. These incredible thoughts and feelings, and the poetry within them, and the love they carry… It's all for me.*"

"They were for you," I said hoarsely. "They still are. I meant every word."

"Because you loved me." Her voice broke, along with my heart.

"Yes."

"You loved me so much that when you came home from Boot Camp, you said nothing." Her agonized gaze pierced my heart. "And Connor and I went straight to bed."

I closed my eyes, all my shame and guilt defeated. When I opened them, she was taking her purse off the couch.

"I have to go now."

As she passed my chair, I took her hand. "Autumn, wait. Can I…? Can we talk more? Please?"

This can't be over.

"I don't know, Weston," she said. "I need to be alone right now."

I pressed the back of her hand to my lips. When I spoke, I pressed the words into her warm skin, praying they'd seep in and find the bottomless well of her generous heart.

"You didn't deserve what happened to you. And I don't deserve another chance. But I'm going to be selfish one last time and ask for one. Because the thought of living without you…" I squeezed my eyes shut, my voice a whisper. "It's fucking unbearable, Autumn."

She stood still as the seconds stretched into eternity.

Silence.

Then she slipped her hand out of my grasp and left, shutting the door softly behind her.

CHAPTER Twenty-Eight

Autumn

I left Weston's place as the night fell in earnest, dark and starless. I hugged myself tight, though I hardly felt the cold. I walked without thinking, just needing to be home in my own space, alone. I shut out Weston's beautiful face, laden with guilt and regret. I needed to sort my own thoughts and feelings first for a change.

I put the key in the lock of my apartment, then realized it was already open. I pushed the door and found Ruby standing in the living room, frantically jabbing at her phone, her luggage stacked near the couch.

Thank God, I thought, tears welling at the sight of my best friend, beautiful in jeans and a soft gray pea coat. When I closed the door, her head shot up and panic lit her eyes.

"Auts, what are you...?" Her gaze darted back toward the hallway to our bedrooms. "I was just trying to text you."

"Oh my God, Ruby, I'm so glad you're here."

I started to move toward her when the toilet flushed in the bathroom.

"Oh, you have someone with you?" Probably a new Italian boyfriend. I couldn't handle this tonight. Not now. I needed Ruby to myself.

Then the bathroom door opened and Connor Drake stepped out.

My stomach plummeted to the floor and my heart pounded above it. Each thudding beat was a puzzle piece falling into place. In ten seconds, I saw the complete picture. It all made sense. I knew exactly where Connor had been all this time.

"Oh my God." My purse fell from my nerveless fingers and my gaze volleyed between them.

"You just *had* to use the bathroom, didn't you?" Ruby muttered out the side of her mouth.

"Hey, Autumn," Connor said. He looked healthy. Tanned and vibrant. A thousand light-years from the broken wreck of a man I'd seen at the hospital.

I staggered back a step. "This is not happening."

"We need to talk," Connor said, coming closer to me.

"Do we?" I asked. "Should we invite Weston over so he can translate for you?"

Ruby covered her eyes. "Oh, God."

"Oh, you knew about that too?" I gave a small, bitter laugh, feeling outside my body. "Funny how I'm always the last to know."

"No," Ruby said in a small voice. "It's not like that. I mean it is, but…shit. Shit. *Shit.*"

She swatted Connor's arm, a small movement dripping with familiarity and intimacy. "This isn't right. We should have… God. Autumn, I'm so sorry…" She took a step toward me and I took a step back.

"Babe," Connor said, "can you give us a minute alone, please?"

Ruby looked at me. "Is that okay?"

"Sure, *babe*," I said. "Why not?"

She grabbed her purse. "I'll just be down at Claire's Café." She started past me and stopped. "Auts, I'm sorry. This is *not* how I wanted to tell you."

"Were you going to write a letter?"

Tears sprang to her eyes and she went out.

"You look good," I said to Connor. "Looks like your arm is healed."

He bent his left arm and then let it drop. He stood tall and strong in jeans, boots, and a smart wool jacket. Radiating a confidence

I'd never seen before, not even in the early days at Amherst.

"How long?" I asked. "The two of you…?"

"I went straight to Italy from here," he said. "But Ruby had no idea I was coming. I just showed up on her doorstep."

"And she let you right in."

"No," he said with a small, fond smile. "She shut the door in my face."

I jerked my head toward the door. "I never got that chance."

His smile fell. "Look, it's a long story, but you need to know we didn't *plan* this, I swear. I needed to get away from Boston. Anywhere. I knew she was in Italy so I went. We were friends for a long time before—"

"Before you started fucking."

He inhaled. "Yes."

I sank down on the couch and clutched a pillow to my chest. "Second time today I've had the earth ripped out from under me. I'm on a roll."

"I'm sorry." Connor moved a small chair closer and sat. "Wes told you about the writing?"

His green gaze was anxious on me. Those eyes had seen me naked, but they'd never witnessed the sleepless nights full of wondering and worrying.

"No," I said. "He didn't *tell* me. You didn't tell me. When did Ruby know?" My voice was even but my arms tightened on the pillow. "Because she didn't tell me either. I'm curious how many people I've been making a fool of myself in front of."

"Ruby didn't know. Not at first."

"But she knew before this afternoon, right? Before I did?" I held up a hand, shaking my head. "You know what? It doesn't matter. Who cares?"

"I care," Connor said. "And Ruby does too. She's been a mess, worried how you'd take it, us being together. She didn't want to hurt you."

"But she didn't tell me about that either," I said. "Everyone has been *so* considerate about protecting my feelings. Truly. Thank you all for trusting me."

Connor's head dropped for a moment. "I was a fucking mess when I left," he said, rubbing his chin. "You saw me. I was a wreck. I had to get out. Get away from my parents. A beach in Italy seemed like a goddamn paradise. I wasn't thinking about Ruby as more than someone who made me laugh when I really fucking needed to laugh. She let me be myself with no pressure to be something else."

"I never put that on you," I said quietly.

"You didn't have to," Connor said. "Not intentionally. You deserve so much and I tried to be *that guy* for a while, but I needed Wes's help."

"You lied to me," I said, my voice trembling. "Both of you lied. And Ruby, too."

"I know," he said. "I'm sorry. I wanted to tell you about the letters before I left but I couldn't. I didn't want to say something that would make it worse. Then when Ruby started mentioning you and Wes were hanging out a lot, I didn't want to ruin anything between you."

I stared at him, not knowing what to do with the amount of information passing around me and behind my back.

"How is Wes?" he asked, his voice gruff. "Is he okay?"

The love and worry for his best friend was in every line of his face. It seeped into the hard shell of sarcasm I was holding around me, dissolving it.

"He's fine," I said. "And I think you should go now. I don't want to talk to you anymore."

"Wait, just tell me—do you still have his letters from Boot Camp?"

"Yes."

His sigh of relief made my blood boil.

"I should've burned them," I said, flinging the pillow aside and shooting to my feet. "You told me you wrote those letters. I asked you point blank and you lied to my face."

"I didn't lie. Not entirely."

"Not *entirely*?" I cried. "Jesus, you are *unbelievable*."

"You asked if what was *in* those letters was true," Connor said. "And I said yes because it was."

"Bullshit."

"They weren't bullshit. They just weren't from *me*. They were from Wes. From his heart. Autumn, he loves you."

"Stop…"

"He's loved you since the beginning. But I was crazy about you and too selfish and blind to see Wes was the better man for you.

LONG LIVE the Beautiful Hearts

And he was too loyal to me to make a stand for himself. He was always putting me first, trying to protect me and...he's just too fucking *stubborn*..."

He smiled a sad smile, his love for his best friend shining in his eyes. And for *my* best friend.

"Ruby and I...we just make sense. We make each other happy. This is the first time I truly don't give a shit what my parents think because I know what's really important in life." Connor looked to me. "Are you and Wes happy?" he asked. "I mean, before all this shit went down. Was it...good?"

Hot tears melted the cold numbness encasing me all night. "We were so good," I whispered. "I'm in love with him."

Connor's face broke into a beautiful smile of heartfelt relief and joy. "God, Autumn, he loves you so much. If you're going to be mad at anyone, be mad at me. Wes didn't write that first poem to get you into my bed. I stole it from him. And when I realized he loved you, I didn't do the right thing, which was tell the truth and walk away."

I stared, exhausted and drained, a thousand emotions battering me.

"Is it too late?" Connor said. "Please say it's not too late."

"I know what's expected of me," I said dully. "You and Ruby are together. Weston and I are together. I should forgive and forget because he loves me now. I should let it all go and everyone will feel better." I cut him off before he could answer. "I've had quite enough revelations for one day. Right now the only thing I know is I want to be left alone."

I started down the hall to my room, but Connor's hand closed on my upper arm. He turned me around and held me gently.

"Don't..." I whispered, my eyes squeezed shut and burning with tears, my arms pressed to my own chest. "I'm so glad you're okay. So relieved, but Connor, I can't..."

"It's okay if you hate me," Connor murmured.

"I don't hate you; I just can't *look* at you."

"I understand, and I'm so sorry. But please, read his letters one more time. Know they came from him and he meant every word."

He let me go, touched my cheek with his palm.

"What's written there is the truth. I swear it."

CHAPTER
Twenty-Nine

Weston

I lay awake listening to the rain fall, drops counting off seconds that became hours. The inability to toss and turn left me feeling even more pinned down and immobile. It wasn't until the deep hours of night that the rain lulled me into a thin sleep, while my exhausted mind turned the body pillow into Autumn. I curled around her warmth and everything was all right. She hadn't left here shocked and betrayed. She still loved me. We were together.

When the cold gray light of dawn filtered through the windows, I woke alone, clutching a cold pillow.

Because it's over, Sock Boy. O-V-E-R.

I tossed the pillow to the floor, threw the circulation blanket off of my legs and sat up. I looked around my wheelchair-accessible state-of-the-art condo and an urge to flee came over me. To do what Connor had done. Get up and walk away. Run away.

Or just fucking *stand up.*

Professor O's words came back to me, like a dream I had a long time ago.

Maybe this is the universe's way of saying you're going to sit down and take it.

I'd been so close to happy, I could reach out and touch it. Wrap my body around it and sleep. But the part of me that watched my father drive away had ruled me my entire life. Constantly running to chase something I would never catch.

And I was just so fucking tired of it.

I knew Autumn was working at the bakery all day today. I didn't want to make a scene or embarrass her, but I had to see her. I had to tell her I wasn't letting her go. Not without a fight. And if it had to be in front of a café full of people, so be it.

I dressed and headed out. It wasn't a short jaunt from my place to downtown. By the time I got to Panache Blanc, the sun was up and a full line of customers waited for Phil and Edmond to fill their orders.

No sign of Autumn.

When Edmond saw me at the door, his face broke into a hesitant, curious smile.

"Monsieur Turner," he said. "I am happy to see you."

"Autumn's not here?"

He shook his head. "She called in sick."

"Damn. Thanks." I started to turn, but he called me back.

"Weston," he said. "I am worried about our girl. When she left here yesterday, she wasn't herself."

Our girl. I nearly told him I wasn't part of that *our* anymore. I bit the words back. A tiny flame of hope was all I had but I didn't want to blow it out.

"Me too," I said and left the bakery. I started the arduous trek up Pleasant Drive to Autumn's apartment. I clung to Professor O's words like a mantra, pushing the wheel rims in time:

Where there's love, there's hope for forgiveness.

My head was down and so full of thoughts, I paid no attention to where I was going. I nearly hit a guy coming the other way, yanking the brake at the last second.

"Fucking Christ, get out of my—" I glanced up at the guy and reality of him punched me in the face.

Connor stood over me, tanned and hearty, his hands shoved in the pockets of a wool jacket.

"Hey," he said. His eyes were clear and lucid. Nothing like the angry, haunted gaze the night he left.

"Hey," I said, my mind now completely blank. I felt my mouth start to smile and my chest open up with relief and happiness. Had I been standing, I would've tackled him, hugged him, let all the old shit between us die.

"What are you doing here?" I asked. "Are you back? For good?"

"Not yet. Visiting. For a few days. But we're coming back in June."

"We?"

He lifted his chin. "Ruby and I."

"Ruby."

The hope I'd been trying to keep stoked wavered and nearly went out.

"Ruby...You and Ruby." I choked out. "Are you fucking kidding me?"

"No," he said. "We've been together a while now. And I love her."

"You love her..." I scrubbed my face with both hands. "Does Autumn know?"

Connor rubbed the back of his neck. "She does now."

"Oh, fuck everything everywhere," I said, slumping.

"Yeah. The timing was shit. Ruby was going to talk to her last night while I skipped out to the hotel. But I needed to take a piss and that's when Autumn came home."

"Last *night?*" I cried. "Are you fucking kidding me?"

And with that, the pitiful flame of hope I had for Autumn and me went up in smoke.

"Wes—"

"Un-fucking-believable. I break her heart and you come along and finish her off. Brilliant." I started to push my chair past him but he blocked the way.

"Jesus, Wes. Wait."

"Move, asshole."

He kept walking backward. "Can we talk?"

"Oh *now* you want to talk?"

"Yeah, I do," he said. "And are you seriously ragging on me for keeping quiet? You? Because that's some bullshit, Wes, and you know it."

I did know it. And it pissed me off even more, this fucked up tangle of lies and secrets and revelations.

"I had to go," Connor said. "I needed help. And not my parents' brand of help. I needed to start over."

LONG LIVE **the Beautiful Hearts**

"But not until your parents dropped six million bucks into your bank account."

"Dude, why are you being such an asshole?"

Because you left. I needed you. You were my best friend, and you left.

"Because you took off for almost a year without saying where you went or if you were okay."

"I kept in contact with my parents," he said. "Jesus, Wes, you saw me. I was a fucking wreck. Headaches and blackouts and every goddamn noise setting me off. Someone would drop a ballpoint pen and it was like a gunshot in my ears." His jaw muscle ticked once before it softened into a smile I'd never seen him wear. "But being with Ruby... It's been so fucking great. I mean, she doesn't put up with my shit and she helped me find counseling and a job... She's amazing. I finally found someone I *fit* with."

"Ruby," I said. "Of all the goddamn women in the world."

"We can't choose who we love," he said. "All the shit we pulled on Autumn? That was on me. I told her I—"

"You talked to her?"

"Last night."

"And?" My hands gripped the rims of the chair to keep from launching out of it and shaking the entire conversation, word-for-word, out of him.

"She was pretty upset," he said. "But I explained what happened and how it was my fault."

"And that made everything all better, right? She believed you, which is why she raced to me, flew into my arms, and all is forgiven." It was the voice of the Amherst Asshole coming through my mouth now. "You made your pretty apology, smiled your charming smile, and now you're done. Your hands are clean, so you and Ruby can waltz into the sunset and leave me with *nothing*."

"What the fuck are you talking about? I tried to—"

"Forget it." I was going to say something truly unforgivable if I didn't end this conversation now. "Go back to your woman. To your money. Open your sports bar and be happy. You suck at misery anyway. Best leave it to the professionals."

"That's right, Wes," he said. "You're the pro at misery. It's what you expected for yourself your entire life. So guess what? That's what you get." His jaw clenched. "You never stood up for yourself.

Not when it counted. And now you can't."

I stared at him. He didn't blink or flinch.

"I'm sorry to put it that way, but it's the truth. You think Ruby and I are the last straw for you and Autumn, but we're not. It's shit timing, I won't lie, but it happened. And—"

"Yeah, shit happens," I snarled, the anger flaring up again. "Sometimes the only thing to do is take your small fortune and live on the Italian Riviera for a year, am I right?"

"I had to go," he said, his tone low. "I couldn't—"

"You couldn't stand to look at me. I remember."

He sighed and looked up at the gray sky for a moment. "I'm sorry I said that. I hate that I said it. But the guilt was fucking tearing me apart. It was me who—"

"Fuck no. I am not hearing this shit again."

I wheeled myself around him, teeth clenched and pure anger powering my arms. My wheels hit a crack in the sidewalk and I lurched forward. Hard. I would've tumbled out of the damn chair if Connor hadn't gripped my shoulder to steady me. The physical contact broke something loose inside me and I whipped my arm away.

"*Don't fucking touch me.*"

"Jesus, Wes—"

"Do you know what it feels like when you say it's your fault I'm in a chair for the rest of my life? Do you?"

He stared.

"Bad, Connor. Really fucking bad. Like your existence is defined by what happened to me and we *both* have to suffer for it. I'm not going to fucking live like that. I've busted my ass too hard and too long to have my entire life boil down to your guilty conscience."

"I get that," Connor said, his voice rising. "And if you'd just shut up for a fucking second… Dammit, Wes, can we get off this sidewalk, go somewhere and talk?"

"Gee, love to, but I'm busy," I said. "I have to go to Autumn's and try to salvage something out of the wreckage we made. And thanks very much for talking to her last night. I'm sure learning that you've been fucking her best friend for months was a great comfort to her."

"Ruby is over there now," Connor said, stopping me.

I turned.

"We're leaving for Boston tonight." The flatness of his voice was worse than his frustration. "She doesn't want to go until she fixes things with Autumn. Or tries to."

His gaze met mine. The connection we'd forged was still there, despite time and distance.

Stay, he told me. *Talk to me.*

I should've stayed. I should've told him I missed him. Those three words would've been easy. Any three words.

I miss you.

I love you.

I'm so sorry.

But I was still running.

"Have a safe trip," I said.

I turned my wheelchair around and went back home.

CHAPTER
Thirty

Autumn

I looked like hell.

Red-rimmed eyes stared back from the bathroom mirror, puffy from crying and ringed with dark circles. I'd lain awake for hours, listening to the rain and thinking about how the night turned out so differently from what I'd hoped. I thought I'd lie in Weston's arms until dawn, his warm body wrapped around mine. Tangled and inextricable and happy.

Instead, I lay alone in a cold bed, tears soaking the pillow.

I shuffled to the couch and fished my phone out of my purse to call in sick to work. Edmond's voice was laced with concern but I dodged his questions and hung up fast.

I bundled up on the couch with a blanket and a box of tissues and turned on cable TV. *Groundhog Day* was on again. I let it play. It was the story of my life, after all. Someone destined to relive the same day over and over, suffering the same mistakes, until they finally got it right and had love. Real love.

Someday, I'll get it right.

I dozed off, waking to a knock on the apartment door. *Groundhog Day* was over and *Sex and the City: The Movie* was playing. A twinge of nostalgia: this was one of Ruby's and my favorites. We didn't have the same taste in much else, but we'd drop everything for Carrie and Company.

Sighing like death, I hauled myself off the couch. Two days ago, I wouldn't dream of opening the door in my condition. I always dressed as nicely as possible, because if you want to be successful, dress as if you already are.

And if you want to get over a broken heart, I thought, *act like it's not shattered into a million pieces.*

I opened the door to Ruby, who looked as if she hadn't slept much either.

Because she was fucking Connor all night.

The thought didn't sting as much as I thought it would. Or, honestly, at all.

"Can I come in?" she asked.

"It's your place," I said. "You don't have to ask."

"I feel like I do. Not to mention you look a little bit like a vampire. Don't vampires have to invite people in?"

"Other way around," I said. "People need to invite vampires. So..." I pushed the door open wide. "Come in?"

"Ouch."

I went back to my couch nest, Ruby following.

"I'm nervous as hell," she said, "but I really want to talk to you."

"Knock yourself out," I said, my eyes on the movie.

"Well..." She sat at the other end of the couch, near my feet. "More than anything, I need you to know I didn't plan anything with Connor."

"I know. He told me last night. He showed up, you were friends—"

"No. I was shocked to see him—"

"Sorry, my bad. You slammed the door in his face. *Then* you became friends and then you started sleeping together. End of story."

"Except it's not the end," Ruby said. "It's the beginning. He and I... I've never felt like this about anyone. And I wanted to tell you a hundred times."

In the movie, it was Valentine's Day, and Miranda had just tearfully tried to apologize to a brokenhearted Carrie for keeping a secret from her for too long.

"Damn, Carrie Bradshaw, I *know*." Ruby grabbed the remote

and shut the TV off. "Can you please just look at me?"

I curled up smaller in my corner of the couch, arms crossed tight, and looked at her.

"I didn't want to hurt you," she said.

"Uh huh," I said. "Heard that before. Why the hell is everyone determined to protect me? Is this the vibe I give off? I'm a fragile little snowflake who melts at the first warm look from a beautiful man? I can't be trusted to handle the truth about anything?"

"You're not—"

"Look, I'm really happy for you and Connor. Maybe someday we can sit down and compare notes about how he is in the sack."

Ruby winced. "Was that really necessary?"

"You tell me."

She glared at me. "What I can tell you is that this isn't you," she said, crossing her own arms. "This sarcastic, don't-give-a-shit act? You *do* give a shit. About everything. It doesn't make you weak, Auts."

"Really? No one trusted me, including *me*. I never trusted myself and it spread like a virus to everyone I cared about. Those two spent *months* duping me. Lying to me. Knowing I'd fall for all that poetic crap because I'm a sap and a hopeless romantic. And you knew it too."

"I didn't know about it until a few days ago. It's the reason we're in Boston. As soon as Connor told me, I knew we had to come back. But I did a shitty job of planning and he was no help. Neither of us knew what to say."

"Story of my life," I muttered.

"I'm sorry, Autumn. For all of it. I really am."

I looked away, my cheeks burning. Being angry at Ruby was only making me feel worse. Every particle in me wanted to launch down the couch and into her arms. Hug her tight and make everything the way it was.

I want my best friend back.

I scrubbed the tears from my eyes. "So? Connor showed up in Italy. Then what?"

She inhaled with relief. "I swear nothing was premeditated. I always thought he was hot and fun, but he wasn't hot or fun when he showed up on my doorstep in La Spezia. He was a mess, drinking too much and not dealing with his PTSD. He thought he could lay on a beach with his six million dollars and all of his problems would magically vanish. But I made him get help. I told him to get a job, to work for both his money and his recovery. And he did. He worked his ass off and I was so proud of him. I watched him come back to life and…that's when I fell in love with him."

She glanced up at my sudden stare. "I'm sorry, Auts, but…" She shrugged and wiped a tear from her cheek. "But it's the truth. I love him."

Ruby never cried. Ruby was never emotional. Ruby never fell in love.

"You love Connor?" I said. "You're in love with him."

"God, so in love, and he—"

A sob erupted out of me. A real ugly cry. Tears streaming, nose running and my breath gasping in shallow hiccups.

"God, Autumn, I'm sorry."

I shook my head from behind my hands over my face. "No, I'm not crying because I'm upset. I'm crying because I'm *happy* for you." I snatched the tissue she held out. "God, what is wrong with me?"

"Nothing," she said, moving closer. "Only that you're sweet and kind and my best friend."

I dried my eyes and blew my nose. "I missed you."

"I missed you too." Now tears spilled over her cheeks and I handed her a tissue. She dabbed her eyes and huffed a long sigh. "I want things to be the way they were. I just want us to be close again."

"Me too."

"And I really want to hug you now."

"Me too."

We embraced tightly, her arms squeezing more tears out of me.

"You're my best friend," she whispered. "And I broke the code."

"I'm in love with Connor's best friend," I said. "Many codes have been broken."

We laughed as we both reached for more tissues and mopped up the flood.

"So…" Ruby said slowly. "You're all right with Connor and me being together?"

I nodded. "It might take a little getting used to. God, I *cheated* on him but now that I think about everything… I understand why it never felt like cheating. Because the real love was always with

Weston."

"Are you going to forgive him?" Ruby asked gently. "Connor said Wes has been in love with you for a long time."

"I feel so tangled up, I don't know which way to go."

"You're tangled up because you're not listening to your heart," Ruby said. "Look, what they did to you sucks, but—and I know this is going to sound really strange coming from me now—Connor had feelings for you too. He really did care about you. It wasn't some cruel game just to mess with you."

"I know."

"Have you read the letters again? Have you read them coming from *Wes*?"

"No. I can't handle them yet. It's too much."

"Well, they might help untangle a few things. Honestly, when you shove aside the bullshit, what's left is Wes is in love with you. He's a brilliant writer who penned you a fat stack of love letters and poems." She waggled her brows. "He's a poet and you didn't even know it."

I groaned.

"Too soon?"

I rolled my eyes at the ceiling. "Good thing I love you."

"I love you too," she said. "So tell me, what do you want? Or need? Connor wants to go to Boston tonight to see his parents, but I don't have to go."

"Has he seen Weston yet?"

"As we speak. I hope it's going well. Connor misses Wes like you wouldn't believe. They have an epic bromance. As Mr. Big would say"—she gestured at the TV—"I can only hope to come in a close second."

"Weston misses Connor too."

"So tell me what happens next. If you need me, I'll stay."

"Go to Boston with Connor," I said. "It'll be a huge moment. Epic. Mrs. Drake loves you and Connor will be so happy."

Ruby beamed and though I didn't want to give her up so soon, I knew I'd made the right decision.

"I'm kind of excited," she said. "Nervous, even."

"Is Connor nervous about seeing his family?"

She shook her head, her dark eyes lit from within with pride. "He's changed so much. They don't have a hold on him anymore. And not because of the trust money. It's something more. Something inside him."

"He's happy," I said. "You make him happy."

She rolled her eyes, but they were shining with unshed tears. "Yeah, okay, take it easy on me." She peeled herself off the couch. "I'm new at the mushy sap stuff."

I walked with her to the door, where she hugged me. "Read the letters when you're ready," she said. "If they make you want to fly to Wes's house and bang his brains out, don't think about it. Just do it."

"That's your sage advice?"

"Always." She gave me another hug. "Thank you for forgiving me."

"It feels better than being pissed off. Anger is exhausting."

"That might be your tangled heart telling you what it wants to do next. Just saying."

She blew me a kiss and left. Without letting myself think, I went to my room and retrieved the hope chest from under the bed.

Cross-legged on the floor, I reread the letters from Boot Camp. Every single one. I tried to reimagine them coming from Weston and waited for a fresh flush of love and exhilaration to sweep me away.

There wasn't any.

Reading the letters the first time, when the words were new and potent, had left their mark. They'd been emblazoned on my heart as Connor's. A signature at the bottom, and it wasn't Weston's.

"Now what?" I whispered.

I went back to the couch, burrowed under the blanket and put another movie on. Rain pattered against the windows, and I slept.

He pulls me gently onto his lap and holds my face. Hands that are hard and calloused but his touch is gentle. Almost reverent. His thumbs stroke my cheekbones as leans in to kiss me. A deep, imploring kiss, full of want and need that I feel in my soul.

He pulls away and I open my eyes.

"I have so much to tell you," I say, and his smile is beautiful. Full of relief and hope.

"Tell me…"

Once again, a knock at the door jolted me out of sleep. This time a smart rapping of knuckles. The windows were dark gray—I'd slept the afternoon away.

I climbed out of the blanket and smoothed down the front of my pajamas. Through the peep-hole, I saw a young man in full Army dress uniform with a hat and white gloves.

My hands trembled as I reached to open the door, needing to orient myself to the present day.

They're home. They're safe. This is not...that.

"Yes?"

"Autumn Cowel?"

"Caldwell."

"I'm Lieutenant Oren Banks, 1st Battalion, Flight Medic Specialist. I was with Connor Drake when we airlifted out of Syria in June of last year."

"All right," I said slowly. "Would you like to come in?"

"No, ma'am. This won't take a minute," he said with a faint Boston accent. "While we were being lifted out, Private Drake gave me something that belonged to you."

"To me?"

He handed me a small, flat box. "Our departure from the combat zone was pretty chaotic. We had multiple injured and one casualty. Anyway, he gave it to me and I stuffed it in my rucksack and... Ma'am, I apologize. I misplaced it after that." His expression grew sheepish. "I forgot all about it, to be honest. I'm so sorry."

Slowly, I opened the box.

"My gear came home with me after the tour," Banks was saying. "My wife stored it in a closet. I did another tour, came home, and while I was sorting out all my stuff, I found...that."

My hands were shaking now. I tipped the box and a small, dirt-encrusted notebook fell into my open hand.

"It was important to Drake that you get it," Banks said. "And we never let a fellow soldier down. I only remembered your first name, a street that starts with an R and Amherst. So it took a while for me to track you down. But here I am. And I'm really sorry about the delay."

"It's okay," I breathed. "Thank you. For everything."

"My pleasure, ma'am." He nodded once and left.

I shut the door and made my way to the couch, my eyes fixed on the notebook's cover. I sank down and opened it.

A sob tore out of me at the first lines. I pressed my hand to my

LONG LIVE the Beautiful Hearts

mouth as I read Weston's words stained with Weston's tears and blood.

For you, I would
bring down the stars,
wreath their fire
around your neck
like diamonds,
and watch them
pulse
to the beat of your heart

For you, I would
capture the candlelight
in the palm of my hand
Give my breath
to give it life
A whisper,
'My love'
So that it may grow
Bright and hot
And burn me

For you, I would
drink the salted oceans
Until their depths
Were swallowed
into the depths of me
How deep it is, this life
This love, for you
I cannot touch bottom
I never will

For you, I would
mine the stony earth
Until it relinquished
The secrets of time
Cracks in the stone
wrinkles of the Earth

As she turns her face
to another new day
And so I wish to live
Every one of mine
With you

For you, I would
be myself
At long last
I would live in my skin
And breathe my words
in my own voice
Tinged with the accent
Of a child calling to a car
that will never stop
And in the fading echo
Nothing remains but the truth
of me
that is the love
of you

I have loved you with both
Hands tied behind my back
Bound with pen and ink
Paper and words
Sealed with someone else's name
until this moment
in which I am nothing
but a man
who loves a woman.
There is nothing left to say
Except to give
all of my heart
For you

My tears joined Weston's on the paper. I clutched the notebook to my heart and inhaled several deep breaths. I looked for more in the book but the pages were empty. But on the back flyleaf in shaky, uneven script:

LONG LIVE the Beautiful Hearts

Autumn,
Wes wrote this and everything else. For you.
-C

Here were Weston's beautiful words, written only for me. And Connor's words giving me the truth. More meaningful than any apology or confession. The poem and its dedication at last set me free from the game that had bound the three of us together. Love for both men washed through me and fell with warm tears onto my lap. I loved Connor. Some part of me always would. But Weston...

God, my love for him wasn't in part, it was my all. The ferocity of it stole my breath. With no confusion or sadness now, my thoughts replayed our time together. The months and weeks and moments we spent learning each other.

It was real.

The love he scratched into a notebook, bound with tears and blood... It's real.

It's mine.

I had to go to him. I set the notebook on the coffee table. Then I thought twice and took it in my room and set it on the bed. It waited patiently as I showered, as I dressed and brushed my hair. I kissed it before tucking it safely in my bag. Then I left.

CHAPTER
Thirty-One

Weston

The rain drummed against the window in my place, hard and relentless. I sat on the couch and stared at the TV, remembering another rain. It had poured in sheets at Boot Camp, soaking me to the bone as I did push-ups with Drill Sergeant Denroy screaming in my ear that I was a shit-for-brains.

He wasn't wrong, Sock Boy.

"Shut up," I muttered.

I was fucking sick of that voice. Sick of the words I spat at Connor and the ones I'd used to lie to Autumn, when the truest words of my heart were on the surface, ready to be spoken. Or written.

But I'd written my greatest poem to Autumn and it hadn't made it out of Syria. The words were gone and I could never get them back. Not the same way I'd written them—with my entire heart and soul, tears and blood on the page.

I was staring through a Red Sox game, when my phone rang with a number I didn't recognize.

"Wes Turner?"

"Yeah?"

"This is Ian Brown."

"Oh, hey, Coach."

LONG LIVE the Beautiful Hearts

"You feeling okay? Sounds like you have a cold."

"No, I'm fine."

"Great. Because I need you healthy and ready to go this Saturday."

"The prelim?" I frowned. "You told me at the last practice I wasn't ready."

"You're not." He chuckled. "Your steering needs work—to put it mildly—but you're fast as hell and I need fast. Zack sprained his wrist. He's out and you're in. Are you up for it?"

You up for that, Sock Boy? Racing around a track in a wheelchair? In front of a crowd—?

"I'm in," I said. "I'll do it."

"Great. Practice on Tuesday and Thursday, as usual. Rain or shine. Hopefully shine."

"See you then, Coach."

A sliver of excitement tried to find me but couldn't quite catch. I wondered if everything would be like that from now on; the bad days worse and the good days shadowed by not having her. Everything would be the same but a little bit shittier. Because I'd ruined us.

Professor Ondiwuje's words echoed in the emptiness.

Fight for you. For who you are. Fight for yourself and what you love. Who you love.

I flipped channels, trying to figure out how to fight for who I loved without hurting them too.

Citizen Kane was on. I picked up my phone and ordered a pizza, then hauled my ass off the couch into the wheelchair. I put a twenty on the table by the door, rolled to the bathroom to take a piss, then transitioned back onto the couch.

It was late afternoon, but the rain clouds blanketing the sky outside made it feel like night. The TV was my only light. It flickered eerie and silver from the black and white movie.

A knock came at the door.

"It's open," I called over my shoulder. "Just leave it on the table. Money's right there."

"Thanks, but I'm not here for the money."

My heart stopped, then took off again as I turned to look at Autumn.

"Can I come in?"

I nodded mutely. She slipped off her coat and hung it on the rack. She wore a dark blue dress that floated lightly around her knees. Raindrops like diamonds clung to her hair.

"Hi," she said, taking something out of her purse.

"Hey." I muted the TV and stared. Jesus, her face was everything my eyes needed to see. I drank her in, my gaze finally coming to rest on the notebook in her hands.

My notebook.

Without even touching it, the memories in its dirty, blood-stained pages swamped me. All the explosions, screams, and gunshots. The heat and the killing. The grenade that blew my life apart and saved me at the same time. The moments before I ran my last race on legs I'd never use again. Words for Autumn pressed against my heart as I ran to save my best friend.

"I thought it was lost," I said.

"It was," she said. "And now it's found." She knelt by my legs and handed it to me. Her eyes were warm and dark and…

Forgiving?

I didn't dare hope. But then what was she doing here?

With trembling fingers, I opened the book and read the poem. The words as real and true on this damp, rainy night as they'd been when I wrote them surrounded by desert sand.

"Look on the back," she said softly.

I flipped the book over, to the shaky handwriting of my best friend, telling the truth—our truth—in his own words. My chest tightened and I sucked in a breath.

"I did," I said hoarsely. "I wrote it for you. All of it. Everything. And I'm sorry." My shoulders rounded over the notebook clutched tight in my fingers. "I'm so sorry I never told you…"

I felt the couch cushions dip, then Autumn knelt beside me, her legs tucked under her. Her arms went around me and I thought I'd die at their soft strength. Her forgiveness seeped into me like sunlight into a dark, cold place shuttered up for a long time.

I clung to her, cried into her. Under my hands, her body trembled with sobs. When she pulled away, her eyes were wet with tears but her gaze was steady. Her voice soft but firm as she spoke.

"What you and Connor did hurt me. And I know you did it for love. Love for both him and me. But I deserve honesty. And respect. I never want to wonder or worry that I'm standing on something that's not there. I deserve something real."

LONG LIVE the Beautiful Hearts

"Yes," I said. "Yes, you do."

"And Weston." Her hand slipped over my jaw. "So do you. You're so much more than that little boy running down an empty street. You deserve to be happy, too. Tell me..." Her voice cracked. "These last few months, were you happy?"

"Yes," I said. "Happy when I thought happiness was impossible. When it should have been more impossible from a wheelchair." I kissed her palm. "A great man told me I had to sit down and be with who I am. No more running. And he was right."

"I love who you are," she said. "I'm so in love with you."

The words sank through my skin, into my bones and down to the marrow. Her love infused every cell and molecule. Even in the half of my body I couldn't feel, I knew it was part of me now.

"God, Autumn," I said, holding her face. "I've loved you for so long. Meeting you in the library that first time felt like a reunion. I've loved you in a thousand lifetimes. Do you feel it?"

"Yes," she whispered. "I've been looking for you my entire life."

"I'm here." Her fingers in my hair then, her hand on my chest, feeling my beating heart that was hers. "I'm right here."

I pulled her sideways onto my lap and kissed her. I kissed her with everything I had. All the words I wrote and all the poetry not yet written. I could write until I had no words left, and it wouldn't be enough.

Autumn's soft, warm body melted against me, her kiss deep and urgent. Taking from me whatever I had to give and giving me all of her in return. Her little sounds filled my mouth, and I breathed them in. Breathed *her* in, my hands tangling in her hair and skimming down her back, feeling every bit of her that was with me because this time it was real.

The deep intensity of our kisses caught fire and she moved to straddle me. Her hands raked through my hair. My hands roamed down her body to the rounded curve of her ass. I pushed and pulled her against me, and she moaned in my mouth.

Sensations I thought were dead stirred below my waist. Nothing familiar; only echoes—signals coming from a great distance, but there, rising up. The area of my injury tingled and sang, the feeling climbed higher, to my chest, my heart, because the greatest desire I had for Autumn lived there. Lust, passion, and love becoming one sensation of overwhelming want.

Her hand slipped between us and stroked the front of my flannel pants. "You're so hard," she whispered against my mouth. "Can you feel it?"

I watched her hand slide again and again over the erection straining against my pants.

"I feel it," I said. "God, I feel you."

She bent to kiss me deep, our tongues sliding and exploring while our hands grew brazen and needy. She reached for the ties on my flannel pants while my fingers went to the buttons down the front of her dress. I was ready to tear it off of her when the doorbell ringing jolted us apart.

"Jesus Christ," I hissed. I sagged against the couch, my hands dropping to my sides.

Autumn gave a little laugh and rested her forehead on mine. "Chinese food?"

"Pizza."

"You'll be glad to have it later." With a last nipping kiss, she climbed off me, answered the door, paid the guy and carried the box to the kitchen counter. Two minutes that felt like a fucking eternity.

"You want to go in the bedroom?" I asked when she stood in front of me again.

She shook her head and began unbuttoning her dress. "I want the couch. I want to finish what we started that night."

Fuck, yes...

I yanked off my T-shirt while she finished with the buttons and pulled the sleeves off her shoulders, one at a time. The dark material pooled at her feet. She unhooked her bra and slid her lacy underwear off her hips and down her legs. Naked in the flickering light of the movie, her skin was luminous and perfect.

"Christ, you're beautiful," I said hoarsely.

She bent and kissed me again, her hair falling over my chest and her mouth tasting so sweet. She put her hands on the waistband of my flannel pants.

"I want you so bad," she whispered.

"Autumn…" My breath was ragged. "I don't know how or…*if* I can do this."

"Let's just try," she said. "I don't care what happens but I don't want to stop."

226

"God, no," I said. "Never stop…"

She helped me strip out of my pants and underwear and tossed them aside. She gazed at the hard length of me with unabashed desire. All thought and worry evaporated as she straddled me, her slight frame perched on my thighs. I stopped thinking about what I could or couldn't do and just *did*.

With a rough sound deep in my chest, I gripped her by the arms and pulled her up to me, taking one small nipple in my mouth. She gave a little cry and gripped the back of the couch. I held where I wanted her so I could suck and bite and kiss each breast.

"Now," she whispered. Begging. "Please…"

I brought her mouth to mine and kissed her while my hands slid down the silk of her naked skin to grip her slender waist that was tiny in my hands. Her long hair brushed my wrists as she settled back onto my thighs.

My hands were on her hips now, my fingers digging in, restraining myself as best I could because this first time would only come once. The twin sensations of love and lust were a tidal wave in me, loving and wanting her so badly I could hardly breathe.

"I've never felt like this before," she whispered, her face wet against mine now.

"Don't cry."

"I don't mean to but everything feels so perfect. Doesn't it?"

I didn't trust myself to speak, unsure whether a sob, laugh, or curse would erupt from me. I kissed her instead while she reached between us. I felt the faint pressure of her hand around me.

"Are you ready?" she whispered.

I nodded, bracing myself. I knew I'd never feel her the way I wanted to feel her. I'd never know the heat and wetness of being inside of her. I'd never feel the completeness of our joining. For a moment I cursed myself for holding back the night before deployment. I could've had her then, could've known what it was like to be inside her. I only stopped because she didn't know the truth.

But now she knew everything.

I held my breath.

She sighed and then gasped. "God…" She settled herself on me, her arms around my neck. "Can you feel me?"

Maybe my memory and imagination were filling in the gaps of what my body couldn't tell me, but Autumn lowered down on me and

227

I felt her. The faint pressure tightened. Grew warmer, until I was deep inside her.

"I feel you," I said. "I can feel this."

Eyes locked, she kissed me, her hair spilling around my shoulders, she moved on me, never breaking our gazes.

Another inhale, another kiss, deeper this time. She broke away with a gasp and her head fell back, ecstasy mounting up in her face.

"Please... Harder." She put her hands over mine. "I need you so bad."

I tightened my grip on her. It was nothing to lift her and bring her back down, hold her deep or move her fast and hard. I watched her take me in her body, over and over, the vision of us translated into sensations I thought were gone forever.

Autumn's hands that never stopped moving over my chest, my shoulders and back, my neck and into my hair... She never stopped giving me sensations I could feel, all the while undulating gracefully on top of me.

"I want to make you come," I said.

"Yes," she whispered tightly. Her face so fucking beautiful in the flickering light. I felt the tension rise in her—an orgasm I was building. Her fingers scraped my shoulders, and her cries grew louder as she held on, rolling her hips against mine.

"Now, Autumn," I gritted out. "Show me..."

"Yes. *Yes...*"

The words choked off as she came, her body contorted as it coursed through her, mouth parted in a silent cry. My thumb stretched to rub circles over her tight knot of flesh to make it last, not letting up until she sagged against me. Her breasts where pressed to me; her heartbeat crashing against my chest as if it were mine.

After a moment, her lips brushed my ear. "Now you."

Our mouths met in a crushing kiss while her hand slipped between my back and the couch cushions. Her fingers found the scarred skin and caressed it. I grunted as a spark ignited.

"Good?"

"Yes...Fuck, yes..."

Her warmth and heat, her sweat and her mouth. Her hand moving over the broken parts of me, bringing life to scarred flesh. She stroked and coaxed while I ground her body on me, building my new version of an orgasm. Part sensation, part memory, part desire, part

228

love. Stanzas built up, one on top of the other, to create the whole.

"I love you," she whispered.

And I came.

Not a white-hot explosion of pleasure. Rather a tightening at my waist, like a fist clenching. Then it loosened, fingers unfolding to release a strange, exhilarating combination of heat and ice. It flooded my chest and thrummed wildly in the tangle of nerves at my injury site. It *sang*. Love and lust in perfect harmony, building and building until the wave peaked and crashed. It washed through my chest, then ebbed away, suffusing me with peace.

I shuddered and let go of her hips. My fingers had left marks on her delicate skin.

Because she's mine, came the primal thought.

And I'm hers too. Until the day I die.

"Oh my God, you came," she said, kissing me. "I felt it."

"God, yes. I felt...everything."

Her palms slid over my jaw. She kissed me again, then wrapped her arms around me. Her skin was slick with sweat, her breath sweet against my shoulder.

Our bodies touched at a thousand different places and I felt every one.

CHAPTER
Thirty-Two

Weston

The rain finally stopped and the track was dry for Saturday's meet. Food trucks were setting up around the field and race officials walked between teams, taking info and passing out numbers. The me from Before would've never noticed an event like this. It would've been invisible to me, as invisible as I sometimes felt. This was a preliminary race before the season began, but it wasn't a kiddie picnic.

This is a life.

My team was one of six comprising a semi-professional league of wheelchair racers who competed in local meets around New England. It was a small league, but Coach Brown was something of a prodigy: several of his racers had medaled in the Paralympics.

My team members were classified as T54—we all had complete mobility from the waist up. Other classifications were reserved for racers with cerebral palsy or higher spinal cord injuries. As the morning drew on, the stands became more populated. Less than what I'd seen in Amherst but not too bad for a prelim.

One of my teammates, a double-amputee named Ron Sellers, gave me a nod as I rolled up. "What's up, Wes?"

He held out his hand in greeting. In my old life, I would've kept my distance. I wasn't there to make friends, I was there to win.

LONG LIVE the Beautiful Hearts

But I was in the After now.

I clasped his hand and gave him a fist bump. "How's it going, Ron? Ready to kick some ass?"

"Always." He laughed. "First race for you. Nervous?"

I tossed my chin at our opponents. "For them? Hell, yes."

Ron chuckled and then Coach huddled us up for a pep talk.

"Turner," he said. "This is your first race. Your job is to not wipe out. That's my one and only coaching directive."

"I'll do my best, Coach."

The late morning was gray and watery after the rains but smelled clean. New. As if so much that was old had been washed away.

I transitioned into my racing chair—a loaner until I earned my own—and tucked my legs under me to kneel. Coach handed me the racing gloves—fat cushions that wrapped around the middle of the hand—and slapped my shoulder.

"You didn't think I was going to leave it at 'don't crash,' did you?"

He crouched beside my chair and looked out over the track, pointing at various spots as he spoke.

"Get a good start. That's going to be your best advantage. Stay out of the inside lane unless you're out ahead. Otherwise, you're going to get crowded in. It'll be harder to keep up, of course, but use your power on the straights to bring it home. Got it?"

In track, the coach told me when to show up and I showed up. I chafed at advice or directions given by older men. The part of my brain insisting I still had a dad somewhere just wouldn't tolerate imposters.

The familiar irritation was there today but faint. Like a bruise from an old wound.

"Thanks, Coach," I said.

"And don't crash."

Mine was the last race of the day—the eight hundred meters. I cheered on my teammates and watched them closely to learn what I could. When my race was called, I changed into my yellow racing shirt. Coach gave me one last chuck on the shoulder.

"Give 'em hell, crazy bastard."

"On it."

I lined up against eight other racers, maneuvering onto lane three. The guy in two looked over.

"Hey. You new?"

The enemy has spoken.

"Yep," I said.

"Awesome. Good luck, rookie."

A hundred cutting, smart-ass remarks were locked and loaded behind my lips.

I gave the guy a smile. "You too, man. Good luck."

Adrenaline surged through my veins at the call to get ready. Eight pairs of arms coiled, ready to spring.

The gun went off.

We pushed at the wheels, everyone slow to get rolling but quickly gaining speed. A good start could win a race.

My start was shit.

I caught up just as the other racers bunched together, crowding me out. Just like Coach said, I had to take an outside lane, which fucked me over on the curve. I was dead last going into the first two hundred meters. I inhaled deep and channeled everything I had into my arms to gain ground on the straightaway and made up two positions.

At the second curve, I disobeyed Coach and moved inside. I could feel the wind from the guys on the other side of me as they pushed at their hand rims.

Distantly, I heard a little murmur of applause and cheers in the crowd.

I managed not to crash or even bump someone, but cold sweat dripped down my back from the effort. On the last straightaway, I saw a hole in the pack and slipped between two racers to escape the crowd. My arms begged for mercy and my lungs were on fire, but I gained another two positions and crossed the finish line behind three other racers.

The me from Before would've been pissed off for losing. Hell, that Wes would've been pissed off for *winning*. But when I crossed the line in 4th place, I knew nothing but pure exhilaration.

And relief I hadn't caused an eight-chair pileup.

The crowd cheered as we rolled by the stands. My arms were lead, but I managed to reach out and fist bump a couple of opponents. Then I heard it...

"You're my boy, Blue!"

My arms dropped by my wheels. My pounding heart nearly

turned inside out as I coasted past the stands, searching.

He was easy to pick out—standing tall while the rest of the crowd had resumed their seats. Still clapping his hands when everyone else had gone back to their phones. He put two fingers to his mouth and whistled. "Way to go, T!"

Holy shit, he's here. He showed up. For me.

Our eyes met and Connor raised a hand, his smile wide but hesitant. I raised a hand back, my pulse ratcheting up into my throat and sticking there in a tight lump.

I joined my team and transitioned into my wheelchair as fast as I could. Coach gave us some critiques and I nodded, not really hearing. A couple of the guys asked if I wanted to go for beers.

"No, thanks," I said, throwing on a sweatshirt. "Another time." I paused a second, then added, "Next time for sure, okay?"

"You got it."

My heart was still thumping when I rolled up to Connor, who stood waiting with his hands jammed in his front pockets.

"Hey," I said.

"Great race, man."

"Thanks. How did you know about this meet?"

His eyes rolled. "Since when have I missed one of your races?"

"Since never," I said, my voice thick. "Autumn tell you?"

"She told Ruby. Who told me."

For a second the awkwardness of our situation settled between us, and we headed down the track, toward the parking lot.

"How are things with her?" Connor asked.

"Great," I said, then decided to cut the bullshit. "She's a fucking miracle, actually. Every day with her is my best day."

"I'm glad, man," he said. "I mean it."

"And Ruby?"

He blew air out his cheeks. "I love her."

"Yeah, you mentioned that the other night."

He laughed. "I know, but I still can't get over saying it. And meaning it. It feels fucking awesome and it's just so easy."

My chest tightened to see him so happy. Almost like his old self, though there was a new depth in his eyes. All soldiers who'd been in combat had it, I thought. Comes with the territory.

"You deserve it," I said.

We continued in silence a few feet more and came to the end of the bleachers.

"Hold up a second," Connor said. He sat on the edge of a seat to put himself eye level with me. "I need to say something."

"No, you don't—"

"Yeah, I do, and you're going to shut up for once and listen."

There was laughter in his voice but he was dead serious.

I shut up and listened.

"I'm sorry I left. I felt responsible for what happened to you. It killed me to see what became of your life, but what tore me up the most was that I couldn't fix it. I couldn't take your injury myself, but I wanted to." His right arm absently wrapped around his rebuilt left elbow. "So I left to try to fix myself, because I wasn't going to make it here or in Boston."

A short silence fell. The chasm between us was right there and dug out of my oldest pain and self-destructing anger. The Drakes thought I propped Connor up, getting him through school and sticking by his side. But the truth was, he had held me together for years, when I would have imploded a long time ago.

"You were right about everything," I said. "About me not standing up for myself. I sabotaged so much that was good in my life because I either felt I didn't deserve it, or it couldn't be trusted. It was probably going to be taken away, so I may as well fuck it up before it does." I looked at him. "Like you. You were the best thing in my life. Starting the day what's-his-name dumped food in my lap. And I never told you."

"You never had to, man."

"I did. Some shit just needs to be said out loud."

Connor nodded. "You saved my life out there. You ran for that fucking grenade and you saved my life."

"I'd do it again this fucking second if I had to. Because you saved my life too. And I don't mean just in Syria."

He frowned for a second, and then understanding dawned slowly in his gaze, and his mouth unfolded into a smile that was everything.

"You okay?" I asked after a thick moment. "I mean…after all that shit?"

"Better." Connor's gaze was on the thick green grass around the track, but I know he was seeing rocky deserts and burned out shells of houses. "So many fucking nights where I thought the gunshots would never stop."

"Yeah," I said. "But we're both still here, right?"

"Yeah. We're still here." He reached over and put his hand on my shoulder. "I love you, man."

The weight of his palm sank into me. I wrote his papers in school. I signed my name on an Army enlistment form. I ran at a live grenade. I turned over the love of my life to make him happy. I did it all because I loved him, but I'd never said the words.

I put my hand near the back of his neck and pulled him to me, forehead to forehead.

"I love you, too," I said, choked by a throat of iron. "Thank you for…" I clenched my teeth for a moment.

Say it. Make it real.

"For you."

Connor nodded against my head. "Same, Wes. Fucking same. Always."

We held still for a few ragged breaths, then let go, dragging sleeves across our wet faces.

"So, ready?"

"Yeah, let's go."

Side by side, we headed to the parking lot.

"You going back to Italy?" I asked.

"In a few days." He glanced around the lot. "Where's your ride?"

"I was going to Uber."

Connor jerked his head at the Dodge Hellcat parked ahead of us. "I'll give you a lift. Just like old times." He knocked my arm. "You must be tired, after all. Coming in *fourth* place is hard work."

"Fuck off," I said. "It was my first race."

"Whatever. You haven't come in fourth since the time you ran the four-by-four-hundred with the stomach flu. Speaking of which, where's the trademark Turner post-race puke?" He shook his head grimly. "I paid good money to watch this race."

I scratched the corner of my eye with my middle finger. "Sorry to disappoint."

His own middle finger rubbed the edge of his sideburn. Then he shot me a grin and the connection between us sang out. A love that ran deeper than friendship, deeper than family. A combat-tested bond that transcended blood and bone.

Soul mates.

CHAPTER
Thirty-Three

Autumn

After my morning shift at Panache Blanc, I went back to Weston's place to shower and wash off the flour and sweat of working a crowded bakery. It had only been a few days, but neither of us could stand to spend the night in our own beds, alone. He came home just as I was wrapping myself in a towel.

"Autumn?"

"In here," I called. "Tell me everything."

Weston rolled into the bedroom, still in his racing attire and sweatshirt and looking like a hunter back from the kill. Goose bumps raised on my arms as his hungry gaze raked me up and down.

"Well?" I asked, over the electric hum in the air. "How did it go with Connor?"

"Fine," he said, his blue-green eyes on my bare legs. "We're good."

"That's it?" I said with a small laugh. "You're good?"

He nodded, moving his chair closer. I retreated until the backs of my legs touched the bed, my heart wild in my chest and the heat already pooling between my thighs.

"Sorry I missed the race," I managed to say. "I wanted you guys to have alone-time."

He took my wrist and hauled me onto his lap. "I forgive you," he said, his voice low and rough with need. His hand slid up under the towel. "And I need you. Right now."

"So demanding," I said, trying to play it casual though I could hardly catch my breath. "You're so bossy in the bedroom."

But he wasn't only one thing, he was many things. Weston was beautifully sweet and considerate in bed too, but it set my blood on fire when he was like this.

My mouth brushed his, breathing the words into him. "Tell me what you want."

He kissed me, hard and demanding. "Get on the bed."

I moved from his lap and sat on the bed, my entire body aching and ready for him. He pushed my knees apart and moved in.

"Lay back," he said. "I'm going to make you come now."

He said it matter-of-factly, a done deal; all I had to do was anything he asked. He moved his chair flush with the bed and pushed the towel up over my thighs. For one second, I only felt the heat of his breath on my skin. Then his mouth descended. At that first touch of his tongue, a jolt rocketed through my body and a cry spilled out of my throat.

"Oh God, Weston…"

The towel fell open as I arched my back into his mouth. My hips bucked under his hands as he worked me over. Biting lightly, sucking, his tongue swirling and licking until it was all I could do to keep from screaming. I writhed but he kept me where he wanted me. Relentless.

"So good," he growled. "Now come, Autumn. Come on my tongue and then I'm going to take you again."

"Jesus," I gasped.

His words alone sent me crashing through that first orgasm. He delved deeper, keeping my body at the mercy of his mouth. I propped myself on an elbow, my other hand making a fist in his hair. He grunted, threw my legs over his shoulders, and then I was done for. I didn't bother stifling the screams. I filled his bedroom with them, until at last he sat up and left me ragged and limp.

"Holy shit." The ceiling swirled above my blurred eyes. "I think I forgot my name."

I blinked a few times, then managed to meet his gaze. The commanding, bossy demeanor was gone and now the heated arousal in his eyes was deeper than physical. My body hummed like a livewire, but I wanted more.

"Come here," I said and scooted backward.

He stripped out of his sweatshirt and T-shirt, revealing his tanned, sculpted beauty.

"You're staring, Caldwell."

"I'm drooling, Turner."

He transitioned from his chair, hauled himself up the mattress and lay his head on the pillow beside mine. We reached for each other at once, all the desperate need deepening into something else. I couldn't get enough of the intense kisses that left no part of my mouth unexplored. My body ached for him. My hands wanted to touch all of him at once.

We broke apart long enough to strip him out of his racing shorts and he positioned himself on his side.

"I'm sweaty," he said.

"Good."

"I want to be inside you," he said, his kiss turning soft and languid, the blue-green ocean of his eyes soft and warm. "On top of you. I want everything…"

He kissed me harder, pushing me onto my back, and used his magnificent arms to move himself over me. I loved the heat of his body, the perfect heavy weight of it, so much of his skin on mine. I needed the completeness of us like I needed air. I reached between us and shifted my hips, tilting them up to take him inside me.

"Weston… Oh my God…"

"Am I crushing you?"

"No. God, you're so deep in me. I love this. I love you."

Weston braced himself on his arms, and in the bright light of day, the lines of his muscles were stark, showing his definition and strength. His forearms were perfection. Fresh heat swept through me at the sight of his shoulders and biceps, the lines of his neck leading to his broad chest, down to the tight ripples of his abs.

"God, Weston," I whispered against his lips. "I can't get enough of you."

His half-smile was heartbreaking in its beauty. I know he still struggled with perceptions of himself, but they were fading. The man who'd based his worth on the failings of someone who should have loved him was slowly being replaced. Emerging from somewhere dark into the light of day.

My ocean eyes and a diamond mind, I thought as we moved and touched and kissed. *God, he's beautiful. So beautiful.*

My hands roamed the broad planes of his back, down to the scarred flesh of his lower spine. My fingers passed over them, feeling the texture change, smooth to rough, over and over.

"God, I love you," he said, his voice gruff as he used his arms to move in me, while I lifted my hips to take him in. "I love you…"

Our movements, a perfect synchronicity, turned desperate. Needy. We had to create our own choreography, but I loved that it was his and mine. Ours. Us.

"No one loves me like this," I said, rising into him, taking him in my body again and again.

"Autumn…"

"I don't want to be loved any other way. Ever again."

He kissed me then, fiercely, and when he pulled away, his eyes were deep and dark. "Get on top," he said. "I need to move you."

He rolled to his back and pulled me on top of him. His hands gripped my waist and he drove me onto him again and again. I rode him hard, and the orgasm that had been simmering in my belly grew to a white-hot flame that Weston stoked hotter and hotter with every thrust.

"Weston, I'm going to…"

"Come, Autumn," he gritted out. "You're going to come. Right now."

I did, my body obeying his potent, coaxing words as the hard length of him bore deep inside me. His words, always Weston's words…

Orgasm ripped through me like a wave, arching my body with its intensity and stifling my voice, my breath, then releasing me as the wave crested and broke.

"Jesus, Weston…yes. Yes…"

His arms—those glorious arms of his—moved me on him, and the raw, animalistic act of him using my body to take his own release built another swift orgasm on the heels of the first.

"Autumn…"

He clenched his jaw, squeezed his eyes shut, and I watched as the wave crashed over him too. The cut of his abs became more stark, his breath shorter. He told me he felt his orgasms in his chest now. All the lust that should've manifested as physical sensation inextricably entwined with the love for me in his heart. I let it flow through me like water, then collapsed down to lay flat over his chest, my head tucked under his jaw. His heart pounded under my ear and his chest rose and fell as he caught his breath.

"So good," I murmured. "God, so good…"

"Is it enough?"

I lifted my head to see his brow furrowed and doubt in his eyes.

"It's good now," he said. "But in a few years…"

"In a few years, in a few decades, I'll feel the same. I don't want anything else."

He stroked my hair. "I'll never be able to come home from work and take you up against a wall. Or bend you over the couch and just…fuck your brains out."

"Wall sex is overrated. And maybe I don't want to be bent over a couch and have my brains fucked out."

"When you put it that way…" His smile faded. "But there might be times when you'll want more than what I can give you."

I traced my finger over his chest, drawing lines and swirls. "No one can give me what you can. What I feel right now is all I've ever wanted, and it's so much more than I could've imagined."

"I love you," he said, taking my face and kissing me deeply. "I love you so fucking much."

"I love you," I whispered. "And I love this. Lying here with you in bed, talking and kissing. It's as important to me as sex. Maybe more."

"Lucky you," he said. "I'm really good at lying around."

"You're good at lots of things. Tell me about the race."

"Fourth place," he said with a shrug.

"Fourth?" I swatted his arm. "Weston, that's amazing. On your first race? Why didn't you tell me?"

"Not important. I just liked being there. And Connor came." His eyes softened. "That was your doing."

"I just pointed him in your direction. Nothing could keep him away from you."

He didn't reply but I could see how the idea touched him.

"Paul called me on the way back," he said after a minute. "He wants to get everyone together for dinner in Boston for Ma's birthday. I think he's going to ask her to marry him."

"That's so wonderful," I said. "*He* is wonderful and he's so good to your mom." I touched Weston's cheek. "Isn't it a good thing?"

Weston nodded. "I think so. There's something I need to do first." His hand was rough and calloused but his touch was soft on my cheek. "Come with me?"

"Anywhere," I said. "Where are we going?"

Weston's eyes hardened. "Home."

CHAPTER
Thirty-Four

Autumn

From what I saw out the Uber car's window, Woburn, Massachusetts was a cute little town. Colonial buildings surrounded by parks and beautiful forest. Weston's hand in mine tightened as the driver turned into a neighborhood adjacent to the freeway, with less green spaces and small clapboard houses huddled close together.

"This it?" the driver asked.

Weston nodded. "Yeah. This is it."

"You want me to wait?"

"No thanks, we're good."

We got out and Weston transferred into his chair. The street was quiet and deserted.

"Which one?" I asked.

Weston pointed at a little blue house with a white roof at the end of the cul-de-sac in front of us. With a rough exhale, he gave the wheels a shove and started down the street. I walked beside him.

"Everything looks so small," he said when we reached the end of the street. "I haven't been back here since Ma had to move us out." His expression hardened as the memories glinted in his eyes.

"It must've seemed bigger to you as a child."

"This is where he was," he said, moving his wheelchair along the curb in front of the house. "Parked right here and then he took off. Ma was screaming and crying."

The neighborhood had made his Boston accent rise up in his mouth. *Ma was screamin' and cryin'...*

"And the bastard didn't stop. I chased him. He had to have seen me in his rearview, but he didn't stop."

Tears welled in his eyes. I waited for him to swipe them away angrily, but this time, he let go.

"He didn't fucking stop." His voice was thick with anger and pain, the words squeezing between the tears. "He kept going. He left her. He left her with *nothing.* And he left us. He left his fucking *kids...* The worst fucking part is... I..." He shook his head, struggling to contain it all. "I still love him. I hope he rots in hell and I still love him."

Weston broke down then, his shoulders shaking. He rested an elbow on his chair's wheel and covered his face with his hand. I moved behind to wrap my arms around him. He rested his head against my shoulder, his tears dampening the sleeve of my cardigan. He cried hard and I held him. Though his pain cut me to the bone, I sensed this was the start of healing. The wound that had festered so long was finally purged clean.

"Sorry," he said, drying his face on his shoulder. "Not much of a trip for you."

I moved around and sat on his lap so I could hold him close and look at him, eye to eye. "This is the best trip I'll ever take."

"Why's that?"

"It may surprise you to know that I'm a hopeless romantic."

"You? Get out of town."

"Since I was a kid, I had a dream about the man I'd love someday. *The One.* I fantasized about what it would be like when I met him, and the fantasy had nothing to do with wedding dresses or castles with knights in shining armor. Instead, I imagined showing him our farm in Nebraska. He'd meet my family and see where I began. And in return, he'd take me to the place where he began, and I'd understand him in that same fundamental way. The two of us, understanding each other like that, was the truest, real love I'd ever have. We'd ever have." I shrugged and touched his face. "And here we are."

"Here we are," he murmured. His gaze swept over the old

LONG LIVE the Beautiful Hearts

house and the empty street. One last tear slipped down his cheek, and I smiled.

At long last, Weston, my love, was right here.

Weston

We checked into our room at the InterContinental Hotel on Boston's waterfront. Paul had made reservations at the Miel restaurant for dinner that night. I changed into a dark gray suit and Autumn wore a deep green dress.

"You're beautiful," I said, tugging at the knot of my tie irritably.

"You're nervous," she said, bending to straighten it for me. "You think he's really going to ask?"

"Think so."

"How do you feel about it?"

I lifted a shoulder. "Not sure yet."

"Well, I think it's wonderful." She kissed my cheek. "Give him a chance, okay?"

I made a noncommittal sound.

We headed down to the restaurant lobby at ten to seven. Ruby and Connor were already there. Connor wore a suit in a lighter shade of gray than mine, and Ruby was in red.

The women greeted each other as if they were picking up a conversation from a few minutes ago. Connor and I clasped hands and hugged. But then he and Autumn faced each other, and Ruby and I simultaneously backed up to give a them little space.

But not too much space, Drake.

"Hey," Connor said, rubbing the back of his neck.

Autumn laughed a little, shaking her head. "Oh for crying out loud..." She reached up and put her arms around his shoulders.

He hugged her back and his eyes fell shut in relief. He whispered something in her ear. I knew it was *thank you*.

The Drakes, including Jefferson and Cassandra, showed up next. The change in Connor's demeanor around them was amazing.

All that old pressure on him lifted, and while I knew having a small fortune helped, the desperate need in his eyes to have his dad's approval was gone.

"Hey, Dad," he said and gave him a hug. "Mom." He kissed Victoria's cheek, then nodded his chin at Jefferson. "What's up, Jeffy?"

Jefferson rolled his eyes. "You know I hate when you call me that."

"Why do you think I do it?"

I made a mental note. *Jeffy it is. From now until eternity.*

My mother, sisters and Paul arrived last, bustling into the lobby like a flock of birds.

"Wow, look at that," Autumn murmured.

I stared with the same thought. Felicia wore slacks and a nice blouse. Her hair was cut short and brushed her shoulders. The wan tiredness of her face was gone, as if she'd gotten a month of solid sleep after years of insomnia.

Kimberly looked so relaxed, I hardly recognized her. My youngest sister had always been guarded and tense, constantly braced for life to jump out of the bushes and pounce on her. Now, even under the same elaborate hair and heavy makeup, she looked calm. Almost serene.

As she bent to kiss my cheek, she laughed. "Take a picture it'll last longer."

Take a pitcha, it'll last longah.

"Don't you give him a hard time," Ma said, swooping down on me. "Lookit you, my beautiful boy."

I was enveloped in her perfume as she bent to hug me. Her bleached hair curled around her shoulders and her acrylic nails were as long and sparkly as ever, but she radiated happiness.

Sock Boy had died on that street in Woburn a few hours before, and it was as if blinders were lifted off of me. I looked to Paul Sheffield—who looked like a fifth grade science teacher dressed for graduation in a suit; mustache combed, his bald head and glasses gleaming in the amber light of the hotel lobby.

And I realized he was responsible for my mother and sisters. Not for their happiness but for giving them a chance at it.

"Don't you men look handsome?" Ma said, stepping back to take in Conner and me. "Seeing the two of you together, oh my God.

LONG LIVE the Beautiful Hearts

My heart is going to burst. *Burst*, I tell you."

"Happy Birthday, Ma," I said.

"Happy Birthday, Miranda," Connor echoed.

"Look at you. Your beautiful smile's back," she said to Connor, pinching his chin in her hand and giving his face a little shake. "And you," she said, turning to me. "Finally you don't got that sour look on your face all the time."

"Thanks, Ma," I muttered.

She turned to Autumn. "That's because of you, you beautiful angel."

"Happy Birthday, Mrs. Turner," Autumn said. "Sorry. Miranda."

"That's better." Ma stepped back to regard the four of us. "So. Quite the game of musical chairs you all been playing, eh?"

"*Jesus*, Ma."

Connor hid a laugh behind his hand, his shoulders shaking. Ruby and Autumn turned identical shades of red.

Paul stepped in. "So long as everybody's happy, right?" He looked to me. "Isn't that what matters most?"

Senator Drake stepped in from the hostess stand. "Our table is ready. Shall we?"

I pressed Autumn's hand to my lips. "Meet you inside."

She bent to kiss me. "Be nice."

"You say that like I have some kind of reputation."

"Imagine that." She rolled her eyes with a laugh and followed the others into the restaurant.

"Hey, Paul, got a minute?" I said.

"Am I in trouble?" he asked but followed me a little off to the side. "Actually, I was gearing up to ask you something."

"You want to marry my mother."

He coughed into his fist. "That's the plan. But I wanted to get your blessing first. Your *blessing*," he said. "Not your permission. No disrespect, but I love her and I'm going to ask. But it would mean a lot to me if you were happy for us. She makes me happy. She's a fighter, you know? She may fight dirty sometimes but she wants the best for everybody all the time, and I love that about her."

"So do I," I said.

"I'm not trying to take the place of your dad but—"

"Paul..." I shifted in my wheelchair, not quite able to meet his eye.

I've already cried like a goddamn baby once today, thank you very much.

"I don't think it would be so bad..." I cleared my throat. "I think I would've been pretty damn happy to have you as a dad."

"Well... Well, that's..." Paul took off his glasses, cleaned them with a handkerchief, and put them back on, blinking hard. "Thank you, Weston," he said, clearing his own throat. "That means more to me than you could ever know."

He stuck out his hand to me. I glanced at it and looked back up at him. A tearful chuckle burst out of him.

"All right then," he said and bent to give me a hug. I hugged back, tightly, and then we broke it up with manly back thumping and surreptitious sniffing.

"Great," he said. "It's settled then."

We went into the dining room where a chair had been moved from the table so I could sit beside Autumn.

"Everything okay?" she asked.

I looked at this woman sitting next to me, her copper hair spilling down her shoulders, framing her perfect face. Those stunning eyes of gemstone green, gold and brown. Sharp with intelligence and kindness—two traits she was going to use to try to fix a little piece of what was broken in the world. My gaze then went around the table. To my mother, who did her best with what she had. The Drakes, who filled in the gaps when she couldn't. Paul, who was the best thing to ever happen to her. To Connor and his love. And back to Autumn again.

My family.

"Everything's how it's supposed to be."

Epilogue

Weston

January, one year later...

"I think I'm more nervous than you," Autumn said, walking beside my chair down the MIT campus sidewalk.

"I know you are," I said. "Because I'm not nervous at all."

"How is that possible?" Connor said, from my other side. "It's ten degrees out and I'm sweating my balls off."

We neared the Johnson Athletics Center, where I'd been commuting from Amherst for specialized rehab for the past three weeks in preparation for today. The trial that Dr. Cerenak had put my name on the list for finally had a spot for me.

We went inside and down the corridors to one of the basketball gyms.

"This is it," I said. I glanced up at Autumn whose face was paler than usual. I gave her hand a squeeze. "You all right?"

She shrugged self-consciously. "I don't know. Just nerves. Don't mind me."

The gym was regulation basketball size but with no spectator seats. Dr. Angie McKenzie and her team of robotic engineers had set up shop there for the last month.

The first time I met Angie, she was dressed in jeans, boots and a T-shirt that read *Surely not everybody was Kung Fu fighting.* I thought she was an intern, but she was a recent Stanford graduate with a double major in orthotics and medical robotics. She was doing her post-grad work at MIT, engineering prosthetic limbs for amputees.

But her real baby was The ExoSuit: a robotic exoskeleton that fit around a paraplegic's hips, legs and feet, allowing them to walk.

Today, Angie wore a lab coat over a gray T-shirt reading THIS IS MY SLUTTY SCIENTIST COSTUME. Her assistant, Carl, was a tall, skinny guy who never said much.

"Heya, Wes," Angie said. Her dark, curly hair brushed her shoulders as she strode over. "You must be Connor and Autumn. I'm Dr. McKenzie, but you can call me Angie. Unless my parents are around. *Doctor* makes them feel better about my student loans. Okay, let's get you set up, Wes. Big day today. Big, big day."

The ExoSuit hung on a frame. It looked like a backpack with mechanical legs hanging off of it, which, technically, it was. This battery-powered machine was going to let me stand up and walk.

"Okay, now I'm nervous," I said.

Connor's hand clapped on my shoulder, and Autumn gave my hand a squeeze.

Angie directed me to one end of the basketball court. She and Carl messed with a computer console on a rolling cart attached to The ExoSuit, then rolled the frame over to me. I scooted to the edge of my chair so Carl could help me slip on the backpack.

"What's that for?" Connor asked.

"This is the battery pack," Angie said as Carl wrapped the straps around my chest. "This bad boy can power the exoskeleton for up to eight hours."

Connor frowned at the wires and metal braces. "Seems like a lot of stuff."

"It is now," Angie said. "But once the Exo adapts to Wes, it'll move better for him. It'll learn how he moves, and then all this apparatus won't be necessary. Just the battery, The ExoSuit, and him."

Connor's eyes widened. "Wes could use this all the time? Instead of the wheelchair?"

"Not quite," Angie said. "Liberation from the wheelchair isn't going to happen overnight, even if you owned an Exo. Not at this stage. Most users still find their wheelchair to be the most convenient.

LONG LIVE **the Beautiful Hearts**

But the technology is only going to evolve. Like an iPhone," she said with a wink. "Newer, better models are in development all the time, to make them smarter, faster and lighter."

Autumn gnawed her lip as Carl handed me elaborate crutches. Each handle had thumb-operated controls.

"The health benefits are what's most important, right?" Autumn asked.

"Heck yeah, they are," Angie said. "The Exo reduces the risk of pressure sores, increases bone density and improves circulation and blood pressure. We just need to get the insurance companies on board."

"They're not?" Autumn asked

Angie shook her head. "All exos are classified as experimental, right now. Insurance won't pay for them." She patted the battery backpack strapped between my shoulder blades. "And this baby isn't cheap, though we're working on that too."

"I want to help," Autumn said. "I'm *going* to help. What can I do?"

Angie beamed. "Wes told me all about you. We should get coffee sometime and have a chat. I—"

"Next week?" Autumn asked. "I'm free on Wednesday and Thursday afternoon. Either one. Or both."

Angie laughed and looked over at me. "You weren't kidding."

"Nope," I said. "She means business."

"I'd love to meet Wednesday," Angie said to Autumn. "Right now, let's get your man up and walking."

Up and walking.

"Holy shit, this is happening," I said.

Angie made a few more adjustments to the braces around my legs and under my feet, then stepped back. "I'm going to initiate The ExoSuit to get you to a standing position. Use the crutches to balance. We'll go slow. Just take it nice and easy. You ready?"

I nodded. My hands gripped the crutch handles so tightly, my bones ached. Autumn and Connor took a few steps back.

"Here we go." Angie pushed a button on her smart pad, and The ExoSuit lifted me out of the chair, straightened my knees, unbent my hips and slowly took me to standing. My vantage rose, higher and higher. To my full height—six feet, one inches tall.

I was standing up.

Holy fucking shit...

I was eye-level with Autumn and Connor, not craning my neck up. Autumn's fingers covered her mouth, her eyes shining. Connor's jaw clenched and he put his hands on his hips. He looked up at the ceiling for a moment, then back to me.

The feeling that rose in me—up from somewhere deeper than my skin and bones, beneath nerve endings that didn't work anymore and those that did—would take a thousand poems to describe, and yet there was only one word for it.

Love. Everything, everywhere.

"How we doing, everyone?" Angie asked gently.

"I am a fucking wreck," Connor said, while Autumn just stared above the hands steepled over her nose.

"Ready to take a step or two, Wes?"

I nodded, not yet trusting my voice. Angie and Carl did a last minute check on the controls at my hands.

"Remember, you'll trigger your own steps," Angie said, indicating the button on the side of the crutch's handle. "When you feel comfortable and balanced, initiate the next step."

"Got it."

"Go slow. I'll be right behind you."

I pushed the button and my left leg took a step. Then the right. For the first time, the faint pressure I could feel in my legs came from the bottom of my feet, my calves, my knees and my hips. The lower half of my body was moving beneath me, taking my upper half with it. A déjà vu or dream of a past life and yet actually happening. Surreal and real at the same time.

Left leg.

Right leg.

Connor was shaking his head. "Holy...shit..."

"Holy shit is right..."

I wanted to fucking cry. Or laugh. Or both, but I had to concentrate on keeping the crutches in time with my steps. The months spent on the parallel bars, prepping my upper body for this, paid off. I kept my balance. I kept walking.

I was walking.

Autumn leaned on Connor's shoulder, crying over her hand as I got closer.

"Way to go, T," Connor said, his voice cracking open.

LONG LIVE the Beautiful Hearts

"You're doing great," Angie said, walking behind me. "Just perfect, Wes."

"How does it feel?" Autumn asked.

"It's unreal. I can feel my blood moving differently."

"He's getting this like a pro," Angie said. "You two want to take a lap with him?"

Connor went to my right side, Autumn my left. I fell deeper into the rhythm of the walking, and we took a slow lap around the gym with Angie and her team watching and taking notes.

"How fast can I go?" I asked.

"Ah, the runner has spoken," Angie said with a laugh. "Don't get too excited, Barry Allen. The suit has a max speed of one-point-one miles per hour."

"It's a start," I said.

Autumn wiped her eye and her brows furrowed. "Who's Barry Allen?"

"*The Flash*," I said. "My rehab specialist is a geek." I shot her an appreciative glance over my shoulder. "And a smartass."

Angie laughed. "Amen, brother. Certified fresh."

I looked over at Connor. No words were needed. Over the telegraph wires, loud and clear, came all his happiness and love.

I looked down at Autumn. *Down* instead of up.

"The top of your head is perfect," I said.

She laughed a little before pressing her mouth tight. I stopped walking and slipped my hand from the crutch handle to touch her face. "You okay?"

Her head nodded, then shook side to side.

I turned to Connor. "Can you give us a minute?"

"Yeah, man." He rested his hand on my shoulder a moment and went to join Angie and Carl.

I looked down at Autumn. "What's wrong, baby?"

"This is good for you," she said. "This is going to help keep you healthy, which means more to me than anything else. And I'm going to get insurance companies to pay for them for everyone. But Weston…"

"What is it?"

"No matter what," she said, her hands running over the straps of the backpack and brushing off lint that wasn't there, the way a woman would smooth down the front of her man's suit and straighten his tie. "No matter what, I love you. I love you in or out of the wheelchair, sitting or standing. I just want you to know that."

"I know," I said, my hands clutching the handles of the crutches. "I do."

She leaned her head against my chest, right in the small square of my T-shirt between the backpack straps. She wrapped her arms around me as best she could, but the bulky apparatus kept me from feeling all of her embrace.

"I can't hold you in this," I whispered against her hair.

"I can still feel you," she said. "And I'm so happy. Are you happy?"

The joy I felt in that moment was pure. And I'd earned it. I'd stood up for myself long before I put The ExoSuit on. If Angie McKenzie had showed up two years ago, I'd have endured months of frustration at the suit's limitations, just to conceal the fear of my own.

I would have used it to keep running.

"I'm happy," I said. "I was happy before I put the suit on and I'm going to be happy when I take it off."

A small sob burst out of Autumn. She pulled away and craned up, stood on her tiptoes to kiss me.

"I knew you'd feel that way but I wanted to hear it out loud. In your voice." Her smile was radiant as she dried her eyes. "Let's keep going."

We continued down the length of the gym. I took one slow step after another with my amazing woman beside me. Her soft fingers wrapped around my wrist since we couldn't hold hands as we walked. Not yet.

But it's a start.

August...

I rifled through the mail, stopping at a plain envelope.

Emerson College, Office of Admissions

"Shit," I muttered.

After I finished my econ degree at Amherst, I went back for

two intense semesters of writing and poetry courses so I could apply to Emerson for an MFA in Creative Writing. The response was finally here, but the envelope was too fucking thin to be an acceptance letter.

I didn't get in.

"Motherfucker…"

Professor Ondiwuje and I had made a pact to open the admissions letter together, but for a second I thought, *Why bother?*

But I'd given my word. Instead of tearing it open and confirming my disappointment, I stuffed it in my backpack with *The Last Song of Africa,* Professor Ondiwuje's poetry collection, then headed over to the campus.

Professor O looked up as I rattled knuckles on his office door. The smile halted halfway on his face when he saw my expression.

"It arrived," he said.

"Yeah, it did." I set the envelope on the table.

He tore the seal and pulled out the letter.

"It's too thin, right?" I said. "If they say yes, you get a fat packet of info, and—"

"Shh. I'm reading."

I rocked on the rear wheels of my chair while he read, his face impassive. With maddening slowness, he set it facedown on his desk, folded his arms and leveled his gaze at me.

"Well?"

"I'm sorry, Wes."

I dropped down to four wheels, my heart dropping too. "Shit."

"But you've been accepted to Emerson College's MFA Creative Writing program."

I stared as he burst out laughing and came around to give me a hug.

"You're *sorry?*" I said, trying to sound pissed, which isn't easy to do through relief.

"I am very happy for you," he said. "But I'm sorry to see you go."

"Me too," I said, "but she got into Harvard."

I never got tired of saying that.

"Of course she did. Lovely Autumn," he said with a smile and crossed his arms over his light gray suit. "The object of your devotion."

"I owe you a lot," I said, my voice thick.

"You owe me nothing. The only thing I want from you is to live your life with truth, honor, and respect for the dreams and talents of your heart." He grinned slyly. "And a signed copy of your first poetry collection after it's published."

I coughed and cleared my throat, not wanting to go, but it was time to go. I had to say goodbye to this man just as Autumn, on the other end of town, was saying goodbye to Edmond, no doubt crying into his apron.

I wasn't about to cry in front of Professor O, but the struggle was real.

From my backpack I pulled my tattered, worn out, dog-eared copy of his poems, *Last Song of Africa.*

"Speaking of which…" I handed it to him. "Would you?"

He held the book in his hand. "Normally, my soul would recoil at the sight of a book—any book—in such a sorry state. But this…" He flipped through the pages of underlined passages and my thoughts scribbled in the margins. "This is an incredible compliment, Mr. Turner."

He took a pen and wrote a few lines in the front pages, closed it, and handed it back. "Keep in touch, Wes," he said. "Please."

"I will."

We embraced and I closed my eyes, gratitude welling up inside me for this man who showed me how to sit in the front row of my own life instead of slipping out the back.

To sit and take it, because it's mine.

I waited until I was outside the Creative Arts Building before I opened the book to his inscription:

For Wes,

A writer, a racer, a warrior poet who shed his armor.

A Twice Born man who emerged from his dark forest to light the way for those who come behind him.

—Michael Ondiwuje

September…

Our new apartment in Boston was a ground floor unit on Park Street.

LONG LIVE the Beautiful Hearts

Rolling distance to Emerson College and a straight shot on the T line to Harvard. The place was small, but it accommodated my wheelchair, especially since we kept the furniture to a bare minimum. We'd taken what was left of the money Connor gave me and made a donation to the Wounded Warrior Project and breathed easier for it. We were going to make it on our own—us two scholarship kids—and our place was furnished with thrift store finds and lots of houseplants.

Autumn graduated Amherst with honors, then spent the summer putting together a comprehensive program to help make the world more inclusive to people with disabilities—those you could see and those you couldn't. The Harvard application review team said it was exactly the right time and place for such a program.

Maybe I was biased, but I tended to agree.

I'd never been more proud in my life to see her open the acceptance letter. Not only acceptance but a full scholarship. And because Autumn was Autumn, she turned her biofuels research over to Senator Victoria Drake, who promised to take up the issue with her colleagues. Now three senators—from Nebraska, Iowa, and Kansas—had championed the cause and were drafting legislation.

"Corn gasoline wasn't my calling," Autumn said, "but I couldn't let my family down."

Translation: if Autumn had to take on a chemistry degree on top of everything else, she'd do it. She worked so damn hard, which made me all the happier to get home that afternoon and tell her what I'd been doing all day.

She looked up from her desk as I came in.

"Hey, you. How was lunch with Connor?"

"Fine." I took off my jacket and hung it on the lower hook of our coat tree. "I had to keep it short, what with the job interview and all."

"You didn't tell me you had an interview today."

I moved next to the desk and kissed her. "I didn't tell you I got the job either. But I did."

She sat back. "What?"

"It's part-time, every morning from eight to noon. My classes at Emerson are stacked in the afternoons, so it's perfect."

Autumn crossed her arms, hardly concealing a smile. "Are you going to tell me what the job is, or are you going to make me run down a list of possibilities?"

"List, please," I said. "Alphabetically."

Autumn swatted my arm. "Talk."

"It's at the VA Boston office," I said. "I'll be working with veterans who've been injured and are returning to civilian life. Helping them with job applications, paperwork, and a little bit of counseling on how to readjust."

"Seriously? God, Weston, that's beautiful." She wrapped an arm around my neck and kissed me. "What about your ExoSuit therapy? And your racing? Will you have time?"

After moving to Boston, I'd had to find a new league. Coach Brown hooked me up with a local chapter out of the Boston Athletic Association. I'd miss him, but I'd still see my old teammates—on the track during competition.

"I'll have time for everything," I said. "More importantly, *you'll* have time."

"What do you mean?"

"Between your scholarships, the Army covering my tuition and now this job, you won't have to work."

Autumn blinked. "I won't?"

"Nope." I rocked back on my rear wheels, watching the news sink in. We'd both been searching for jobs—Boston was a hell of a lot more expensive than Amherst—but the one I'd landed that afternoon paid more than I thought it would.

"Weston…" She stared at the pile of work on her desk.

"You can devote your time to saving the world, not waiting tables at Cheers."

She shook her head. "God, I love you."

"I know." I pulled her into my lap. "I love you too."

"And I'm so grateful you'd do that for me," she said, planting a kiss under my ear.

"Yeah? How grateful?" My hand slid under her dress, up the smooth skin of her thigh. "Take-the-rest-of-the-afternoon-off-and-get-naked grateful?"

She nipped at my earlobe, her warm breath on my skin. "I was thinking ride-you-in-this-chair-until-you-come-inside-me-so-hard-we-both-fall-into-a-coma grateful." Her lips blazed a trail of kisses along my jaw, until she reached my mouth. She sucked my lower lip between her teeth, then pulled away to look me in the eye. "How's that sound?"

LONG LIVE the Beautiful Hearts

My hand slipped higher between her legs, rubbed against her damp heat. "Sounds like I should go out and get three more jobs."

We stripped out of just enough clothing to get at each other. She rode me hard in the wheelchair, then let me move her how I wanted until she came undone—twice—in my lap, her nails digging into the back of my neck and her cries filling the apartment.

Afterward, she lay against my chest, still straddling me, our breaths in sync and our hands skimming over one another. Finally, she extracted herself and we put our clothing back together.

"Speaking of Cheers," I said.

"Were we?"

"Connor's grand opening is coming up next month."

Autumn tugged at a strand of hair. "His place is across the Common from the Cheers bar. Do you think it's too much competition?"

"No, I meant he's like the Ted Danson character. A bar owner who doesn't drink."

"Yeah, he is," she said. "I'm so proud of him."

"Me too," I said. "And the party is supposed to be something special. Everyone will be there."

"Can't wait," she said. She kissed me and headed down the hallway. "Going to shower; then we need to go out. We have so much to celebrate, I don't even know where to start."

The bathroom door closed and I smiled. I had an idea.

October...

With his father's blessing, Connor named his sports bar Drake's Bar & Grill. The location couldn't be better—on Province Street near the Orpheum Theatre. His customers would include hungry theater-goers after a show let out. For me, it was a short ride on the T from Emerson. I could visit him after class whenever I wanted.

On the night of his grand-opening, Autumn had class until five and said she would meet me at the bar. My last class got out at three. I went home, showered and changed into a gray suit with a blue-green paisley tie. Riding the T to Drake's, my hand checked the pocket of my suit jacket a thousand times, making sure the little box was still there, along with the poem wrapped around it.

I rolled across the threshold of Drake's, and Connor stepped out of a circle of friends to meet me. "Well, what do you think?"

I stared around me, at a loss. I'd seen the bar and grill at various stages of redesign but never the finished product. The floor was tiled in giant alternating red and green diamonds. The booths upholstered in the same green, while the furnishings were deep, reddish wood that gleamed under hanging lights. TVs lined the walls at intervals, and three more gigantic flat screens hung behind the bars' shelves of bottles and glasses. Bruins, Sox, and Patriots posters and pennants filled the wall space. The entire place felt rich and dark but not overly fancy.

But what struck me hardest—in this expensive city with high rent—was that Connor gave up valuable floor space to make wider aisles. And my goddamn eyes stung when I saw that the main bar had two levels—one set with high barstools, the other at a lower height with chairs. Low enough for guys like me to sit at without the bar coming to my chin.

"Connor, man, this is unbelievable…"

"The bathroom is accessible too," he said. "And I don't mean it meets the bare minimum requirements. I don't want you—or anyone—to ever come here and feel like it's *almost* good enough. I want it to be more than good enough. Because that's how it should be, right?"

"Right," I said. "A haven."

The smile that split Connor's face nearly broke me.

"Yeah," he said gruffly. "Exactly that."

We let the moment breathe for a second, and then he chucked me on the shoulder. "Come on, let me show you around."

He gave me a tour of the place, which included pool tables in the back and three dartboards. Then I parked the chair at the lower level bar. Connor went around to his side and poured me a beer.

"You look like you need it," he said with a laugh. "You ready?"

"I've been thinking…"

"Oh shit, here we go."

He propped both hands on the bar, a rag over his shoulder. He looked *born* to be standing there and I was so goddamn proud of him. I knew the journey began back in Italy, when Ruby made him get a job. He worked first as a bar back, then a bartender, before being promoted to manager. He'd learned the ropes of the business by working his ass off—in a different language, no less—instead of paying someone else to do it.

"This is your night," I said. "It should stay that way."

"It will be *more* my night if you ask her here," he said, glancing around. "This place is fucking perfect but it needs to be christened, you know? To get its start in the best way. Okay?"

He looked so happy. He beamed a new version of his mega-watt smile. It had all the welcoming inclusion of the old one, but the blithe, all-is-right-in-the-world aspect was gone. He'd seen firsthand that not all was right in the world. But he was still here, still smiling, and there was a kind of perfect poetry in that. An experience of pain and loss that made everything he loved more precious.

I knew the feeling.

Ruby arrived shortly after I did. She and Connor kissed, then stood together talking a moment. Arms wrapped around each other, their eyes looking nowhere else. Then she smacked a last kiss on his lips, wiped the lipstick off with her thumb, and joined me.

"Looking sharp, Turner," she said, taking in my suit. "What's the occasion?" She winked at Connor behind the bar. "Something happening here tonight I should know about?"

I glared at Connor over my beer but he waved his hands innocently.

"I'm *kidding*," Ruby said, oblivious. "I just mean it's nice of you to dress up for la festa del mio bellissimo amante. This place turned out pretty swell, don't you think?"

"It's okay," I said, loud enough for Connor to hear while he made last minute checks on his bar stock. "The owner though…"

"The owner's a saint," he said. "He lets in any old asshole off the street."

I laughed so hard I forgot to flip him the finger.

The party kicked off at seven. Only Connor's close friends and family were invited, yet the place was still near capacity. My mother, Paul, and my sisters arrived and gathered around me at the low bar where I nursed my one beer, growing more nervous by the minute. Where was Autumn?

"My God, Connor, baby," Ma said. "This place is just special;

that's what it is." She looked radiant and healthy, her hair freshly done and her nails as glittery as her wedding ring. "If I were still a drinking gal, this would be my watering hole."

Paul shook my hand and bent to give me a hug. "Gee, you don't look nervous at all," he said over the music blaring from the sound system. "Not one bit."

I let out a breath, genuinely relieved to see him. Aside from Connor, Paul was the only one who knew what I planned to do that night. He'd come with me to help me pick out the ring.

"What if she hates it?" I said. "What if she says no? This is the rest of her life…"

"Stop thinking so much, Wes," Paul said. He put the beer back in my hand and clinked his soda water to it. "Let me be the first to say congratulations."

His optimism didn't erase the nagging worry that turned over and over in my gut.

The Drakes arrived, followed by Jefferson and Cassandra. Cassandra was six months pregnant and she held her stomach protectively, as if just being near alcohol were bad for the baby.

I hid a smile into my beer and nearly spilled it all over the front of my suit when I saw Autumn come in. She wore a black dress with a white band at the top and around the hem. Tendrils of her hair fell out of a twist and clung to her cheeks in ribbons of red gold.

She paused to turn a small circle, gazing at the bar in awe. Then she found me in the crowd and rushed over.

"I'm so sorry I'm late," she said, kissing me. "The T was delayed and—Oh my God, Connor, this is *amazing*…" She knelt on the chair I'd been saving to hug Connor over the bar, then climbed back down to kiss Ruby on the cheek.

"This place is incredible. I can't believe how great it all turned out. Congratulations."

"Thanks, Auts," Connor said. "Can I get you something? Pear cider?"

"Yes, please—" She stopped. "You're kidding. You have it?"

"Of course I do," he said and poured her a pint. "What kind of joint do you think I'm running here?"

Autumn sipped her drink. "Better than Yancy's." She glanced at me. "You okay, honey?"

I nodded. "Yep."

L O N G   L I V E   the Beautiful Hearts

Nope. This isn't it. This is all wrong.

Victoria Drake gave a small, Congressional-sounding speech but finished with a more emotional toast to Ruby and Connor's happiness. Then Mr. Drake took command of the room. I held my breath, but his speech was just complimentary enough that I didn't feel the urge to kill him. The Drakes were proud of Connor in their own way, but the real triumph was that Connor didn't need their approval. He was happy and they were happy he was alive and healthy. When you stripped all the crap away, that's all that mattered.

All the toasts done, Connor looked to me, eyebrows raised.

It's time, his look said.

But it wasn't. Drake's was a nice sports bar, but it was still a sports bar, and the reality slapped me upside the head.

Are you fucking out of your mind? You're going to ask a girl like Autumn to marry you with six different TVs blaring ESPN and the scent of hot wings in the air?

I made a slashing motion with my hand and shook my head. Connor came over and leaned in while Paul and Autumn talked politics a few feet over.

"I can't," I said. "Not here. I'm sorry man, but…this is your night."

Connor's night, not ours. And while I loved him more than blood, Autumn and I needed to start our life together, just the two of us. After all that had happened, nothing felt more important.

"You sure?"

I slapped his shoulder. "I'm proud of you, man. You did it. And it's going to be great. I can feel it."

"Uh huh," Connor said, watching me. Then he grinned. "This isn't her."

"No," I said. "It's not."

"Well, you were always the expert on romance."

"You got that right." I leaned over and he leaned down for a quick hug. "Love you, man."

"Love you too. Get out of here. Both of you."

After a few delays extracting ourselves from my mother—and a meaningful exchange of looks with Paul—Autumn and I stepped out into the warm night.

"I'm glad you wanted to head out," Autumn said as we made our way down Tremont Street. "I love Connor's new place, but sports bars aren't really my thing."

I inwardly rolled my eyes at myself for nearly screwing up the most important moment of my life.

But shit, now what?

I had no plan B. Nothing clever or special. Not even a dinner where a waiter could set down a champagne glass with the ring floating inside. Hell, the diamond was so small, she'd probably swallow it with the champagne and not even notice.

I glanced up at Autumn walking beside me, looking fucking radiant in black and white, a small smile playing over her lips. She wore that smile almost all the time. I didn't think she even knew it was there. It was just her happiness shining through and I wanted to capture and keep it. Protect her at all costs, for the rest of my life.

Starting now.

"Autumn—"

"Oh, look," she said. "It's open."

I followed her gaze across the street to the Boston Public Library. Cones of amber light illuminated the Renaissance Revival-style building of gray stone and arched windows. A crowd of people in suits and dresses were exiting the front steps.

"Looks like some sort of event is letting out," I said.

"Let's sneak in," Autumn said. "Just a peek. I've never seen the library at night and this one's so incredibly beautiful."

"You want to crash a library party?" I said, a smile spreading over my lips. *It's perfect.*

"Hell, yes," she said. "We're even dressed up. They'll never suspect a thing."

We crossed the street and took the wheelchair ramp up to the entrance. Autumn stuffed her pocketbook into my hands and I tucked it behind my back. We approached an usher who was wishing people a goodnight as they departed.

"I'm so sorry, but I left my purse inside," Autumn said. "I just need to run in and grab it. Won't take a minute."

"Of course," the usher said and stepped aside to let us pass.

I glanced up at Autumn, who looked pretty happy with herself. "Done this before?" I asked. "Your name *is* Autumn, right?"

She laughed. "Once or twice."

We entered the main hall of the library and stopped dead, staring at the immense, vaulted ceilings of coffered plaster, gold roses

LONG LIVE the Beautiful Hearts

at the center of each square. The walls were lined with old, beautiful books, filling the space with that distinctive smell of time and history captured on old paper. Two rows of wooden desks were illuminated by small table lamps with green shades. Gold light splashed against the dark windows that lined each wall.

"So beautiful," Autumn murmured.

"The most beautiful," I said, watching her.

We slowly moved down the main aisle, taking in the Renaissance-style paintings and antique chandeliers. No one bothered us.

"Reminds me of where we met," Autumn said. "In the Amherst library. You were so cold to me at first. Trying to mess with my head."

"I liked you," I said. "Immediately."

She smiled as we came to a shelf of books. She pulled out and old, leather-bound tome and fanned its pages open. "You were reading Ayn Rand and you said feelings were like tonsils."

"True, but I hadn't been reading Rand first," I said, my throat already thick. "It was Whitman."

Autumn stared. "Oh my God... You're right. You were reading..."

"Poetry," I said. "I was reading poetry."

Her mouth fell open and she looked back into the memory. "That's right. And I liked you too. And then..."

Then Connor showed up and our lives took the forks and turns and twists into our own paths—into dark forests that sometimes felt impossible to survive. All leading to this moment, *creating* this moment with this woman and my ability to love her with my unbroken soul, even if my body wasn't.

"I wouldn't change a thing," I said, taking Autumn's hand. "Not one moment."

"Neither would I." Autumn set the book back on the shelf, her eyes shining. "Let's keep going."

We walked out of the library and into a courtyard where graceful statues danced in a small fountain. The walkway was wide, lined with green grass. Footlights lit up the quiet building around us.

And we were alone.

I pushed my wheelchair, she walked beside me, and we made our way around the fountain. Lit from below, the water splashed gold and blue, reflected against the dark of Autumn's gemstone eyes.

265

"Come here," I said.

She sat sideways in my lap, and her arms went around my neck at once.

"Such a perfect night," she said, her fingers in my hair. "I love everything about it. And I love you. A million times, I imagined what it would feel like to love someone like this. I never came close. Not once."

"Me neither," I said. "I didn't think this kind of happiness was in the cards for me. And I didn't think I could make someone else happy too."

"I am," she said. "You did."

I reached into my suit pocket and pulled out the small box wrapped in a poem written on vellum and tied with dried paper string.

Autumn's hands flew to her mouth.

"I know you said pretty words don't mean anything unless there's something real behind them." I set the box in her hand. "I figure if they were wrapped around a ring…"

A little laugh burst out of her as she unwrapped the poem with trembling fingers. I watched her read it, her exquisite face rendering the precise moment the words reached her heart. Tears filled her eyes and spilled over, and when she got to the last line, she set the paper in her lap and wordlessly held me tight. Her entire body melding to mine.

"You haven't even gotten to the jewelry yet," I said, my own throat thick.

She sat up, wiping her eyes. "As if I need more."

"I want you to have more." I opened the box to show her the antique ring, set with a small diamond surrounded by intricate filigree. "Autumn… Will you marry me?"

She stared at the little ring and I had a moment of doubt, which quickly dispelled when I saw myself reflected in her dark eyes.

"Yes," she whispered, then inhaled. "Yes, Weston. I want nothing more in the world than to marry you. Nothing else. Just you."

I nearly knocked the ring box onto the ground kissing her. Kissing the sweetness of her and the salt of her tears—or maybe they were mine. Kissing her gently but with every ounce of my being, to seal my promise to love her forever.

She held the poem in her right hand as I slipped the ring on her left. It fit perfectly over her delicate fingers and glinted in the light of the fountain.

LONG LIVE the Beautiful Hearts

"It's stunning," she said. "And this…" She held up the poem. "This is…"

"Only a small part of what I feel." I held her face in both hands, my thumbs brushing her cheeks.

"Autumn," I said. "I have so much to tell you."

Long may the light
That shines in your eyes
Burn.
Until the gold melts
the heavy armor I carry.
It thaws the ice in my veins,
and illuminates
every dark corner
of my heart.

Long may the touch
of your hand
press deep into the earth,
sealing broken cracks.
And my scars,
Etchings on gravestones,
marking where all that was dead in me
lies buried,
Awakened instead
by your fingertips,
nerve endings singing
ecstasy
where there had been nothing.

Long may your voice
Echo in the hearts
of those who love you.
It sings in mine loudest
when you say my name,
it singes my skin
when it slips from your tongue
in the heat of a dark night
as our bodies strive

to revel and reveal
all that burns between us.

Long live the beautiful hearts
Like yours
That beat with infinite depth
Canyons of forgiveness
Cathedrals of beauty and love
Their doors wide open
A haven to weary runners
Whose race has ended.

Long live the twice born hearts
Like mine.
It beats only for you
My love
Unending and infinite,
I will take you with me
Into the next life
And a thousand beyond that
Always.
Forever.

—All my love,
Weston

THE
End

Author's *Note*

Isabel once took an inventory of my books. She wasn't permitted to read them, of course, but she was invested in them as an artist and as a person who cared deeply about social issues, diversity, and inclusion.

She quizzed me: "Do you have characters who aren't white?"

Yes, I said.

"Do you have characters who are gay?"

I do.

"Do you have characters who are disabled?"

I told her I had written a character who is blind.

"What about in a wheelchair? And the story can't be ABOUT him being in a wheelchair. He just is."

That, I told her, I did not have. And so she gave me *that look* of hers. The one that said, "Come on, Mom. Get to work."

I'd already had an idea for a book inspired by Cyrano de Bergerac. In the play, Cyrano believes he is not worthy of love based on a physical characteristic (his big nose). I had planned to create my Cyrano who felt he was unworthy of love because of his own inner demons. When Isabel brought up the wheelchair character, I didn't immediately know it was Weston.

War does damage to those brave enough to endure it, and it made sense to me that my soldiers wouldn't be spared. Weston's self-imposed "unworthiness" was never going to be about his disability.

Rather, his disability was an aspect that helped him to know his worth. It's not *about* him being in a wheelchair. It's about him (and Connor and Autumn) finding their own worth through the love they feel and experience with others.

For me, living in the After and still making my way through the dark forest, one of the guiding ideas that has kept me going is not that 'everything happens for a reason' but that things happen the way they are meant to happen. Even if *what happened* is unimaginable. I thought writing this book would be impossible. I thought my writing would be forever changed or even silenced. Instead, every part of it, every plot point, every emotion, every word is right where it is supposed to be. The book wasn't written, it was unearthed, as Stephen King says, in the backyard of my own experience. It was meant to be exactly this, and that is how it saved me. I cannot yet write the full story of *what happened,* but with Isabel's help, Before and After, I wrote this duet.

One Before. One After. Just as it was meant to be.

Thank you for reading.

SNEAK Peek

He fled to escape his demons and landed on her doorstep.
He wasn't supposed to be there.
She wasn't supposed to let him in.
They weren't supposed to fall in love.

Una Bella Anima (Beautiful Hearts Book 2.5)
A novella, coming this December

More from Emma Scott

Bring Down the Stars (Beautiful Hearts Book 1)
*I was not expecting to feel so lost. So emotional. So desperately in love
with EVERYONE AND EVERYTHING about this novel." -Angie &
Jessica's Dreamy Reads*

Amazon: https://amzn.to/2Mra71M

In Harmony
"I am irrevocably in love with IN HARMONY." —**Katy Regnery,
New York Times Bestselling Author**
"Told through Shakespeare's masterful Hamlet in the era of #metoo, In
Harmony is a deeply moving and brutally honest story of survival after
shattering, of life after feeling dead inside. If you've ever been a victim
of abuse or assault, this book speaks directly to you. This is a 6 star
and LIFETIME READ!!!--**Karen, Bookalicious Babes Blog**

Amazon: http://amzn.to/2DyByBK

Forever Right Now
You're a tornado, Darlene. I'm swept up.

LONG LIVE the Beautiful Hearts

"Forever Right Now is full of heart and soul--rarely does a book impact me like this one did. Emma Scott has a new forever fan in me."
--*New York Times* bestselling author of *Archer's Voice*, **Mia Sheridan**

Amazon: http://amzn.to/2gA9ktr

How to Save a Life (Dreamcatcher #1)
Let's do something really crazy and trust each other.

"You're in for a roller coaster of emotions and a story that will grip you from the beginning to the very end. This is a MUST READ..."—
Book Boyfriend Blog

Amazon: http://amzn.to/2pMgygR
Audible: http://amzn.to/2r20z0R

Full Tilt
I would love you forever, if I only had the chance...

"Full of life, love and glorious feels."—**New York Daily News, Top Ten Hottest Reads of 2016**

Amazon: http://amzn.to/2o1aK1o
Audible: http://amzn.to/2o8A7ST

All In (Full Tilt #2)
Love has no limits...

"A masterpiece!" –**AC Book Blog**

Amazon: http://amzn.to/2cBvM26
Audible: http://amzn.to/2nUprDQ

Never miss a new release or sale!

Subscribe to Emma's super cute, non-spammy newsletter:
http://bit.ly/2nTGLf6

Follow me on Bookbub: http://bit.ly/2EooYS8

Follow me on Goodreads: http://bit.ly/1Oxcuqn

Follow me on Amazon: http://amzn.to/2FilFA3